DEED *to* DEATH

D.B. Henson

A TOUCHSTONE BOOK
Published by Simon & Schuster
New York London Toronto Sydney

For Tim

Touchstone
A Division of Simon & Schuster, Inc.
1230 Avenue of the Americas
New York, NY 10020

This book is a work of fiction. Names, characters, places, and incidents either are products of the author's imagination or are used fictitiously. Any resemblance to actual events or locales or persons, living or dead, is entirely coincidental.

First Touchstone trade paperback edition July 2011

TOUCHSTONE and colophon are registered trademarks of Simon & Schuster, Inc.

For information about special discounts for bulk purchases, please contact Simon & Schuster Special Sales at 1-866-506-1949 or business@simonandschuster.com.

The Simon & Schuster Speakers Bureau can bring authors to your live event. For more information or to book an event contact the Simon & Schuster Speakers Bureau at 1-866-248-3049 or visit our website at www.simonspeakers.com.

Manufactured in the United States of America

10 9 8 7 6 5 4 3 2 1

Library of Congress Cataloging-in-Publication Data

Henson, D. B.
Deed to death / D. B. Henson.—1st Touchstone trade paperback ed.
p. cm.
"A Touchstone Book."
1. Women real estate agents—Fiction. 2. Nashville (Tenn.)—Fiction. I. Title.
PS3608.E59D44 2011
813'.6—dc22

2011011936

ISBN 978-1-4516-4960-4
ISBN 978-1-4516-4961-1 (ebook)

DEED *to* DEATH

1

Alvin Harney stretched his left arm out of the window and tapped the beat to an old Rolling Stones tune on the truck door. He bobbed his head as he sang the song off-key. There was no working radio in the truck, just a melody in his head and the crisp morning breeze in his face.

Except during a thunderstorm or hard downpour, he always drove with his window open. Even in winter when frost coated the Tennessee hills and most people cranked their heat up as high as it would go, Alvin kept the driver's-side window of his white Ford pickup rolled down. The cold never seemed to bother his fifty-year-old bones.

It made him feel alive.

This morning the air felt even fresher than normal. A heavy spring rain had fallen during the night—a cleansing deluge that had hammered the gray dust from the surface of the gravel and forged deep puddles across the road leading to the construction site.

The pickup rocked as Alvin splashed through the pools, the spray coating his arm with a fine brown mist. At the end of the road loomed a massive skeleton of steel and concrete, which, under his guidance as lead superintendent, would soon be transformed into the largest and most luxurious hotel in the posh Nashville suburb of Blanton Hills.

Alvin was usually the first to arrive at the site. It gave him the opportunity to review the progress from the previous day and then make adjustments to ensure the project remained on schedule. Not the bigwigs' schedule, dreamed up in a boardroom somewhere—his own schedule, honed into shape from years of hard work and experience.

He took pride in bringing projects in well ahead of the expected completion date, an ability that had garnered him a sterling reputation in addition to fat bonus checks.

Today, however, he was not the first to arrive.

Alvin wheeled his pickup into the parking area next to a black Dodge. Nico Williams sat on the tailgate eating a biscuit sandwich, a Hardee's sack in his lap. He swung his legs in unison with each chew.

Nico was new on the job. This was his third day. At first glance, he was not what you would expect a construction worker to look like. But for a man of around 250 pounds, he was extremely agile.

Agile and quiet.

On two separate occasions, Alvin had turned around to find Nico standing directly behind him, close enough to butt heads, never once having heard him approach. Nico reminded him of a big yellow tomcat stalking its prey.

Alvin never liked cats.

He turned off the ignition, got out, and slammed the pickup's door. The wet gravel crunched under his work boots as he rounded the corner of the truck bed. He nodded at Nico. "Hey, how's it going?"

"Can't complain."

As Alvin passed, Nico stuffed the last of the biscuit into his mouth, wadded up the paper sack, and tossed it into the back of his truck. Leaving his tailgate down, he followed Alvin to the double gates in the security fence.

Alvin removed the padlock and let the gates swing open. "So what got you here so early?"

Nico shrugged. "Just trying to make a good impression on the boss." His Cheshire grin revealed bits of what looked like either steak or sausage between his tobacco-stained teeth.

"Uh-huh. Well, here comes your chance." Alvin gestured toward the silver BMW X5 making its way down the access road. "That's Scott Chadwick. He's the man who designed the hotel, and he and his partner own all of this." Alvin waved at the SUV as it crawled through the gates, but the hard-hat-clad Chadwick stared straight ahead, a cell phone glued to his ear.

"Seems like a real nice guy."

A smirk had replaced Nico's grin, and Alvin wasn't sure which irritated him more. He turned and watched the BMW disappear around the corner of the hotel. "Well, actually he is, but he's probably got a lot on his mind right now. He's getting married in a few days."

"You don't say."

"I'll bet that's her on the phone, giving him her honey-do list."

Nico pulled a red bandanna from his pocket and tied it around his blond crew cut before slipping on his hard hat. "You married, Harney?"

"I used to be." Alvin hooked the padlock onto the open gate and headed for the construction trailer.

The trailer was one of three at the site used for offices and meeting space. The interior was small but adequate. A metal desk, a blueprint cabinet, and a bank of file drawers, topped with a copier and fax machine, filled the left side of the room.

On the right, a card table and four folding chairs were set up in front of a kitchenette complete with a coffeemaker, microwave, and miniature fridge. The plot plan and drawings of the front, rear, and side elevations of the hotel plastered the walls.

Alvin fired up the coffeepot and then settled at his desk. Through the open door, he could see Nico standing near one of the portable toilets talking on his cell phone. Probably getting his own honey-do list.

Alvin checked his watch. It was 5:15—about thirty minutes before the crews started trickling in. He opened his notebook to the day's agenda. He was glad Scott had arrived at the site early. They needed to go over several changes in the lobby's interior.

The hotel was being fast-tracked, Alvin's favorite type of project, though some considered this risky. He loved the challenge of coordinating all the phases of construction simultaneously. The project began with a preliminary design, and then the builder made modifications as the construction was completed.

In order to fast-track a building, you had to have a first-rate architect. Otherwise you could end up with the plumbing or electrical wiring in the wrong place. In Alvin's eyes, Scott Chadwick was the best. Alvin had worked for a countless number of design/build firms before signing on with Chadwick & Shore, but none of the contractors had earned the level of respect he held for Scott. And it wasn't just his boss's architectural skills that he admired. Scott always made Alvin feel that his opinions mattered—that he was more than just an employee.

The pungent aroma of the freshly brewed coffee permeated the trailer. Alvin glanced up and saw Nico standing at the door.

"Think you could spare a cup?" Nico asked.

Alvin checked his watch again. "Yeah, I think so, but don't expect it to become a habit."

He filled three cups and handed one to Nico. He placed the other two on the trailer steps along with his notebook, just long enough to close and lock the door, and then he set out to find Scott.

The hotel consisted of a twelve-story tower flanked by two five-story wings set at forty-five-degree angles. Designed to cater to an upscale crowd, the rooms were mostly suites, each equipped with a working fireplace and an elaborate bath. The hotel would also house two gourmet restaurants and a nightclub.

Alvin walked into the lobby area expecting to see the building's owner, but he wasn't there.

"Scott?" Alvin's voice echoed through the empty structure.

Maybe he was still outside.

Alvin crossed the lobby and peered out the doors that opened onto the rear courtyard and pool area. He could see Scott's car parked about a hundred feet away.

Still carrying the coffee, Alvin stepped onto the plank that served as a makeshift ramp from the door of the lobby to the ground. He was halfway down when he saw Scott Chadwick.

The coffee cups slipped from his hands.

The scalding liquid soaked through the front of his jeans, but Alvin didn't feel a thing.

2

Toni Matthews dialed the number for the fifth time.

"This is Scott Chadwick; you've reached my voice mail."

Why didn't he answer his cell phone? He wasn't answering his private line at the office either. She glanced at the clock on the bedside table: 7:23. Did he have an early meeting this morning? She couldn't remember.

"Hi, it's me. I was wondering if you could meet me somewhere. I left my briefcase in your car last night, and the file for my nine o'clock closing is in there. Call me when you get this. I love you."

She couldn't show up for the Barton-to-Collins closing without that file. Everything was in it—the termite inspection, the septic letter, even the keys to the house. And this was one property transfer she really didn't want to postpone. The sale of the Bartons' home was her final order of business for the next three weeks. She wanted to get it over with as soon as possible so she could spend the rest of the afternoon concentrating on last-minute wedding details.

It was hard to believe she would be married in less than seventy-two hours. There was a time when Toni was certain she would remain single forever. Not that she hadn't had meaningful relationships before. She'd had strong feelings for several different men during the course of her twenty-nine years. But in the past, she'd always managed to keep a sliver of distance between herself and them, sheltered by an invisible wall of protection. She'd cared for them, but never let them get too close. Never gave them the opportunity to break through that wall.

Then she met Scott, and everything changed. She remembered the first time he'd asked her out two years ago. She'd turned him down. The second time he asked, she'd turned him down again. Not because she didn't want to go out with him, but because she was afraid to say yes. She somehow knew from the moment they met that he was the one man she wouldn't be able to keep outside the wall. And she'd been right.

He was the only man who had ever truly understood her. He never pushed too hard. He never tried to change her or mold her into something he wanted her to be. Instead of stifling her independence, he acknowledged her freedom. She remained a whole person, never feeling that she was sacrificing a part of herself in order to be with him.

Scott never played games. His love was solid. Constant. He loved her as she was, for who she was. And when it came to loving him, she held nothing back for the first time in her life.

Toni returned the phone to the nightstand and shifted her focus to the mahogany-framed photo on the left, taken the previous summer in Cozumel, Mexico. Four faces smiled back. Scott, deeply tanned with gold streaks in his sandy hair; Scott's business partner, Clint Shore, wearing sunglasses and holding up a Corona; Jill, Clint's wife, lithe and blonde and as beautiful as any runway model; and Toni sitting in the front, clad in an emerald-colored sundress.

The shot was definitely not her best picture. But no matter how plain she felt it made her look, oddly, it was one of Scott's favorites. He said it showed her natural beauty—though she wasn't convinced she had any. Still, he loved the look of her long auburn hair falling across her bare shoulders and the glow the sun had painted on her nose and cheeks.

But Toni liked the photo for a different reason. It was a reminder of the best summer of her life. Clint and Jill owned a house on the beach, and the previous June, they had all spent two perfect weeks snorkeling, sunning, and relaxing. On the last night, after a quiet dinner for two, Scott had asked her to marry him.

The phone rang.

"Scott?"

"Toni, it's Eva Collins."

"Hi, Eva. Are you ready for closing?"

"Exhausted is what I am. We've been driving all night. Let me tell you, it's a long trip from Savannah with three kids and two U-Hauls."

Toni laughed. She'd met the Collins's children. All boys—aged two, four, and five years. "I can only imagine."

"I just wanted to check in and make sure everything was still on schedule."

"Everything's fine. The Bartons moved out over the weekend, and I had the carpets cleaned yesterday. You'll be able to move in right after closing."

"I really appreciate how you've taken care of things. You're the best real estate agent we've worked with, and we've worked with quite a few. Thank you so much."

Toni hung up the phone. It was already seven thirty and she hadn't heard from Scott. She had to get that file. Knowing him, he was most likely out at the hotel site. He'd practically been living there the past few weeks. He'd probably left his cell phone in the car and had no idea she was trying to reach him. It could be hours before he checked his messages. She would just have to take a chance and drive out there.

It was eight o'clock by the time Toni reached the construction site. As she made the sharp turn onto the access street, a white van barreled down the center of the road toward her. She jerked the wheel and veered off the gravel, her right tires plowing into fresh mud.

You idiot, stay on your side of the road. You're going to kill somebody.

After the van had safely passed, Toni pulled back onto the gravel and continued down the road. There were three police cars in front of the hotel and a uniformed officer at the gate. The construction crews were huddled in groups a few feet away. She wondered what had happened. Had there been a fight between the workmen? Had some of them been arrested?

She left her car in the parking area and walked toward the workers, dodging mud puddles along the way. It was the first week of April, and the old nursery rhyme echoed in her mind. *April showers bring May flowers.* Looking at the raw red-clay earth surrounding the construction site, it was hard to imagine the lush greenery that would soon line the drive and walkways leading to the finished hotel.

She thought about the people who would stay here. Perhaps travelers from the North who had longed to visit the Grand Ole Opry, or peewee football players who had convinced their parents to bring them to a Tennessee Titans game. She imagined the hordes of conventioneers who would be lured by the beauty of the city on the Cumberland River. What a difference just three more months would make.

A man in a red T-shirt, standing by himself, gazed upward toward the roof of the building.

"What's going on?" Toni asked him. "Why are the police here?"

When he looked down, she could see the man's face was ashen. He cleared his throat before he spoke. "A guy did a swan dive off the top floor."

"You're kidding."

"No ma'am. Wish I was."

A man had died, and she'd been worried about something as mundane as a closing. No wonder Scott hadn't returned her call. He had far more important things to deal with. "When did it happen?"

"Early. I got here right before six, and the police were already here. They're not letting anybody in."

"Did you know him, the man who jumped?"

"Not real well, but yeah. He owns the construction company."

Toni's stomach lurched. "What?"

"It was Scott Chadwick."

Her throat went dry, and for a moment, she forgot how to breathe. "Who told you that?" she demanded.

Startled by her tone, the man shrugged. "I . . ."

Toni shouted, "Who told you that?"

The man backed away, eyeing her as if he was unsure how to answer.

He couldn't be right. This had to be just a rumor somebody started. Like the game where you tell someone a secret, and by the time it gets around the room, it's morphed into something unrecognizable. She had to get inside. She'd find Scott, and he'd tell her what really happened.

Forgetting the mud, she ran toward the gate. The officer on guard caught her before she could get through. "I'm sorry miss," he said. "You can't go in there yet."

"No, you don't understand—I need to get inside." She jerked her arm free and tried to push past him, but he held her back.

"Just calm down—"

"Dammit, let me go!"

She saw Clint on the other side of the fence and called out to him. "Clint!"

When their eyes met, it was as if he didn't even recognize her. He hesitated for a second and then, seeming to realize who she was, headed for the gate. He nodded at the officer. "Let her in."

"I'll have to get her name first."

"This is Toni Matthews," Clint told him. "She's Scott Chadwick's fiancée."

The officer stepped aside and Toni rushed through the gate. "Where's Scott?" she said. "I need to talk to him, right now."

Clint pulled her to him and wrapped his arms around her. "I'm so sorry."

"No." She pushed him away. "Don't you dare tell me that Scott's dead."

"Toni, I'm sorry, but it's true."

She searched his face for some sign that this was all a mistake, some kind of sick joke. A harmless prank taken too far. Instead, she saw the truth in his soft brown eyes—a truth she was not ready to accept.

Hot tears spilled from her eyes, scorching her cheeks. Her strength seemed to leave her all at once, and her knees began to buckle. Clint caught her and held her close, gently rocking her from side to side as violent sobs wracked her body. When she was finally able to catch her breath, she pulled away from him, determined to stand on her own. "I need to see him."

"Toni, you can't. He's not here."

She remembered the van that had passed her on the access road. It must have been the medical examiner. "Then I'm going to the medical examiner's office or wherever it is they took him."

"I don't think that's a good idea. Not right now."

"I'm going."

Toni had started to head back to the gate when she caught sight of a familiar sandy-haired figure standing a few yards away, his back toward them. Relief flooded through her. They had been wrong after all. Scott was alive. She had never before experienced such a rush of joy in her life. She pushed past Clint and ran toward him. "Scott!"

Clint was right behind her. "Toni, wait—"

She grabbed the man's arm, and he turned around. Her chest tightened and the feeling of weakness returned. It wasn't Scott's face that met hers; it was the face of his younger brother, Brian Chadwick.

"Toni, this is Detective Russell Lewis," Clint said. "He just wants to ask you a few questions."

The way Clint was looking at her reminded her of the way one would look at a small child when trying to explain something too adult for a young mind to handle. She was sitting at a folding table in one of the construction trailers. He had somehow managed to get her here, and although she had been vaguely aware of his presence, she remembered nothing about the trip from the front gate. Had no idea if she walked or had been carried.

Someone—she wasn't sure who—had put a glass of water in front of her. She stared at the cup and tried to make sense out of what she'd been told. Only there was no way to make sense of it.

Clint moved behind her chair and put his hands on her shoulders, but his touch barely registered. Her body had gone numb. Nothing seemed real; it was as though she was trapped inside a bad dream—the kind of dream where you want to run, but no matter how hard you try, you can't move. She had the urge to shake herself, to do something—anything she could to wake up from this nightmare. To open her eyes and see Scott sitting beside her.

"Miss Matthews?" The voice was a deep baritone. She looked up to see the man she assumed was the detective standing expectantly before her. Middle-aged and dressed in a plain brown suit, he had thinning hair and kind hazel eyes. She wanted to connect with those eyes, wanted to make him understand how wrong they all were.

Without rising, Toni shook the detective's hand. She nodded but realized she couldn't yet speak. Her throat had closed up, strangling her words.

The detective pulled out one of the metal chairs and sat down facing her. "I'm really sorry for your loss, and I understand how hard this is right now, but I need to ask you a few questions. I need your help to piece together what happened here this morning."

Toni nodded, still not trusting her voice.

"Now, I understand you had a party last night."

She shook her head. "No. No, it wasn't a party." When she spoke, her voice sounded hollow in her own ears, as if it had come from outside her body and she was merely a wooden puppet mouthing the words of a ventriloquist. "We had our rehearsal dinner. We're getting married on Friday."

Toni noticed Detective Lewis and Clint exchange glances, and she realized how crazy she must seem. "I meant, we planned . . . we planned to get married," she said.

The detective nodded and slid his chair closer to hers. He motioned for Clint to step back, as if somehow giving her space would make her more comfortable. But nothing anyone did would make her feel comfortable. Not now.

"How did Mr. Chadwick behave at the dinner?" the detective asked. "Did he do or say anything out of the ordinary?"

"No." She shook her head. "He was fine . . . everything was fine."

"Did you notice anything different about his actions over the last few days? Did he ever seem distant or preoccupied?"

Toni looked down at the tissue in her hand. She had forgotten she was even holding it. She twisted it around her index finger, wondering what she should say. What she *could* say that wouldn't be taken the wrong way.

"Miss Matthews?"

She cleared her throat. "There were a few times when it seemed that something was on his mind, but that's not unusual. This hotel is a big project; of course, he would be preoccupied with it."

She watched the detective scribble something in his notebook. She knew he was making a psychological profile of Scott—trying to justify his death as a suicide since everyone was saying he had jumped.

"What happened after the dinner?" he asked. "Did you go straight home?"

"Yes."

"Did you argue?"

The eyes that had previously held kindness were now full of accusations. "What?" She couldn't believe what he was implying. "Just what in hell are you trying to say?"

This was all too much to take. She needed to get out of there; she needed some air. She attempted to push her chair away from the table and accidentally knocked over the cup of water.

Clint stepped between Toni and the detective. "That's enough. She doesn't have to do this now. It can wait."

Toni tried to stand, but her legs wobbled. As the room began to spin and darkness threatened the edges of her vision, she sank back into the chair. A cold sweat broke out on her forehead, and she realized she was going to faint.

She closed her eyes, held onto the table, and took several deep breaths. She felt Clint's hand on her arm. His strong grip steadied her, helped her hang onto consciousness. She opened her eyes. The room had stopped spinning, at least for the moment.

"I'm taking you home," Clint said.

"No. No, you don't have to do that. I'll be fine." She wasn't sure who she was trying to convince—Clint or herself. But she had to stay. She couldn't leave, not until the detective knew that there had to be an explanation other than suicide for what had happened.

"The answer is no," she said. "Scott and I never argued that night. We were happy—both of us. There's nothing I could have said or done that would've caused this." Her eyes began to fill with tears.

"I'm sorry," Detective Lewis said. "I never meant to imply that you did."

Clint knelt beside Toni's chair. "Are you sure you're ready to answer questions right now? Why don't you let me take you home?"

Toni wiped her eyes with the tissue. She stared at the puddle of water that had dripped from the table onto the dusty green floor. She thought about the detective and wondered if he had a family—a wife, children. How would he feel if he were sitting where she was now? If someone he loved was gone? Would he realize how absurd the questions sounded, how they added to her pain?

But their roles weren't reversed. He wasn't the one who'd lost everything; the one being forced to recount events that didn't matter. He didn't know her, and he didn't know Scott. He was just doing his job, following a routine. And the sooner she answered his questions, the sooner he could start trying to find out what had really happened.

She nodded. "I want to get this over with."

The detective turned his gaze toward Clint, as if daring him to speak. "We're almost done here." His hazel eyes then locked on Toni. "Just take your time and try to remember. Last night, did Mr. Chadwick do anything unusual, anything out of the ordinary?"

Toni took a deep breath. Should she be truthful? Would the detective try to twist things around, use the events of the previous night to help strengthen his case? She hesitated for a moment, but then decided it didn't really matter what she told him. Once he did a full investigation, suicide would be ruled out. "I woke up during the middle of the night—around two, I think. Scott wasn't in bed, so I went downstairs and found him in the study."

"What was he doing there?"

"Just sitting at his desk, staring at the computer. He's got this screen saver that's a slide show of some vacation pictures we took in Mexico."

"So he was looking at the pictures?"

"No, not really looking at them—more like he was looking *through* them, if you know what I mean. He had a strange expression on his face, like he was off in another world."

"Like he was mulling something over in his mind?"

Toni nodded. "I asked what he was thinking about, but he said it was nothing."

"And you didn't believe him?"

"No. I thought maybe he was having second thoughts about the wedding. When I asked him, he pulled me onto his lap and told me he loved me." Toni's voice broke, and she swallowed a sob as tears rolled down her cheeks.

"It's okay. Take your time."

Clint handed her a fresh tissue, and she wiped her face. "He told me there were a few problems with the hotel. I asked him if I could help, but he said no, that it wasn't anything serious. We talked about the wedding and our honeymoon trip to Tahiti, and then he got out his blueprints and I went back up to bed."

"Did he tell you what the problems were?"

"No."

"What about this morning? Did he say anything else?"

"He was already gone when I woke up."

"What time was that?"

"Around six."

"Did he usually leave before you got up?"

She shook her head. "No, not usually, but I just assumed he had an early appointment."

The detective scribbled something else in his notebook and then closed it. "Thank you, Miss Matthews. I think I have everything I need." He started to rise.

"Wait." Toni stopped him. "There's one thing you need to get straight."

"What's that?"

"It doesn't matter how things look, or what you think about Scott's mental state. There's no way in the world he jumped off that building."

Detective Lewis exchanged another glance with Clint. "And how do you know this?"

"Because I knew him—just as well as I know myself. No matter how many problems Scott may have had, he would never even consider taking his own life. I'm not sure exactly what happened up there this morning, but I do know one thing: it was an accident—it had to be."

Brian Chadwick stood alone at the main entrance to the hotel and watched Toni as she emerged from the construction trailer with Clint at her side. His arm was around her, supporting her, as if he thought she wasn't strong enough to stand on her own. But Brian knew better. He knew not to underestimate her.

Toni might be many things, but weak was not one of them.

He'd been taken off guard when they'd met the night before. She was nothing like the woman he'd imagined. He'd expected to meet a blonde playmate type—all body with not much going on upstairs. But his memories of the kind of women his brother preferred were now twelve years old. Scott had only been twenty-two back then. His tastes had apparently changed with age.

Not that Toni wasn't attractive. She was—but more in a girl-next-door kind of way. More Mary Ann and less Ginger.

It wasn't only her appearance that had surprised him. Toni possessed a quick wit, an acute business sense, and an easygoing personality. It wasn't hard to see why Scott had fallen for her. Brian remembered how they'd looked together, the happiness he'd seen in his brother's eyes—the eyes of a man who thought he had a whole lifetime of special days ahead of him.

But what his brother had planned didn't matter, just as Toni's beauty and intelligence didn't matter. What concerned Brian now was her attitude. Toni was a woman who knew exactly what she wanted and was determined to get it.

And that just might prove to be a problem.

3

Just before eleven o'clock on Friday morning, on what should have been Toni's wedding day, the white hearse glided past the iron gates into the cemetery followed by a steady stream of cars, lights on. She rode directly behind in a dark blue Mercedes driven by Scott's best friend and attorney, Mark Ross. He had both hands on the wheel, his attention on the hearse.

Although Toni had not seen him cry, his dark-brown eyes were bloodshot, and his face appeared older than his thirty-three years. She wondered what he was thinking. Was he replaying his last moments with Scott? Had he said everything he'd wanted to say, or did he have regrets?

Mark reached over and took her hand. "We're going to get through this. You know that?"

She didn't want to get through it. She wanted to bolt from the car and run from the cemetery. She wanted to scream to the heavens how unfair life was. She wanted the rest of the world to shut up and leave her the hell alone. She wanted Scott. "No. No, I don't know that."

He took an audible breath, and she could tell he was holding back his emotions. "We'll lean on each other."

She knew Mark would be there as long as she needed him, and Jill would be as well. The two of them had been her rocks the last few days. She never could have made it this far without them. They'd cancelled the wedding caterer and florist and notified all the people on the guest list. They'd even returned all the gifts. But most important, they'd held her hand as she made the funeral arrangements. She was lucky to have friends who cared, who understood.

Mark had been Scott's best friend since childhood. His mother had worked for the Chadwick family, and they practically grew up in the same house together, just like brothers. It was Mark who had introduced her to Scott.

Mark had seen the advertisement for a condo she had listed in one of the real estate magazines two years earlier. He took one tour of the place and decided to sign the contract. After closing, she'd stopped by to deliver a housewarming gift, and Scott was there.

Toni would never forget the first time she gazed into his blue-green eyes. With that one look, he'd pulled her in, and she knew her life was about to take an unexpected turn.

She thought about the last time they were all together—the night of the rehearsal dinner. She could still see them all gathered at the table. Scott on her right with Brian seated next to him. Jill on her left, next to Clint, and then Mark. It had been such a carefree night. None of them knew how fast everything would change.

Mark parked the car and led Toni up the slope toward the grave site. Her heels sank into the soft earth with each step, as if the souls of the dead below were trying to pull her down into their decaying coffins. The thought of Scott lying in a wooden box in the cold ground sent a chill coursing through her. Then she reminded herself that Scott was no longer in his body. He had long since moved on to a better world—a world where there were no more tears, where death could no longer sting.

They paused at the top of the rise to allow Clint and Jill to catch up with them. Although Toni had been comforted by the couple only minutes before at the funeral home, each gave her another lingering hug. Death has a way of bringing out a need to feel close, a need to hang on to those you love.

"I still just can't believe it," Jill said. "I never would have thought in a million years that we'd lose him this way."

Had she heard Jill right? Toni knew of the rumors that were circulating around the area, but they were light-years away from the truth. She'd been aware of the whispers at the funeral home, picked up snippets of conversation when no one thought she was listening, and noticed the obvious silences when she walked into a room. But no matter what people were saying, she'd expected more from her best friend. Jill couldn't believe the lies, could she?

"What way?" Toni asked.

Jill opened her mouth to speak, but no words came out.

Mark put his arm around Toni's shoulders. "Come on. We need to go."

"No. No, I want her to tell me what way she's talking about."

"Toni, I'm sorry," Jill said. "I really didn't mean that the way it sounded."

Although the medical examiner had listed Scott's death as a suicide, Toni didn't believe it for a second. Until now, she didn't think her friends did either. She shifted her gaze to Clint and then Mark.

As she studied their faces, the realization of their feelings hit her full force. "I don't understand any of you anymore. Am I the only one who sees the truth here? Am I the only one who even knew Scott?"

Jill tried to pull Toni into an embrace, but Toni pushed her away. "No. Just leave me alone." She turned and headed toward the grave site.

The casket, covered in white roses, rested beneath a green canopy tastelessly emblazoned with the name BLANTON HILLS FUNERAL CHAPEL in large white letters. In front of the coffin, the director had arranged a couple of dozen chairs, each of them now filled, in neat lines on top of a thin, turf-type carpet. Toni sat in the front row between Brian and Mark, Clint and Jill just behind them. The rest of the large group stood to the rear and sides of the canopy.

When the last of the mourners had filtered in, the minister took his place behind the lectern. "We are gathered here today to pay our final respects . . ."

Toni wasn't listening. Today was supposed to be the day she and Scott married, the day they had planned for months. She closed her eyes. *I shouldn't be here*, she thought. *None of us should be here.*

Instead, at this very moment, she should be in the bridal dressing room at the church, slipping into her custom-made gown. Laughing as she checked for the tenth time to make sure she had the customary requirements of something old, new, borrowed, and blue. She should be waiting to follow Jill down an aisle strewn with rose petals. Waiting to join Scott at the altar. Waiting to stand before the very minister who was now at the lectern. The words he spoke were not the words she should be hearing. Instead of death, he should be speaking of life, of new beginnings.

An involuntary sob escaped her lips. Brian shifted in the seat beside her. Toni brought her handkerchief to her face, avoiding his gaze. Although she hadn't actually sat down and talked with him at length yet, he probably felt the same way as everyone else. After all, he'd not seen or spoken to Scott in years. If Scott's closest friends didn't believe his death was an accident, why should Brian?

Toni returned the handkerchief to her lap and glanced at him. Brian's resemblance to Scott still unnerved her. They had the same sandy hair, the same build. But their eyes—their eyes were different. Scott's beautiful blue-green eyes had been full of laughter and warmth and put everyone at ease the moment they met him. But there was something unsettling in Brian's storm-gray eyes. Something just below the surface. Something she couldn't quite fathom.

Hearing the minister speak her name, listing her as a survivor, Toni was once again aware of the service.

"Today, we thank our heavenly father for allowing Scott to be a part of our lives," the minister said. "Though our hearts are heavy, Scott would want us to remember him not with sadness, but with the joy that he brought to us while we were still together."

4

Toni and Mark rode home from the service in silence, an obvious tension between them. It wasn't because Mark hadn't attempted to smooth things over. He'd tried to talk to her several times before they left the cemetery, but she was still too hurt to listen. When they reached Toni's door, he blocked her from going in. "Look at me," he said.

She did. His eyes reflected more than just the sorrow of losing his best friend; their depths seemed to reveal an inner conflict. Had she read him wrong earlier? Was he just as confused by the ruling as she had been? Maybe it was time to hear what he had to say.

"Scott loved you," he said. "Nothing else matters. It's not important what anybody else thinks or says."

She shook her head. Why couldn't he understand? "What other people are saying about Scott might not matter to you, but it matters to me. I want him to be remembered as the strong man he was, not as somebody who took the coward's way out." She pushed his arm aside and slid her key into the lock. "And another thing—if you thought Scott was capable of hurting himself, why didn't you tell me?"

"There weren't any signs. I never expected this to happen."

"Then why in hell are you so sure it wasn't an accident?"

He bowed his head. "I'm *not* sure."

Dozens of cars had followed them from the service and now lined Toni's driveway and street. A woman in a blue dress whose name had temporarily slipped from Toni's memory neared the house. The deli tray she carried appeared large enough to feed a hundred people. In the sunshine of the clear spring day, with her graying hair loosely twisted atop her head, she gave the impression of a lady attending a garden party, not a funeral luncheon.

Toni turned her attention back to Mark. Was he just humoring her? Telling her what he thought she wanted to hear? "Let's just get inside, okay? We can talk about everything later."

She'd been home only a short time, and already the house was packed with people. As they greeted Toni, she noticed they all wore the same mask—a look that said they were all privy to a terrible secret, one they dared not share. They were all probably thinking the same thing—that Scott would rather be dead than marry her. They pitied her, and that was the last thing she wanted.

She kept circling through the foyer to the living room, family room, kitchen, and then dining room—not wanting to sit, afraid to stop moving. If she let herself be still, her mind would break free of its distractions. She'd be forced to face the truth that Scott was really gone, that he wasn't coming back, and that she'd be living the rest of her life in this big house alone.

She picked up a sprig of parsley that had fallen from one of the trays onto the dining room table. She glanced to her right and noticed Jill watching her.

The whole time Toni had been making her rounds, Jill had refused to leave her side. She was becoming as irritating as a cocklebur. "You don't have to keep following me," Toni told her.

"Was I following you? I thought I was just mingling and being sociable."

Toni met her friend's eyes for the first time since they left the grave site and immediately felt ashamed. The love and concern were obvious. Jill had done everything possible to help her since Scott died, including insisting she spend the past two nights in the Shores' guest room. And what had Toni done to thank her? She'd jumped down Jill's throat. "I'm sorry I yelled at you."

"Now don't you even give that another thought, because I'm not."

Jill pulled her close. As they hugged, Toni felt tears well up inside her again, the dam threatening to break. She fought them back; she had to be strong. She couldn't allow her guests to see her fall apart. She ended the embrace, thankful that the air was now clear, thankful she had a friend willing to put up with her.

Toni wandered from the dining room and was about to begin her circuit again when she caught sight of Brian down the hallway. She was glad he'd been able to return to town and see his brother one last time, and she hoped that they had settled all their differences.

She joined him at the door to the study. "I never got the chance to thank you. For coming home for the wedding, I mean. I know it meant a lot to Scott to have you here."

"Thanks for the invite."

Toni nodded. "So how long are you staying?"

"Oh, I don't really know yet. A few days maybe."

"Good. Since you'll be around for a while, we should spend some time together. I think it would probably help both of us to talk about Scott. We could have lunch or something."

Have lunch? What was wrong with her? she wondered. The man had just lost his brother and that was all she could think to say?

She knew she should try to offer Brian some comfort, try to help him the same way her friends had helped her, but something was keeping her from connecting with him. It was strange: he was almost the mirror image of Scott, yet he shared none of his brother's warmth. "Well, I should get back to the other guests, so just make yourself at home. If you need anything—"

"I'll let you know."

After all the guests had gone and Clint had left to drive his parents home, Jill and Mark insisted on staying to clean up and put all the food away. Toni knew why they were really there: they were afraid that if they left her alone, she'd come unglued.

Maybe they actually think I'm unstable enough to kill myself, she thought.

Toni threw back the comforter and slid out of bed. Although her friends had ordered her to take a nap, she couldn't rest. Her body felt drained, but her mind refused to allow her to sleep. The bed was too big, too empty without Scott. And every time she closed her eyes, she pictured him lying broken on the cold concrete at the construction site. Her doctor had written her a prescription for a sedative, but she was hesitant to take anything. She hated the way drugs made her feel, hated not being in complete control.

The phone rang. She started to pick up, but then decided to let Jill or Mark answer it. She didn't feel like listening to someone else tell her how sorry they were. She went to the bathroom and noticed she'd left the closet door ajar. She pushed it the rest of the way open and stared at the racks where Scott's clothes hung.

On the left, he had arranged his polo shirts and jeans. Khakis, sport coats, and casual slacks and shirts hung in the middle, his suits and dress shirts on the right. Next to his tie rack, he'd hung a group of suits meant for the cleaners. She ran her hand down the sleeve of one of the jackets and then slid it off the hanger. The lining still held Scott's scent.

She wrapped the jacket around her shoulders, closed her eyes, and breathed in his cologne. She imagined his arms around her. If only she could feel them one last time. She dropped to the floor and let the flood of tears loose, cried harder than she ever remembered crying, sobbed until her eyes and throat ached. When she'd finally shed all the tears her body could produce, she pulled herself up, went back into the bathroom, and splashed cold water on her face.

The best part of her life was over. She'd never before felt pain as intense as the pain she felt now—not even when her father died; at least she'd been prepared for that. Maybe she'd let herself become too happy. She should have known better, should have kept that wall of protection up. But she'd never once thought that Scott would leave her. However, the blame was not his—he wasn't at fault. And she wasn't willing to let him go without finding out what had really happened. She had to see for herself.

She dressed in jeans and an Auburn University sweatshirt, combed her hair, and headed downstairs. Jill must have heard her milling about because she met her on the landing.

"And where do you think you're going?" Jill asked.

"I have to get out of the house for a while. If I don't, I'm going to go nuts."

"Come and sit down in the den and talk to me. You know, I understand how you're feeling."

Except for Clint, Jill had no family either. She was an only child and had lost both of her parents several years earlier. Still, Toni wasn't really ready to talk about Scott, not until after she knew exactly how he'd died. "Where's Mark?" she asked.

"He just had to run out for a bit, but he's coming back later."

"Are the two of you taking shifts now or something?"

"We just think it's best if you have your friends around for a while. That's all."

Toni decided to let it go. She knew they were just worried about her. "Who was that on the phone?"

"That was one of the clients we did some work for a few months ago. He's been out of town and he just heard about what happened." Jill worked with Clint and Scott at Chadwick & Shore Construction. She had a real estate broker's license of her own and handled all the sales contracts for the firm. She also oversaw the company's property management division.

"I'm glad I didn't pick up."

Toni made her way to the study with Jill at her elbow. The paper bag sent over from the medical examiner's office was still where she'd left it the day before, on top of Scott's desk. Amid the neatly arranged sketches of the hotel, it looked strangely out of place, as if someone had packed a giant lunch and was counting the minutes until noon. She sat down at the desk and stared at the bag. Scott's personal belongings—everything he'd had with him when he died—were inside. New tears slid down her cheeks as she unfolded the top.

"Why do you want to open that now?" Jill asked.

"Because . . . I have to."

Toni withdrew the gold watch she had given Scott for Christmas. She could still see the look on his face when he opened the gift, like a child opening a long-awaited toy. Now the crystal was broken, and one of the hands was missing. She removed his wallet and his cell phone, and then his Italian leather loafers. The shoes were slightly dusty now, but still looked almost as new as the day he'd bought them. In the bottom of the bag, along with some loose change, she found what she was looking for: Scott's keys.

"Now why on earth do you need those?" Jill asked.

"Because I'm going to the hotel."

"What in heaven's name for?"

"I have to see where he died. I have to find out for myself how it happened."

Jill nodded. "I understand, but I'm not about to let you go there alone."

Toni maneuvered her red BMW sedan down the access road to the hotel. She remembered the last time she'd driven this route. She'd had no idea that Scott's body lay inside the van that had nearly plowed into her. As she pulled up to the gate, the empty structure loomed before her, dark and foreboding. Clint had given all the workers the day off to attend the funeral, and the site was deserted.

Jill stayed in the car while Toni unlocked the gate with Scott's key. Then she drove around behind the building and parked where the gravel gave way to red clay—the same spot where Scott had parked the day he died.

The ground at the end of the drive was still soft from the recent rain. Toni and Jill crossed from the gravel to the concrete slab poured for the courtyard on their tiptoes. When they reached the spot where Scott had fallen, Toni sank to her knees, fresh tears filling her eyes. Although one of the construction crews had cleaned the concrete with muriatic acid, a faint brown stain remained. Scott's blood.

Jill draped her arm around Toni's shoulders. "Why don't we do this another day?" she asked.

"No. No, I'm okay. I need to do it now."

Toni dried her tears on her sleeve, and they continued toward the rear entrance of the hotel. The absence of workers and the odd silence made the building seem eerily solemn, like an ancient temple erected by slaves in honor of some long-forgotten god. When they reached the plank propped against the foundation, Jill motioned for Toni to go first.

She inched her way up and stepped into the lobby. The musty odors of tile grout and drywall mud hung in the air. Tiny particles danced in the sunlight streaming through the windows and then disappeared into the shadowy corners. Tiled with marble and containing an elaborate fountain at its center, the lobby was nearly finished. She remembered how hard Scott had worked on the design. Now he would never see it completed.

Toni sat down on the edge of the empty fountain and imagined how it would look in a few months. She could almost hear the water spraying out of the jets and falling into the pool below, could almost see the copper pennies and silver-colored nickels and dimes that would soon dot the bottom. It reminded her of the fountain outside the bank where her father used to have his account, years ago in their small hometown in Alabama.

Every Friday afternoon he'd pick her up after school, and she would go with him to deposit his paycheck. He always had a penny ready for her to toss into the fountain. He told her that if she closed her eyes and made a wish, one day it would come true. She'd whispered the same secret wish every week for ten long years, hoping and praying that it would come true. It never did. Now she knew better than to believe in wishes.

Toni and Jill left the lobby and climbed inside the construction elevator, a metal cage in a shaft mounted to the outside of the building. They held on as the rickety lift creaked and groaned its way to the twelfth floor. Neither of them spoke. They knew they were retracing Scott's final steps, seeing what he saw in the last moments of his life. When the elevator jerked to a halt, Toni pushed open the gate, and they emerged into the hallway connecting the four penthouse suites.

Each floor of the hotel was at a different stage of completion. Here at the top, the rooms were little more than steel framework zigzagged by electrical wiring and plumbing pipes. They entered the room on the back side of the hotel. Toni knew from Scott's drawings that this suite was the largest of the four. When finished, it would contain over three thousand square feet of living area, three working fireplaces, a formal dining area, two bedrooms, and two lavish baths with jetted tubs. They made their way past ladders and buckets through the main room and out onto the terrace.

The terrace, boasting a heated lap pool and hot tub, ran the entire length of the suite, with additional doors opening to the bedrooms. Toni walked to the boundary, a concrete wall roughly four feet high and over a foot thick. The police had found Scott's hard hat sitting on top of the wall, as if he had taken it off knowing it wouldn't protect him from what was about to happen.

With Jill watching her, Toni stood on her tiptoes and leaned across the wall as far as she could. Although Scott was half a foot taller than her, she couldn't imagine him falling over a barrier of this height. She knew he would never climb on top of the wall. No one involved in the construction industry would be so careless. So how had he gone over?

Toni surveyed the ground below. She could see Interstate 65, the Blanton Hills Mall, and, in the distance, the hills of Brentwood. She wondered if anyone could see her. If anyone had seen Scott that morning. She pulled away from the wall, turned, and sank to the floor, her back against the cool concrete.

"Are you all right?" Jill asked.

Toni nodded. But she wasn't. She wouldn't even be close to all right until she figured out what had gone on here. Unless they were sitting on top of the concrete wall, it would be next to impossible for anyone to fall accidentally from the terrace. They would have to jump.

Or be pushed.

That's crazy, she thought. Why would anyone want to kill Scott? Jill was looking at Toni with a puzzled expression, but Toni dared not tell her friend what she was thinking. She didn't have the energy to defend her reasoning. Still, it was no crazier than the notion that Scott could take his own life. Why would he?

The hotel was a presale project just a few months from completion. He was doing great financially, and he was about to be married. Even if he'd stopped believing in the possibility of a heaven and a hell, even if he'd decided that when you die you just go to sleep and feel nothing, that you just cease to exist, why would he want to leave this life? It didn't make sense. He had too much to live for, had worked too hard to get to where he was.

Of course, no matter how honest, no one could get as far as Scott had in the business world without making a few enemies. Had he made someone angry enough to commit murder?

Jill squatted down beside her. "Don't you think we've seen enough for today?"

They returned to the elevator and began the bumpy descent to the ground. Toni glanced down at the floor and noticed the glint of gold metal in the far corner. She steadied herself against the back wall and slowly moved to the other side.

"What are you doing?" Jill asked.

Toni pointed. "I see something over there."

The object, wedged in a small gap between the elevator floor and the steel frame, was all too familiar: a gold pen engraved with the initials SAC. *Scott Aiden Chadwick.*

"Isn't that Scott's pen?" Jill asked.

Toni nodded.

How did the pen end up in the elevator? She knew Scott had it with him the night before he died. He'd used it to sign the check at the restaurant. He always kept the pen in the inside pocket of his jacket. It would have been hard for it to slip out, and she couldn't imagine him trying to write while the elevator was moving.

Maybe he hadn't been alone. Could he have struggled with someone? Could they have fought hard enough to knock the pen out of his pocket?

As the elevator rumbled to a stop, she slid it into her purse. She wasn't sure what had taken place the day Scott died. But one way or another, she was going to find out.

They returned to the car, and Toni drove toward home. She never even noticed the dark green sedan following a short distance behind.

5

Toni had just gone to the kitchen to take some aspirin when the doorbell rang. Her head ached and her thoughts were churning. An imagined scene played repeatedly in her mind like a bad movie. She kept seeing Scott on the terrace, fighting with the dark silhouette of a man, struggling as hard as he could to survive, and then being thrown over the wall. She tried to block the images, tried to focus on happy memories, but nothing worked. She could find no way to make them stop.

She poured herself a glass of ice water and debated answering the door. Less than an hour had passed since Jill had left, and she really didn't feel like talking to anyone else. She wasn't in the mood to put on a brave face and listen to platitudes. If she ignored the visitor, pretended she wasn't home, maybe they would go away.

The bell rang a second time. Toni shook three pills from the bottle, popped them into her mouth, and then washed them down with the water. She hoped the aspirin was strong enough to stop the throbbing in her head. What she really needed was rest, but at this point, sleep seemed impossible.

The bell rang again. Toni closed her eyes and pressed the cold glass against her forehead, then slowly wiped it across her brow. The persistent ringing of the bell changed to pounding on the door. Whoever it was was determined. She put down the glass and walked into the foyer.

"Toni, open up. I know you're in there."

Mark's voice. She cracked the door open. He had a grocery bag in his arms and another at his feet. "Did Jill send you?" Toni asked.

"No, Jill did not send me. I'm here because I wanted to see you."

Toni stood in the doorway, not moving.

"Are you going to let me in?" he asked. "Or do I need to build a campfire on the lawn?"

Toni shook her head and pulled the door the rest of the way open.

He walked past her, carrying the groceries to the kitchen. "I come bearing steaks," he said.

"Do you even realize how much food is left over from this afternoon? There must be half a dozen casseroles in the refrigerator."

"Um, congealed tuna. Think I'll pass." Although Mark was making an attempt at humor, he couldn't hide the worry in his eyes.

"Thank you for coming over. I appreciate it, I really do, but there's no need for you and Jill to babysit me."

"I get that. But you're not the only one who lost him."

Toni had never before felt so selfish in her life. What was wrong with her? All she'd thought about was what *she* had lost, how *she* would manage. She'd just assumed Jill and Mark had been trying to help her. It never even occurred to her that the time the three of them had spent together earlier in the day might have been a comfort to them—that they needed her.

Mark slipped off his jacket and tie and draped them over a chair in the breakfast room. After turning up his sleeves, he took a glass bowl from the cabinet next to the refrigerator and began mixing the ingredients for the steak marinade.

Toni realized she was glad he'd come over. Maybe he needed to talk, needed someone to listen and care about how he was feeling. She wanted to be that friend. She wanted to be there for him the same way he'd been there for her.

If he hadn't stopped by, she probably would have spent the night wandering through the house, thinking about all the planning she and Scott had done. Remembering how happy they were when they'd moved in just two weeks earlier.

Scott had designed the house with children in mind. He'd worked endless hours on the plans, going over every detail with her, pouring his soul into creating the perfect home for their family. When he'd first showed her the blueprints over a year ago, she had no idea the house was meant for them. He'd kept her in the dark, letting her believe it was for a client; after all, they weren't even engaged then.

In addition to the master bedroom, there were five other bedrooms he'd hoped to fill with little ones. He'd also built a huge playroom over the garage. Scott had his heart set on a large family, often joking that he wanted his own baseball team.

At first, she'd been terrified at the thought of having children. She had no role model, no idea of how to be a good mother. But Scott was persuasive; he convinced her that all she had to do was love them. The rest would take care of itself. Now it no longer mattered.

She was sure her friends would advise her to sell the house; it was far too big for one person. But she couldn't bear the thought of letting it go. It was more than just wood and brick to her. It was a monument of Scott's love, the only thing she had left.

Toni reached into one of the bags and pulled out a head of lettuce, a bunch of carrots, a cucumber, and a container of plum tomatoes. "I'll make the salad," she said.

Mark smiled. "Go easy on the carrots."

After dinner was over and the dishes rinsed and piled into the dishwasher, Toni and Mark headed to the family room and switched on the television. One of the satellite channels was rerunning the original Austin Powers movie.

Once they'd settled on the sofa, Mark turned down the volume with the remote, his face somber, and turned to Toni: "There's something I need to tell you."

Toni squeezed one of the throw pillows tight against her chest, bracing for more bad news. "What? What is it?"

"Brian's attorney called me this afternoon. He's contesting Scott's will."

"Can he do that?"

"I'm afraid so. It's all about the wording. Scott left his estate to his wife, Toni Chadwick, not Matthews."

"Okay, so what difference does that make?"

"To a judge, it could make all the difference in the world. You and Scott were never married. Brian is his only living relative, and so he may have a claim on the estate."

On the screen, Dr. Evil was soaring through space in the Big Boy. Toni wished she could escape from her own problems as easily. At least she knew how to resolve this one. "It's okay; I want Brian to share in the inheritance. Call his attorney in the morning, and tell him I want to work out a settlement as soon as possible. Tell him Brian can have half of everything."

"Well, that's the problem. Brian doesn't want to share."

"What? What are you saying? Are you trying to tell me that he wants it all?"

"Yes."

Toni shook her head in disbelief. "Is he insane? He's had no contact at all whatsoever with Scott for the past twelve years. Now he expects to just waltz in here and take everything? What about this house? It's part of the estate. Does he want it too?"

"Don't get upset." He put his hand on her arm in a reassuring gesture. "We'll fight this. I'm almost certain you'll get to keep the house."

"Almost?"

Still clutching the pillow, Toni rose and walked to the french doors that opened onto the patio. The sun had gone down two hours earlier, and with the outside lights off, all she could see was her own reflection.

Should she just let Brian have the inheritance? What real difference did it make? She could sign over everything except the house. After all, it had never been about money with Scott. He could have been a pauper, and she would have loved him.

She had a successful career and was financially secure on her own. But what about Brian? She had no idea what kind of salary a magazine writer earned. Whatever the amount, he had managed on his own up until now. So why would he contest the will? Was he in financial trouble? Did he simply think that his blood entitled him to the money? Or was it greed?

Scott's estate was valued at $12 million, not including his interest in Chadwick & Shore. She wasn't sure what the business was worth, but it would probably add a substantial sum to the total. A thought struck her like a lightning bolt.

What if Brian had been the person in the elevator with Scott? The one who'd pushed him off the terrace?

When she thought about it, it made perfect sense. If Scott had died just a few days later, he and Toni would have been married. Brian would have had no claim on the estate.

Toni felt Mark behind her. She turned away from the french doors. "There's something I need to know. Scott told me they fought just before Brian left town, but he clammed up when I asked him about the reason. He brushed it off and said it wasn't important, that it didn't matter anymore, but I always wondered why he didn't want to talk about it. Did it have something to do with a woman?"

"No. Not a woman."

"Then what?"

"Did he ever talk about his sister?"

"He just told me how she had died as a child during some kind of surgery. Talking about Caitlin always seemed to upset him, so I tried not to bring it up much."

"*Surgery*'s not really the right word for it."

"What do you mean?"

Mark ushered Toni back to the sofa. "Scott adored Caitlin, and she idolized him. When she was sixteen, she got pregnant. She was too ashamed to tell Scott, so she went to Brian."

"How old was Brian then?"

"Eighteen. Old enough to find a clinic over in Murfreesboro. It was near the university there and had a reputation with the college crowd. It was the kind of place that didn't ask questions and didn't keep any records."

"An abortion clinic?"

Mark nodded. "Brian didn't know the doctor was a drunk, that he'd lost his medical license. There were complications, and Caitlin died."

"But Scott blamed Brian anyway?"

"Yeah. And that's not all: I think he also blamed Brian for the death of their parents."

"Hold on a minute. Scott told me his parents died in a car crash."

"They did. But Scott's father was in bad health when Caitlin died. He'd had a heart bypass the year before. It was just a few weeks after Caitlin's death when they had the accident. He just drove right off an embankment. The police couldn't figure out why. At first they thought maybe he'd fallen asleep, but when the autopsy came back, it showed he'd had another heart attack."

"And that caused him to lose control of the car."

"Right. Scott thought the stress from Caitlin's death was just too much."

"Were Scott and Brian close before Caitlin died?"

"I thought so. But they had the fight right after their parents' funeral. I'm sure they both said a lot of things they later regretted. Brian ended up leaving town the same day."

Toni let go of the pillow and drew her knees up to her chin. A new pain had wormed its way inside her chest. Scott should have been able to share his family problems with her. She'd confided everything about herself, down to the very last detail. She thought Scott trusted her completely. Had she been wrong?

She had always assumed the fight had been over a woman and that he had resisted talking about it because he feared hurting her or making her jealous. Now she didn't know what to think. "I don't understand why he couldn't tell me."

"Like he said, it must not have mattered anymore. If it did, he wouldn't have invited Brian to the wedding."

"I'm the one who invited Brian to the wedding, not Scott. I didn't even tell Scott about it at first because I was afraid Brian would say no, and I didn't want to make things worse."

"I don't know then. But he never talked to me about Brian either."

Toni sighed and leaned her head back against the sofa. In a way, she almost felt sorry for Brian. If he was anything like his brother, he probably blamed himself as much as Scott had—maybe more. Carrying that kind of guilt all those years must have been a living hell.

Although money alone seemed motive enough for Brian to want Scott dead, Toni wondered whether there could be more. Could his motives run deeper?

She was sure Brian had tried to help Caitlin the only way he'd known how. Not only must he feel responsible for her death, but for the loss of his parents as well. And instead of receiving the understanding and forgiveness he probably longed for, he must have felt exiled from the only home he'd ever known.

A sentence handed down by his brother.

Over time, the wound of guilt he bore could have festered into resentment and hatred—hatred for Scott. By inviting Brian to the wedding, Toni had unknowingly given him an opportunity for revenge.

Toni grabbed Mark's arm. "I don't care what it takes or what kind of legal maneuvering you have to do, but I want you to convince that judge not to give Brian one cent of Scott's money."

Mark looked at her in surprise. "A few minutes ago you wanted to give him half. What changed your mind?"

Should she tell him? If she let him know she suspected Brian of murder, would he think she was crazy?

Although he hadn't said it out loud, Mark acted as though he believed Scott had taken his own life. Before she started making accusations, tried to convince him otherwise, she needed some kind of proof, some solid evidence to back up her claims. "I've just got a bad feeling about the whole thing," she finally offered.

"What do you mean?"

Toni picked up the remote. "I really don't feel like talking about it anymore. Can we just forget about Brian for now and watch the rest of the movie?"

Mark stared at her. It was obvious he wanted her to explain, but he let it go. "Sure. Turn up the sound."

To the north in Belle Meade, Clint Shore sat on an antique sleigh bed, goose down pillows propped behind his back and an open computer on his lap. He stopped typing for a moment and took a sip of pinot noir from the glass on the bedside table. "So how's Toni holding up?" he asked, his question directed toward the master bathroom.

Jill appeared in the doorway wearing a teal silk robe, a silver hairbrush in her hand. "She's not doing too well, I'm afraid. After you left, she insisted on going down to the construction site to see where Scott died. As long as she lives, I don't think she'll ever be able to accept the fact that he killed himself. Instead, she's convinced that it was some kind of freak accident."

"Well, then, maybe you should humor her. Maybe you should just let her believe whatever she needs to in order to put it behind her and move on."

"Is there any chance she's right?"

Clint returned his fingers to the keyboard. "No."

"You didn't see anything that morning that could have caused him to fall?"

Clint's forehead wrinkled. "Jill, the police have checked out all the angles; they've reconstructed every move Scott made. I don't want to believe it any more than you do, but if they're satisfied it was suicide, then so am I. We just have to accept it and let it rest."

Jill tilted her head to the left and slid the brush through her long blonde hair. "I guess you're right."

"I know it's hard to think about work right now, but I need you to write up the contract to buy Scott's share of the company. We need to get it done as soon as possible. I want everything in place before I approach Toni."

After ten years of working with a partner, Clint would now be the sole owner of Chadwick & Shore. He knew it was no secret that Scott's absence would be a major blow to the business. It would take a while for it to recover. Clint would have to make some adjustments, but he was up to the challenge. He had long since wanted to take a more active role. Although the shift in power was under terrible circumstances, this was his chance to prove himself—to show the world what he was capable of doing.

Although Scott had been the primary designer, there were two architects on staff. Now they would be working on *his* designs. From now on, the visions created, the legacy built of brick and stone would be *his.*

His alone.

Jill placed her brush on the table and took a long drink of Clint's wine. "I'll start on it first thing Monday."

Clint pointed toward the computer screen. "Come here and look at this. I'm making a list of possible new names for the business. What do you think about Clint Shore Enterprises?"

"What I think," replied Jill as she opened her robe and let it fall to the floor, "is that it's time to turn off the computer."

When the closing music began and the credits started to roll, Mark realized he couldn't remember exactly how the movie had ended. Instead of paying attention, he had been going over legal strategies in his mind, trying to recall a precedent. He had decided to consult with a probate expert on Monday. It might be a difficult fight, but he was going to do everything in his power to ensure that Toni retained Scott's estate. Or at least the majority of it.

He stretched and looked over at her. She had drifted off to sleep, her head on a throw pillow. He was glad she was finally getting some rest. He doubted she had slept at all during the past two days. He inched his way up off the sofa, careful not to wake her.

Toni had a rough battle ahead and not just with Brian. However grueling, that would be the easy part. Toni had to battle the pain of losing Scott, a fight that had already left a permanent scar. It would take time, but he knew she would win this war. She was one of the strongest people he had ever known. She was a survivor.

Mark found a quilt in the closet of the guest bedroom and draped it over Toni. She looked so peaceful, like an angel. "Sweet dreams," he whispered.

The intruder watched the blue Mercedes pull around the drive and then speed down the street. Luck was on his side; Mark Ross was gone.

For a while, it had looked as if the attorney might stay until morning. It was one thing to do the job while Toni was at home. The intruder had no choice in that. He had to get it done tonight; he'd already wasted too much time. But he didn't feel comfortable with two people in the house. The odds of him getting caught would have been doubled.

He slipped his night vision binoculars back into their case and checked his watch. He would give her another hour. By then, she would more than likely be asleep.

The house was a newly constructed brick Georgian located in an exclusive subdivision in Blanton Hills. Situated on five landscaped acres, the home came complete with a pool, hot tub, and tennis court. He had scoped out the property before nightfall. Having determined the lights at the rear and side of the house were set to be motion activated, he had devised a route to avoid them.

He already knew about the security system. He knew the brand and the model, and he'd come prepared to disarm it, or so he thought. He had brought along a small receiver designed to capture the electronic pulses transmitted through the air whenever someone entered in the alarm code. After picking up the signal, the device would display the numbers. But so far, the box hadn't registered anything. Either the system wasn't armed, or the receiver had stopped working. He figured he would find out when he reached the house.

After an hour had passed, he dropped the binoculars at the base of a tree and pulled on a black stocking cap. He looked up at the sky. The winds were coming in from the southwest, pushing a thick canopy of clouds across the full moon. He hoped the clouds would block the moonlight long enough for him to reach the house.

Sliding the backpack containing his tools over his left shoulder, he emerged from his hiding place, a clump of mature evergreens at the edge of the property. He paused for a moment, scanned the street for approaching cars, and then slipped across the lawn, going from tree to tree until he reached the garage.

The foundation shrubs pulled at his jeans as he picked his way between and then behind them. He needed to stay as close to the walls of the house as he could, or he would set off the motion detectors. Keeping his back to the brick, he rounded the corner of the garage and made his way along the rear wall of the house.

When he reached the first window, he turned around. The blinds were open, allowing him to see inside the kitchen. The alarm keypad hung next to the door leading to the garage. Again, he was lucky. All the lights were green: the system was off.

He hoisted himself up onto the patio and squatted beside the glass doors to the breakfast room. The moon sliced through a break in the cloud cover, partially illuminating the patio. He froze, crouched in the shadow of the roof overhang.

When the moon had safely hidden itself again, he unzipped his backpack and removed a penlight, a pair of latex gloves, and a small wooden box. The box contained a metal object resembling a dentist's tool. But the device hadn't been created for oral torture. Instead, it was an electronic lock pick. He pulled on the gloves, clasped the penlight between his teeth, and went to work. He opened the deadbolt first and then the knob lock.

With his tools tucked away again in the backpack, he eased open the door and crawled across the threshold. He pushed the door closed and sat still on the tile floor of the breakfast room, listening. The only audible noise was the low hum of the refrigerator. It seemed his wait had paid off.

The first thing he had to do now was locate her. He didn't feel comfortable starting the job until he knew exactly where she was. Until he could be reasonably sure she wouldn't surprise him. He removed the Beretta 9 mm from the holster on his belt and crept through the kitchen and up the back staircase. He paused briefly at the top of the stairs, again listening for any movement. Detecting none, he decided to turn left.

He wasn't familiar with the second floor, and the first room he came to was a bedroom. Obviously a guest room. The bed was still made up, and no clothes were hanging in the closet. The adjoining bath was also empty. The next room was huge, seeming to span the entire area of the four-car garage below. There was no furniture here; it was probably intended to be a recreation or media room. He made his way back down the hall and past the stairs he had used, checking each room.

Once he cleared a room, he closed its door. The last room he came to, at the end of the hallway, was the master bedroom. The door was open, revealing a sitting area with a love seat and two chairs. He stood still in the doorway, trying to pick up the sound of breathing.

Silence.

He eased into the room. To the right, a four-poster bed stood awash in moonlight. But the bed was empty, and the pillows and comforter undisturbed. The door to the master bathroom was open as well, the lights off. He checked the walk-in closet. Nothing. Where was she? He knew she had to be in the house. Mark Ross had driven off alone.

He returned to the first floor and checked the dining room and then the formal living room. Just past a powder room on the left, he came to a set of closed double doors. The only closed doors he had encountered so far were closets. He'd never been in this room before, but he knew it wasn't a closet.

Keeping his pistol raised, he turned the knob with his left hand and nudged one of the doors open. He slipped inside. He noticed the silhouettes of several tall pieces of furniture as he turned to check behind the now open door.

Directly in front of him stood the shadow of a man.

He dropped to a crouch, ducking behind one of the pieces of furniture, the Beretta aimed toward the shadow. The man was gone.

His eyes darted across the room. Unlike the previous rooms he had visited, the blinds here were closed. However, enough moonlight peeked through that the objects around him began to materialize into familiar forms. He touched the piece of furniture beside him. The metal was cool against his skin. It was not a chair, as he had first thought. It was a weight rack—the kind that holds round iron plates.

He could now clearly make out a stationary bike, a treadmill, and several weight machines. Mirrors paneled the side walls from the floor to just below the ceiling.

He realized the man he had seen was himself.

He left the exercise room and continued to comb the house. He finally found her in the family room, asleep on the sofa. He stood over her, studying her as she slept. Her breathing was slow and methodical. Her eyes flitted back and forth beneath her lids, lost in that deepest state where dreams become reality.

In the glow of the moon, she appeared almost childlike. Alone and vulnerable. The thought of killing her flashed through his mind, but he stifled his rage and pushed the thought away.

Now was not the time.

He returned the Beretta to its holster and backed out of the family room, easing the double doors closed.

Brian Chadwick had work to do.

6

Morning sunlight streamed through the window, warming Toni's face and waking her. She opened her eyes, disoriented at first, unsure why she was in the family room. Then she remembered: Mark had been there; they had been watching a movie. At least she had pretended to watch.

Her eyes might have been on the screen, but her mind had been far away. She had spent most of the night trying to come up with a way to gain some kind of evidence against Brian. She knew so little about him that she wasn't sure exactly where or how to begin.

Toni yawned, stretched, and forced herself up off the sofa. The stress of the past few days was finally catching up with her, weighing her down. She was tempted to spend the entire Saturday curled up under the quilt, staring at the television. Feeling sorry for herself. Being what her father used to call a poor-me-baby. No one could blame her. Wouldn't most people do the same? But she knew from experience that self-pity never solved anything. It only made things worse.

Toni folded the quilt and returned it to the guest room. She went into the kitchen, dropped two slices of bread in the toaster, and grabbed a bottle of Coke from the refrigerator. She needed the caffeine. Her cell phone, a Droid X, was on the kitchen counter. She'd switched it to silent mode before the funeral and up until now hadn't wanted to turn the ringer back on.

When she woke the phone, it showed several missed calls and two text messages from Jill.

Jill had sent the first message right after she'd left the day before:

Just spoke 2 Mark. On his way. Call me.
Luv, J :)

So Jill *had* asked Mark to come over. Maybe he didn't need her shoulder after all. The second message had been sent just an hour earlier:

Don't want to call the house and wake U. Call me.
Luv, J :)

Toni decided to text Jill back, let her know she was okay, and that she would call her later in the afternoon.

The bread popped up in the toaster. Toni took a plate from the cabinet and coated the toast with a thick layer of blackberry preserves. But when she took a bite, the bread stuck in her throat, making her want to gag. The breakfast she ate nearly every day tasted like cardboard today.

She threw the toast in the trash and went upstairs to shower. She was starting to feel anxious. There was no reason for her to hang around the house alone. She might as well go in to the office. She could do a little research on Brian while she was there.

McKay-Wynn Properties was located in Blanton Hills near Interstate 65 in the Magnolia Springs Office Park. Toni parked her car in the spot reserved for her as the top producer and entered the large glass building. Shannon, the weekend receptionist, was at the front desk. Unlike some other real estate agencies, McKay-Wynn kept its office phones staffed seven days a week, a difference that made their listing owners very happy.

When Shannon saw Toni walk in, she stopped writing and put down her pen. "Toni? What are you doing here?"

Toni smiled. "Well, the last time I checked, I worked here."

"I meant—" Shannon's gaze fell to the floor.

"It's okay, I know what you meant. I just need to keep busy right now."

Shannon nodded.

Toni walked past her to the elevator and hit the call button to open its doors. She got on and pushed the button for the third floor.

Along with the reception area, the ground floor of the building housed the administrative offices, a full kitchen, and six private conference rooms. The second floor contained a training room where the managing broker held the weekly sales meetings, a computer room that allowed agents to access the multiple listing service, and a large bullpen area with agents' desks arranged back-to-back. The company reserved the third floor for the private offices of the top producers.

The elevator bell chimed, and the doors slid open. Toni's office was at the end of the hallway, her name on a wall plaque just beside the door. She breezed through the outer office past the two vacant desks belonging to her assistants, Janet and Cheryl, and then entered the second door to her own private corner office.

She noticed an express package on the side of her desk with a return address she didn't recognize. She put down her purse and briefcase and opened the box, spilling the packing peanuts across the floor. Inside was a package wrapped in white paper with a large cream-colored bow. Obviously a wedding gift. There was an envelope taped to the top. Toni opened it and read the card:

> *Toni—*
>
> *I saw your wedding announcement in* The Tennessean. *You looked absolutely beautiful. I am so happy for you.*
>
> *We're living in Memphis now. Bob decided to open another restaurant. His son is running the one in Nashville. I would love to see you sometime.*
>
> *Mom*

She had scribbled her new address and phone number at the bottom.

"And as usual, you're a little too late, Mother."

Toni tossed the unopened gift into the trash and turned on her laptop computer. She pulled up her favorite search engine and typed in Brian's name in quotes along with the name of the Washington, D.C.- based news magazine he worked for, *The World Revealed.* When she pressed Enter, a sea of hits filled the screen.

The magazine kept extensive archives online. There were articles written by Brian going back as many as five years—a lot to wade through. Stories on fraud in the meatpacking industry, political corruption, and organized crime, to name a few. What caught her eye was a seven-part exposé on a man named Edward Sheffield, a CIA assassin-turned-traitor. The article went into great depth regarding Sheffield's covert activities, including detailed information on his CIA training.

A chill prickled the tiny hairs on the back of her neck.

Brian knew a professional killer.

Toni printed the entire article; it might come in handy later. She wished she had access to Brian's personal information. She had come across a short biography listing his educational background and various awards he had earned, but could find nothing damaging. She would have loved to call a loan officer and have them pull a credit report, but to do that, she needed Brian's social security number. For now, she would just have to keep digging on her own.

There was a quick knock at the door, and Dana Dawson stepped into the office. Her mass of red hair was piled on top of her head with tendrils streaming down the sides of her face. She was wearing a light blue skirt and a boxy jacket reminiscent of Jackie Kennedy.

Fresh out of school, Dana had joined the agency less than a year earlier. They had clicked right from the start, and Toni had become somewhat of a mentor to the younger woman, sharing all the little secrets she'd learned on how to succeed in the business. She had taught her how to land an appointment from a cold call, explained that the expired inventory sheet—a listing of houses that had been on the market with other companies and failed to sell—was one of the best sources for new clients, and helped her practice her listing presentation.

Dana was a fast learner and a natural at sales and had already closed enough deals to afford the payments on a new C-Class Mercedes. She pulled Toni into an embrace. "I'm surprised to see you here," Dana said. "How're you feeling?"

"I'm okay."

"Are you sure? You know if there's some work that needs to be done that I'll be happy to take care of it for you."

"To be honest, I just needed to get out of the house. Work is a good distraction."

"Well, since you're here, I might as well tell you about your listing on Coldwater Court. I've got a buyer who's interested, but she wants the dining room drapes. I know it says in the MLS that they don't stay. I just put the contract on Janet's desk; I figured she could call them and try to work something out."

"If the money and terms are right, it probably won't cause a problem."

"Good." Dana noticed the package Toni had thrown away and pulled it from the trash. "What's this?"

"That's a wedding gift from the woman who calls herself my mother."

"Oh. Does she know about . . ."

Toni shook her head. "No. I don't know if she does or not."

"Would you like me to call her?"

Dana was aware that Toni and her mother didn't get along, but she didn't know the details as to why. That was one of the things Toni had shared only with Scott. "No, she'll find out soon enough."

Dana's cell phone rang and she placed the package on the edge of Toni's desk. "I have to take this, but I'll check back in on you later. You call me if you need anything—anything at all, okay?"

Dana closed the door behind her.

Toni stared at the package. She might as well open it, even though she intended to return whatever was inside. She slipped off the bow, pulled off the top of the box, and lifted out a Baccarat crystal vase. It was exquisite. And yet to Toni, it was about as desirable as a plague of locusts.

Why doesn't she get it? Toni thought. *She was never around when I needed her. So why does she think I would want her in my life now?*

Her mother had left one morning in November when Toni was only six years old. It was the day after her birthday, two days after Thanksgiving, and Toni woke up early. She went into the kitchen to help her mother with breakfast by stirring the pancake batter, a Saturday morning tradition. Instead, she found her father sitting at the table alone, his head cradled in his hands, sobbing. It was the first and only time she had ever seen him cry.

It took hours for him to find the words to tell her that her mother was gone. That she was not coming back. But he was quick to explain that it was not Toni's fault. That she had done nothing wrong.

Beginning that day, her father had raised her on his own, the best he knew how. Afraid of having his soul crushed again, he never remarried. He made Toni the focus of his life. He was the one who stayed up all night by her bedside when she had the measles. He worked twelve-hour days to put food on the table, clothes on her back, and to make certain she had all the things a young girl needed.

He did everything imaginable to ensure her life was as happy and normal as it could possibly be, including putting some money away to help pay for her college education. And when he became ill, Toni alone comforted him.

Against his protests, she took a semester off from college and cut a few hours from her job waiting tables in order to spend more time nursing him, willing him to live. But the cancer had been merciless, quickly spreading throughout his body. He succumbed to the disease the year she graduated.

Her mother, however, had left her by choice. She had never said goodbye, never explained anything. She just disappeared. No matter how many wishes Toni made when she threw pennies in that stupid fountain, her mother never came back. She never called. Not until the afternoon of Toni's twenty-first birthday—the day she reappeared at their front door. But by then, it was too late.

For some reason, Toni thought, her mother didn't seem to understand the concept of time. She didn't understand why Toni couldn't welcome her back with open arms and allow her to pick up right where she had left off, as if she had done nothing wrong.

Over the years, her mother had made a few attempts to set things right. When Toni had moved from Alabama to Tennessee, trying to make a fresh start, trying to leave the bad memories behind, her mother had followed. But Toni wasn't interested—not then and not now.

Her mother had sent a few birthday and Christmas cards and an occasional letter filled with the details of life with her second husband. Each one made Toni cringe. What had been so wrong with the life her mother had left? Why hadn't Toni and her father been good enough?

Tears of anger stung her eyes—anger at her mother, anger at her father's cancer, anger at losing Scott. With all the strength she could summon, she hurled the vase against the wall, shattering it into a million shimmering slivers.

The intercom buzzed. It was Shannon. Toni cleared her throat, took a deep breath, and pressed the answer button.

"Yes?"

"Are you taking calls?" Shannon asked her.

"Who is it?"

"Someone wanting information about your listing on Red Oak."

"Give it to the agent on floor duty. Oh, and Shannon, could you send up a broom and a dustpan? I've had a little accident."

"Yeah. I'll have somebody bring it right up."

"Thank you."

Toni swept up the mess as best she could, but only a vacuum would be able to pick up all the tiny shards buried in the carpet. Fortunately, the janitorial service scheduled their cleaning on Saturday nights. They should have better luck.

She carried the broom and dustpan into the outer office, leaned them against the wall, and then walked back to her desk. She gathered the pages of the exposé from the printer, opened her briefcase, and started to shove them inside. She stopped short when she saw a stack of listing paperwork she had completely forgotten about.

The house belonged to Josh Martin, a man she had once dated. After a few months, it became obvious they weren't romantically suited for each other, but they had remained friends. She had met with Josh the day before Scott died. He wanted to take care of all the paperwork necessary to get his home on the market before Toni left on her honeymoon.

He had postdated the listing forms because he was leaving town on business and didn't want the house shown until he returned. With all that had happened, the new listing had been the furthest thing from her mind.

Toni pulled out the forms and the small brown envelope containing two keys to Josh's house. One of the keys she stashed inside a lockbox. The other she left in the envelope.

She flipped through the MLS information, property condition disclosure, advertising sheets, and various other forms, making sure everything was completed and signed. Then she paper-clipped it all together and stuck it into a file folder with the key envelope. She attached a sticky note to the outside of the folder informing Janet and Cheryl about the special circumstances of the listing. Then she threw the lockbox into her briefcase along with Brian's article.

She turned back to the computer and started to close her search engine. On the screen, she spotted an item she had somehow overlooked and clicked on the link. Unlike the others, Brian had not written this article. Instead, in this particular story, he was the subject.

Her pulse quickened as she read the headline.

7

The phone rang twice.

"Hello?"

"Did you take care of it?"

"Everything's clean. I replaced the hard drive."

"What about backups?"

"I checked. There were none."

"Are you sure?"

"Positive."

The line went dead.

JUDGMENT AGAINST REPORTER FOR $2.1 MILLION.

Toni quickly scanned the article printed in the *Washington Times* a few months earlier. It chronicled a lawsuit between Brian and a midwestern meatpacking company. She remembered reading the story he had written accusing the management of bribing federal inspectors and knowingly shipping ground beef contaminated with salmonella and *Listeria monocytogenes* to fast food restaurants across the nation.

The company had sued, claiming Brian's allegations were false. They charged he had planted evidence while working undercover at the plant. Based on the testimony of two employees who claimed they had witnessed Brian's activities, a judge had ruled in the company's favor, finding Brian guilty of slander and ordering him to pay damages.

Toni clicked the print icon.

The story was exactly the kind of information she was looking for. Realtors were required to carry errors and omissions insurance, which would pay a portion of the damages if they ever found themselves on the losing end of a lawsuit. She wondered if reporters had any type of coverage. Either way, the article reinforced her suspicions.

Brian had a financial motive for murder.

Toni searched through her purse looking for the card the police detective had given her at the hotel. It had somehow lodged itself between the pages of her checkbook. She dialed the number for the Blanton Hills Police Department, printed below his name.

"I need to speak with Detective Russell Lewis, please."

"One moment," a female voice answered.

She put Toni on hold. After two verses of a Muzak version of the Beatles' "Hard Day's Night," the voice came back on the line. "I'm sorry, Detective Lewis isn't here. Can I take a message?"

"Do you know when he's expected back?"

"Just a minute." This time, instead of putting her on hold, Toni heard the woman cover the receiver with her hand, and then the sound of muffled voices in the background. "He's not due back on duty until Monday morning. Would you like me to leave a note for him to call you?"

The day and a half she would have to wait seemed more like a century. "No, that's okay. Thanks." She hung up the phone.

Toni knew the evidence was circumstantial, but she felt it was worth pursuing. She only hoped the detective would agree.

Mark climbed on the treadmill and set the speed at four miles per hour. He would walk at this pace for approximately three minutes before increasing to a slow jog and then finally to a six-mile-per-hour run. He followed the routine every other day, Monday through Saturday.

On the days he didn't run, he worked out with free weights. Although muscular, he stopped short of the bulked-up look common among the other men at the gym. His goal was to be fit, not a Schwarzenegger clone.

He twisted in his earbuds and plugged them into his iPod. He ran his thumb over the click wheel and scanned through the music. He pushed Play when he reached the album he had downloaded that morning by the band of the moment.

Something bordering on heavy metal blared in his ears. He couldn't quite make out the lyrics, but he didn't care. It was just background noise to him. Something to keep his momentum up, help propel him into the endorphin zone.

As he picked up his pace to five miles an hour, a petite brunette, dressed in a sports bra and running shorts, passed in front of the treadmill. She flashed him a smile and then a coy wave. Mark nodded and raised his hand in a greeting.

She was a regular, usually in the company of a blond bodybuilder who, he had assumed, was her boyfriend. Today she appeared to be alone. He didn't know her name, but her lithe form had occupied his mind more than once during his workouts.

His gaze followed her as she made her way to the drinking fountain. She removed the lid from her sports bottle and began filling it with water. She glanced up, made eye contact, and then quickly looked away. Mark turned his attention to the treadmill controls, increasing his speed to a run. When he looked up again, she was heading toward him. She smiled, took a sip from her bottle, and then hopped on the treadmill next to his.

She raised the incline and began walking at a leisurely pace. All the while, she kept glancing in his direction. Mark fixed his eyes on the TV screen built into the treadmill. It was funny watching the Darling clan mouth a hillbilly song on *The Andy Griffith Show* while he was listening to some wanna-be rocker murder a guitar.

Any other time, he would have pulled out his earbuds and initiated a conversation with the brunette. It was obvious she was interested. But aside from the fact that he didn't enjoy talking while he was trying to run, he just didn't feel like starting anything. He wasn't dating anyone seriously, and if he had seen her here alone a week ago, he would have been quick to ask her out. Now the desire was gone. It was strange.

Lately, the only person he could think about was Toni.

Mark had been married briefly. He and Emily had met the first year of law school. They were happily married for a time, blissfully even. Then he found out she was having an affair with one of her professors. He had always been faithful, had taken his vows seriously. When he found out she had strayed, he could no longer bear the sight of her.

He had met several interesting women since Emily, but none he wanted to grow old with. None who could make him forget the past and dare to take another shot at marriage. He preferred the single life. He could see whomever he wanted, whenever he wanted, without any complications.

So why did he keep finding himself wanting to spend time with Toni? No matter how hard he tried, he couldn't seem to get her out of his head. He told himself it was because of Scott—that he felt a responsibility to help her get through the pain. But he knew that was a lie. The truth was simple: Toni was the kind of woman who could make him want to try again. She was worth all the risks.

And that scared the hell out of him.

Brian sat low in the rental car, a blue Mustang convertible, the top up, his head covered by an Atlanta Braves baseball cap. He kept his eyes trained on Toni's car, parked in the lot across the street. She had surprised him by going out so early. He thought for sure she would sleep in.

He had arrived at her house around nine o'clock and found that she was already gone. But he had no trouble locating her, thanks to the satellite tracking device he had installed on the underside of her car the night before. The instrument came equipped with mapping software, which allowed him to monitor her whereabouts using the Internet.

Brian lifted the lid of the cooler on the floorboard of the passenger's side and pulled out a Coke. He ripped open a bag of chips. He had been sitting in front of Toni's office for nearly five hours. It was well past lunch, and his stomach was letting him know it.

Not only was he hungry; his legs were getting stiff. He had just turned thirty, but after hiding out in the trees the previous night, and sitting nearly motionless in the car all day, he was starting to think he was getting too old to be doing surveillance. This time though, he didn't have a choice. It wasn't a story that was on the line. It was his life.

Around four o'clock, Toni walked out of the building and got into her car. Brian had hidden a listening device under her seat. When she started the engine, music from her radio blared through the receiver—Boston singing "Don't Look Back." He hoped she would take the song's advice.

He waited for her to pull out of the parking lot and onto the street before falling in behind.

Toni opened the glass door of the Sub-Zero refrigerator and stared inside. She had a choice to make: tuna casserole number one, tuna casserole number two, some kind of shepherd's pie dish, or a green bean casserole. Not one of them looked appetizing.

She was clad in one of Scott's T-shirts that fell to mid-thigh, and the cool air brought goose bumps to her bare legs as she stood and contemplated the selections. She pulled open the freezer drawer and found a lone pint of chocolate ice cream. There wasn't much else to eat. She hadn't been to the grocery store in over a week—not that she ever bought a lot of food. With their busy schedules, she and Scott had pretty much lived on restaurant fare.

She grabbed a spoon from the cutlery drawer and opted for the ice cream. She hadn't eaten since the failed attempt at toast that morning, and she was starting to feel a little sick. She threw the lid in the trash and headed for the family room. Before she could eat the first bite, the doorbell rang. She peeked out the sidelight. It was Mark.

Toni stuck her spoon into the ice cream container and opened the door. She wondered if Jill had called him again. She'd talked to her best friend an hour or so earlier and found out one of Clint's brothers had been rushed to the hospital for an appendectomy. Since Jill was otherwise engaged, she'd probably laid a guilt trip on Mark and ordered him to come over again. "Back so soon?"

"Get dressed. We're going out," Mark said.

"I really don't feel like going anywhere tonight, if it's all the same to you."

"What's that you're eating?"

Toni smiled and hid the ice cream behind her back.

"Yeah, I know," Mark said. "That's why we're going out."

They drove to Santini's, Toni's favorite Italian restaurant, and ordered an extra-large pizza with spicy beef, mushrooms, green peppers, and black olives. The delicious scents of garlic, tomato sauce, and various meats wafting from the kitchen caused her mouth to water, and she realized how truly hungry she was.

Toni sipped her soda and let her gaze travel across the room. As usual, the place was packed. All of the tables, topped with white linen cloths and accented with a single red rose, were filled. She couldn't help but remember the last time she'd been here with Scott. It was the week before the wedding, and they had been so happy. Neither of them knew that their time together would be so short.

"Tell me what Scott was like when he was growing up," she said.

"Let me see. He was athletic—practically lived outdoors. And popular. He always had about a dozen girls swarming around. And he never could resist a challenge. He excelled at everything he ever did. Everything always came easy for Scott."

"I really wish I could have known him back then." Toni picked up a mushroom that had fallen from her pizza. "Were you close to Brian?"

"Well, he was always around. But he was three years younger. He had his own group of friends. Why do you ask?"

"You know me—I want to be prepared, that's all. I just need to know who I'm up against."

"Don't worry about that. I have a feeling we'll win."

The inheritance was not what was on her mind. She couldn't care less about the money. The only thing that interested her was finding out what really happened to Scott. And it seemed that Brian might be the only one who knew the answer.

"Was Brian anything like Scott?" Toni asked.

"In some ways. But he was quieter. He played sports the same as Scott, but he also liked to read. He was always making up stories. He had a great imagination."

"Did he have a temper?"

"That's a strange question. What's going on in that head of yours?"

"Well, if things go his way, Brian stands to gain a substantial sum of money from Scott's death. I was just thinking, What if it wasn't an accident?"

Mark reached across the table and took her hand. "Toni, you have to let this go. Brian had nothing to do with Scott's death. You can't keep looking for someone to blame. I know you don't want to believe it, but Scott's the one and only person responsible."

"That's not true."

"I'm sorry, but it is."

Toni pulled her hand away. "Excuse me."

She got up from the table and headed for the restroom. She didn't care what Mark thought; she had to keep digging. Brian was responsible—he had murdered Scott. And she was going to prove it.

8

After spending Sunday with Mark, streaming movies from Netflix, on Monday morning, Toni went down to the Blanton Hills Police Department and asked to see Detective Lewis. The officer at the front desk gave her the once-over before he picked up the phone and dialed the extension. She could guess what he was wondering: *Is this woman a criminal, a victim, or a jilted lover?*

"There's a Toni Matthews here to see Lewis," he said into the receiver. "Okay. Yeah." He put the phone down. "Detective Lewis is with somebody right now. If you'll have a seat, we'll let you know when he's finished."

The waiting area was empty. Toni sat in the chair nearest to the front desk, pulled the *Washington Times* article from her purse, and read it again. If a judge had been convinced that Brian was capable of planting evidence just to get a story, then she should be able to convince the police that he might be capable of more. She could get Detective Lewis to reopen the case and question Brian as a possible suspect.

Did they even ask his whereabouts at the time Scott died? And why was Brian at the hotel that morning? Clint hadn't even had time to contact her before she arrived. How did Brian know? How did he manage to get there before she did?

"Miss Matthews?" The officer at the desk motioned for her. "Detective Lewis is free now."

Another officer led her down a hallway to a pale green room filled with metal desks arranged in groups of four. The detective's desk was off by itself in the far right corner.

"Hello, Miss Matthews." Detective Lewis held out his hand. Toni shook it and then sat down in the chair he offered. "What can I do for you today?"

"I need to talk to you about your investigation into Scott's death."

"What's on your mind?"

"You need to reopen the case because I know it wasn't an accident, and I know he didn't commit suicide."

The detective shook his head. "Miss Matthews, I can assure you that we did a thorough investigation—"

"He was pushed."

Detective Lewis sighed and scooted his chair back. "Wait here. I'll go get the file."

Toni looked around the office. Three other policemen were in the room. One was talking on the telephone; another was typing something into a computer. The third man was wading through a stack of papers on his desk. Another police officer came in and handed a message to the man on the phone. She smiled at Toni and then left again.

After a few minutes, Detective Lewis returned with the file. "Now, you were saying?"

"Scott's death was not an accident, and he didn't jump. He was pushed off that balcony."

The detective leafed through the file. "That's impossible. We have two witnesses who were there when Mr. Chadwick arrived at the scene. He entered the building alone."

"Someone could have been waiting for him."

"Miss Matthews—"

"Did you know that Scott's brother, Brian, is contesting the will? Do you know that he's in financial trouble?"

The detective sat back and rubbed his right temple. "I understand that this is hard for you to accept, but we've ruled out homicide. There was nothing at the scene to indicate foul play. Mr. Chadwick took his own life."

"No. No, he wouldn't do that."

"We have evidence to the contrary. We have a statement from his business partner, a statement from his attorney, we spoke to—" he stopped short.

"Who? Who did you speak to?"

The detective quickly closed the file as if there was something in it he didn't want Toni to see. "His business associates—and they all indicated the same thing. Mr. Chadwick was very distraught over a business deal, and he even mentioned the possibility of suicide as a way out. It's unfortunate that no one took him seriously."

"No, they're wrong. If Scott ever said anything about killing himself, then it was only because he was joking."

Detective Lewis moved the closed file from his lap and placed it on the desk. "How long had you been acquainted with Mr. Chadwick?"

"I've known Scott for two years. Why?"

The detective picked up a picture frame and turned it toward Toni. Inside was a photo of an attractive woman, probably in her late forties, with short brown hair. "This is my wife, Barbara. We'll be celebrating our twenty-ninth wedding anniversary next month. I love her more now than I did the day we were married. But no matter how close we are or how much I love her, there are still things she doesn't know about me. Things she'll never know."

Tears of frustration threatened Toni's eyes, but she managed to hold them back. She realized that no matter what she said, Detective Lewis was not going to change his mind. He thought she was completely delusional. There would be no help from the police. She was on her own.

"Can you at least give me the names of the two witnesses who saw Scott that morning?" she asked.

He glanced inside the file. "The lead superintendent, Alvin Harney, and one of the workmen, Nico Williams." The detective started to rise indicating that their conversation was over.

"Can I borrow your pen?" Toni reached across the desk knocking the file onto the floor. She rushed to help the detective pick up the scattered papers. She didn't see much, only a name.

Gloria Keith.

Detective Lewis put the file under his arm and handed Toni his pen. He shot her an accusing look. He knew that spilling the file was no accident. Toni jotted the names down on a sticky note and stuffed it into her purse. She gave the detective back his pen. "Thank you for your help." *Or, rather, lack of it.*

"Do yourself a favor, Miss Matthews. Go home, have a good cry, and then get on with your life."

"Oh, I've cried—I've cried more than enough. Now it's time I did something about it."

Toni left the police station and drove north on Interstate 65 toward downtown Nashville and the offices of Chadwick & Shore. She remembered the first time she'd driven into the city, right after her father had died. She'd made the decision to leave her painful past and the small Alabama town she'd called home for twenty-three years to begin a new life.

Like so many other hopeful souls arriving in the metropolis known as Music City, she had come to live out her dreams. Her first sighting of the battalion of tall buildings standing sentry on the bank of the Cumberland River—silvery columns against an azure sky—had filled her with anticipation.

She'd marveled at the unusual architecture of the AT&T building, the tallest in the state. She would later learn the skyscraper had been dubbed the Batman Building by the local residents due to its resemblance to the superhero's mask, the twin spires rising toward the heavens reminiscent of his pointy ears.

Her first night in town, she'd walked along Second Avenue and down Lower Broadway checking out bars and restaurants like the Bluegrass Inn and the Honky Tonk Grill, where you could dine on a fried bologna sandwich, a MoonPie, and a Goo Goo Cluster. The streets bustled with tourists, natives, and newcomers like herself, and she was immediately swept up in the excitement pulsing through the city where dreams could come true.

She'd had hardly any money, but was quick to drop whatever she could spare into the hats of the performers who belted out country songs and strummed their guitars on the sidewalks, their talent waiting to be discovered. But unlike so many of them whose hopes had been crushed, who'd returned home with nothing but empty pockets, she'd found all she'd come for and more.

She'd made it. She was one of the top-selling agents in the area, and until just a few days ago, her life had been close to perfect.

She picked up her cell phone and dialed her assistant Janet. "How're things going this morning?" Toni asked.

"Well, Dana brought in a contract on Coldwater Court and the sellers countered, but it looks like the buyers have decided to accept."

"Dana told me about that offer. Good job. Oh, I almost forgot, there's also a contract on my desk that needs to be initialed."

"I found it, and I've already called the homeowners. They've agreed to the change, and Cheryl is going to run the contract out to them this afternoon."

"Okay, good. It sounds like the two of you have everything under control. I won't be in the office today, but if something comes up, you can reach me on my cell."

"Will do. And Toni—"

"Yeah?"

"Cheryl and I just want you to know that if you need anything . . ." Her voice started to break before trailing off.

"I know. And I appreciate it."

Detective Lewis returned the Chadwick file to the proper cabinet. Fortunately, he had thought to remove all the photos taken at the scene before going in to meet with Miss Matthews. She had knocked the file off the desk on purpose, and he was glad she hadn't seen the shots of the deceased. They weren't the type of images you wanted etched into the mind of the bereaved. She was having a hard enough time as it was.

He had seen the same type of scenario played out a thousand times during his thirty-year career in law enforcement. The details were always slightly different, but the underlying theme remained the same. A loved one was convinced that the defendant, or in this case the deceased, was beyond reproach. That somehow the police were wrong. They misunderstood the person in question.

He remembered one woman in particular who had stood by her boyfriend, believing he was innocent up until the very day of his execution. It didn't matter that he had confessed to raping and murdering seven teenage girls. She claimed the police had framed him, that they had coerced him into giving a false confession.

Toni Matthews was suffering from the same blind faith. He knew she wouldn't be satisfied until she had conducted her own mini-investigation. She was an intelligent woman. It shouldn't take her long to gather all the facts. He wished he could have gotten through to her. That she had listened to him. He only hoped she could handle the information she would uncover.

Some things she was better off not knowing.

Chadwick & Shore Construction was located on Commerce Street across from the AT&T building. Toni pulled into the parking garage, below street level, and stopped at the guard station. The attendant noticed the green and gold parking sticker on her windshield and raised the security arm to let her through.

She parked in Scott's space, next to Clint's Mercedes, and rode the elevator to the lobby. The twenty-three-story building housed several companies, with the offices of Chadwick & Shore filling the top three floors.

Toni crossed the lobby and entered the second elevator along with a well-dressed woman and a small child with strawberry-blond hair. The little boy, not more than five years old, held a package wrapped in bright red paper.

"My daddy works here, and he's gonna take us out to eat," the boy said. "Today's his birthday and he's really old, like fifty whole years. He's a cow nut."

"An accountant," his mother corrected.

Toni smiled. "Really? I'll bet you've got something special for him in that box."

"No, this is just a stupid ole shirt that my mom got for him at the store this morning."

"Oh, I see. What did you want to get him?" Toni asked.

The boy's blue eyes sparkled. "He really needs a puppy."

The elevator dinged, and the woman led the child out. "Bye," he called.

"Good-bye," Toni said.

The image of the little boy tugged at her heart. He looked exactly the way she had pictured her own son would look. A perfect blending of herself and Scott.

When she reached the twenty-first floor, Toni stepped out into the reception area of the construction firm. Five men, dressed in dark suits, occupied the twin leather sofas and one of the wing-back chairs. Each wore a grim look. *Bankers,* Toni thought. An administrative assistant was serving them coffee and pastries.

Toni nodded at the receptionist behind the front desk as she made her way to the elevator that would take her to Clint's office on the twenty-third floor. She got on and pushed the button. A young woman she didn't recognize, her arms loaded with file folders, rushed toward the elevator.

"Hold the door, please!"

Toni stuck her hand out, and the doors slid back.

"Thanks," the woman said.

"No problem."

The woman bit her lip as if she was trying to think of something to say. "I was really sorry to hear about Mr. Chadwick. We all were. He was a great person to work for."

"Thank you. I appreciate your saying so."

When the doors opened at the top floor, the woman disappeared around the corner. Toni continued on toward Clint's office.

His secretary was away from her desk, and the door to his office stood ajar. Toni tapped on it. When she received no answer, she peeked inside.

The office was empty. She returned to the secretary's desk and scribbled a note for Clint to call her. She marked it urgent and put it on the top of the other messages in his box.

As she was leaving his office, she ran into Jill in the hallway.

"Toni, I'm so glad you're here. I was just getting ready to call you and see if you wanted to have lunch," Jill said.

"Yeah, that sounds good. Do you know where Clint is? I need to talk to him about something."

"He's in a meeting right now, and he probably won't be free for another couple of hours."

Toni glanced at her watch. It was almost eleven o'clock.

"Why don't we go out to lunch, and you can talk to him when we get back," Jill said.

They walked to Demos', a steak and spaghetti place at the corner of Commerce and Third Avenue. Although the restaurant had just opened for the day, it was already starting to fill up. The hostess led them to a table by the front window with a view of the parking garage across the street. As soon as they were seated, their waiter appeared, recited the day's specials, and took their drink order.

"Did you get any sleep after Mark left last night?" Jill asked.

Toni nodded. She'd gotten more than she'd expected.

"I'm sorry I had to be at the hospital all night Saturday, but you know how much of a worrier Clint's mother is. Even though the doctor assured us that the surgery was routine, she was really upset. I just couldn't leave her like that."

"Don't be sorry; she's your family. You needed to be there—not just for her but for Clint."

"You're my family too."

Toni could feel tears rising in her eyes. With all the crying she'd done, it was a miracle her body wasn't completely dehydrated.

"You okay?" Jill asked.

Toni nodded and took a deep breath. She needed to tell Jill about the information she'd dug up on Brian—about the judgment against him.

She'd already told her about the will, but she'd held back on her suspicions of murder. She'd been afraid what her friend would think, that she would doubt her sanity, but sitting here with Jill now, she felt it was time to confess her feelings. Toni was just about to spill it all when the waiter returned.

He carried a tray with two soft drinks and a basket of bread. He placed them on the table. "Are you ready to order?" he asked.

"I'll have the medallions of sirloin," Jill said.

After he had taken their orders, the waiter disappeared again. He'd been gone only a second when a lady in a beige pantsuit spotted Jill. Jill introduced the woman and her male companion to Toni, and they exchanged pleasantries.

Once the couple had moved on to their own table, Toni scanned the room. Right away, she picked out three people she recognized, and all of them knew Scott. She wondered whether the crowded restaurant was the right place to talk about Brian. Maybe it would be best if she waited until after they left.

"So what did you want to talk to Clint about?" Jill asked.

Toni hesitated. It was hard to explain to her best friend that her husband might have lied to the police.

"Was it about the business?"

Toni tilted her head. "Well, um . . ."

"If you're worried about it, don't be. Clint was going to call you; he was just waiting for the right time. We didn't think you'd be ready to discuss it yet."

"Discuss what, exactly?"

"He wanted to talk to you about buying Scott's share of the business. Since you have a career of your own, we didn't figure you'd want to deal with the construction company too."

"I don't know. I haven't even thought about it."

"You know he'll make sure you get market value. We're working on an appraisal right now."

Toni's thoughts started to spin. The business had been the last thing on her mind, and she had no idea what she wanted to do. Everything was happening too fast. "It may not be mine to sell," she said. "There's a chance Scott's half might go to Brian."

"Now don't you worry about that. Mark's consulting with the best probate attorney in the state, and Brian won't get a dime."

"I'm not completely convinced of that yet."

The waiter interrupted with a salad for Toni and a cup of soup for Jill. "Can I get you anything else right now?"

"I think we're fine," Jill said.

Toni poked at her salad with her fork, her mind on her meeting with the police detective.

"Is there something else bothering you?" Jill asked. "You seem a million miles away."

"I went down to the police station this morning and talked with Detective Lewis, the officer who investigated Scott's death. He said he took statements from Clint and from some of Scott's business associates and that someone told him Scott mentioned suicide."

"And you think it was Clint?"

"I hope not, but he's never come out and said that he doesn't believe it, so I have to wonder."

Jill took a sip of her soup, and then patted her lips with her napkin. "I don't think Clint would ever say anything like that, but there is something he doesn't want you to know."

"What?"

Jill hesitated, a worried look in her eyes.

"Tell me. Whatever it is, I need to know."

Jill nodded. "You're right. It is time you found out." She glanced around the restaurant and then lowered her voice. "Scott was in trouble."

9

Clint adjusted his tie, took a deep breath, and walked into the conference room.

The group of men assembled around the table represented five different lending institutions. Each held a note on at least one of the projects currently under construction with Chadwick & Shore—projects that Scott had spearheaded. With him gone, Clint knew the bankers were questioning the solidity of the company. He had to do everything in his power to quell the lenders' fears before they turned to panic.

Financing strategy was like playing with dominos. If any one of the banks decided to call in its loans, the others would follow. But if he could steady the shakiest, keep it from toppling, they would all stand.

"Gentlemen," Clint said. He shook each of their hands, taking note of the icy mood that pervaded the room. "I'm glad you could all make the meeting."

"We wouldn't miss it. And as I told you at the funeral, Clint, you have my condolences. I know everyone in this room agrees that Scott Chadwick was a fine man, and we're all saddened by this loss." The man who spoke was Tyler Armstrong. His bank held construction loans on a strip mall and a condominium complex just south of Nashville.

The other men nodded and offered their own words of sympathy. As the room quieted, Tyler regained the floor. "As much as we've all enjoyed doing business with Chadwick & Shore, it's no secret that we're a bit nervous given the manner of Scott's death."

"There's absolutely no reason to be anxious," Clint said. "I'm sure that once we're finished here, once you see what the company has planned, your minds will be put at ease."

The eldest of the group, Randall Clarke, shook his head. "Rumor has it that Chadwick & Shore is in financial trouble," he said.

"I've never put much stock in rumors," Clint said. "Neither should you."

"When a partner commits suicide, it does make one wonder," Randall said.

The other men nodded in agreement.

"I can assure you," Clint said, "Scott's problems were his own and had nothing to do with Chadwick & Shore. The company is financially sound, as you'll see from the presentation."

Clint dimmed the lights and then flipped the hidden switch that controlled the huge wide-screen LCD monitor on the wall at the other end of the table, turning it on. A cable running beneath the floor connected the monitor to his laptop computer. He clicked the file icon on his desktop, and the presentation began.

After a brief introduction, images of ongoing projects flashed across the screen. Details such as estimated cost, sales price, and date of completion accompanied each. Clint watched the men in the glow from the monitor. Their faces remained solemn.

Pompous sons of bitches. It was his business that paid their salaries and their mortgages, and sent their kids to college. Not so long ago, they had competed viciously for the opportunity to work with Chadwick & Shore. And they would again. They would beg for the chance. Clint would make sure of it.

Scott and Clint had started the business right after college with very little money. Chadwick & Shore had grown into a multimillion-dollar company, surpassing everyone's expectations—especially those of Clint's father.

Clint's parents owned a plumbing business. Although it had always somehow managed to pay the bills, Shore Plumbing had never amounted to much. In Clint's opinion, his father lacked the drive necessary to create a successful company. He was satisfied just *getting along*, as he called it. And Clint's two older brothers seemed content to follow in that tradition.

But since early childhood, Clint knew his life would consist of greater things. He wasn't about to spend his time snaking out toilets or pumping septic tanks. He wanted nothing to do with the family business. Instead, while in high school, he got a job at an electronics store in the mall.

He worked nights and weekends, earning commissions on each stereo and television he sold. He became quite the salesman. And instead of blowing his money on pizza and beer like his friends did, he followed the advice of one of his father's clients and had it invested in mutual funds.

He kept his grades up, graduating as valedictorian, and landed a scholarship to Vanderbilt. It was there that he met Scott. He knew he had found the right person to help him build his own fortune. And they had done just that.

Now, with Clint solo at the helm, free to explore his own ideas, the company would soar even higher. He'd no longer have Scott to hold him back, to stifle his creativity by telling him all the reasons that his concepts wouldn't work.

Developments in the pipeline, under contract but not yet begun, filled the screen next. Clint noticed Tyler Armstrong discreetly entering something into his smartphone. The ice was thawing. They would all be vying for the financing on the new projects before they even left the building.

Graphs and a detailed report showing the earnings and profit projections for the next two years marked the end of the presentation. Clint turned up the lights and switched off the monitor. He passed out bound material detailing the information from the presentation. As he handed each man a folder, he noticed a change in their countenance. Even Randall Clarke looked impressed.

"As you can see," Clint said, "Chadwick & Shore has a very bright future ahead. Together, we will continue to profit from our endeavors."

Tyler Armstrong stood up. "We all know that Scott was the driving force of this company. Without him, what assurance do we have that the projects will be completed on time?"

Because Scott had been hands-on with every aspect of their projects, they somehow seemed to think Clint was incapable of running the business alone. He wished he could tell every one of them to go to hell. However, he sensed that he had all but won their loyalty. He couldn't let a seed of doubt slip in now.

"Scott Chadwick was the front man, that's true," Clint said. "However, the real force, the gear that makes the clock tick, is on the inside, behind the scenes. Let me make myself clear, gentlemen. I am, and always have been, the heart and soul of this company."

Jill stirred her soup. "Scott didn't want you to know either," she said. "He didn't want you to worry."

"Worry about what? Tell me what was going on," Toni said.

Jill put down her spoon. "Scott—all of us—we almost lost everything."

"What are you talking about?"

"When we first met with AlquilaCorp, the company under contract to purchase the hotel, they insisted that Scott add certain architectural elements into the design. The sales contract they signed was based on those initial plans and specs. But when the hotel went up, Scott had to make some structural changes to the plans to ensure the building would be sound. When the head of AlquilaCorp found out, he threw a fit and threatened to back out of the contract."

So that's what was on Scott's mind the night before he died. How could he have kept this a secret from her? How could Jill? "Why didn't you tell me any of this?"

"Scott asked me not to."

The answer galled her. "Well I really don't see how one deal falling through could cause Chadwick & Shore to lose everything."

"Because of the construction loan. The bank agreed to the loan only because we already had a contract on the hotel. If they ever found out the buyer had cancelled, they'd call in the note. If that happened, it would cripple the company. We'd have to sell off all of our assets, maybe even declare bankruptcy."

"As long as you were making the interest payments, I don't see why you couldn't just wait it out and find another buyer."

"It's not that simple. You're used to the residential market. There's always another buyer ready to purchase a new home if the contract falls through—everybody needs a place to live. But finding a buyer for a luxury hotel is a whole other ball game. The bank knows that. They would foreclose on the loan, and when the word got out, the other banks we deal with would call in their notes too. They would all scramble to get out with as much of their money as possible, as fast as possible."

"So why does Clint want to buy half of a company that's on the verge of bankruptcy?"

"Because the deal didn't fall through. The afternoon Scott died, we reached a compromise with AlquilaCorp. If Scott had waited just a few more hours . . ."

The waiter returned with their entrees and a fresh basket of bread. Toni hadn't eaten one bite of her salad.

"Is something wrong with your food?" the waiter asked.

"No," Toni said. "It's fine."

"Then I'll leave it with you." He removed Jill's soup bowl from the table. "Enjoy." He headed back toward the kitchen.

Toni stared at her chicken. The possibility of losing the contract on the hotel might send some people over the edge, but not Scott. She had never known him to run away from his problems; he always faced them head-on. "You've known Scott for five years; you know how strong he was, how he never gave up. Do you really think he could have killed himself?"

"When we applied for the construction loan on the hotel, they required us to sign personal guarantees. If the bank had foreclosed, they could have taken all of Scott's personal assets, including your house."

"You didn't answer my question."

Jill dropped her gaze, studied her plate for a moment, and then looked directly into Toni's eyes. "The last thing in the world I want to do is hurt you. But I have to be honest, because I'd want you to be honest with me."

Toni knew what Jill was about to say, and she didn't want to hear it.

"I do think he committed suicide," Jill said. "I'm sorry."

They finished their meal in silence, neither of them knowing what to say. They were on opposite sides of the situation, each believing her view of the world was the right one.

Toni moved her food around her plate, barely eating anything. After the waiter had cleared their dishes, Jill reached across the table and touched Toni's arm. "I know how hard this was for you to hear, but I can help you get through it if you'll let me."

"I just don't understand how you can be so sure."

"Because my mama did the same thing."

"I thought your mother died from cancer."

"She was dying of cancer, but it was an overdose that killed her. She just couldn't handle the treatments anymore—they made her so weak and sick. She just wanted the pain to be over once and for all."

"But Scott wasn't in pain."

"There's pain in humiliation and in the fear of losing everything you've worked your whole life for."

The waiter brought their check, and Jill insisted on paying.

As they walked back to Chadwick & Shore, the sidewalk bustled with hungry souls, all hurrying to get in and out of one of the restaurants before their lunch hour was over. The traffic crawled bumper-to-bumper beside them.

The temperature had climbed into the seventies underneath a clear sky. The sun warmed the top of Toni's head and she wished she had worn a lighter-weight suit. When they reached their building, she remembered a question she had wanted to ask. "Who's Gloria Keith?"

Jill slowed her pace. "Gloria Keith?" She shook her head. "I don't know. The name doesn't sound familiar to me. Why do you ask?"

"Her name's in Scott's file at the police station."

"What did the detective say about her?"

"Nothing. I wasn't supposed to see it, so I didn't ask him."

"Maybe she was one of Scott's secretaries or a temp or something. Our clerical staff changes so often, I can't keep up."

"Maybe."

Toni pulled open the door of the office building and let Jill enter first.

As Jill turned to the right toward Chadwick & Shore, Toni veered to the left.

"Aren't you coming up to see Clint?" Jill asked.

And hear the same story repeated? Toni thought. *What good would that do?* "No. Just tell him I'll talk to him later." Toni started to walk toward the garage elevator.

"Wait," Jill stopped her. "I can't stand leaving things like this. You know that you're the sister I never had, and I couldn't bear to lose you."

Toni didn't know what to say. In a way, she could understand the reason Jill was so quick to accept that Scott committed suicide because she'd been through the same thing with her mother. But even knowing that and even though she loved Jill, she still felt hurt and betrayed. "You won't lose me."

Jill's lips formed a smile her eyes did not reflect. "I have to run by the hospital after work, but I'll call you, and we can get together after that."

"Sounds good." Toni continued toward the elevator.

She really had no desire to spend an evening with Jill and Clint. It was funny how quickly things changed. Just a week ago, she, Scott, Clint, and Jill had been the closest of friends. Now it felt as if those days never existed and they had never known Scott at all.

She took the elevator to the garage and walked to her car. She noticed Clint's Mercedes was gone. His meeting must be over. She slid into the driver's seat and buckled her safety belt. Her cell phone rang. A glance at the caller ID display revealed it was Mark.

"Hi, Mark," Toni said.

"Hey, where are you? I hope you're not working today."

"No, I'm just running some errands."

"I thought you might want to meet for lunch."

"Actually, I just ate. I had lunch with Jill."

"Really? That's good."

"Uh-huh."

"Well, how about dinner later?"

She knew Mark had better things to do than to keep babysitting her.

She had already consumed enough of his free time since Scott died. She couldn't keep imposing on him. She had to let him get back to living his own life.

"I've already made plans for tonight," she lied. "How about a rain check?"

"Oh. Okay. I'll call you later then."

Toni hung up the phone and drove out of the parking garage and onto Commerce Street. She dug into her purse and pulled out the sticky note from the police station. She read the names.

Alvin Harney.

She remembered Scott mentioning him, saying that he was the best lead superintendent in the business. The other name she didn't recognize.

She turned left on Fourth Avenue and then merged onto Interstate 40. She opened her sunroof and turned on the radio. Voices from the talk station filled the car. A local financial advisor offered words of encouragement to a caller overwhelmed by credit card debt. Too depressing. Toni switched to the classic rock station.

American woman . . .

She cranked up the volume. Forcing all thoughts from her mind, she traveled down the highway toward the hotel, singing along with The Guess Who.

Two cars back, a green sedan followed.

10

Toni paused inside the open gate to the construction site. The last time she had been here, the hotel was deserted. Now the structure swarmed with workers. She imagined this was the scene that had greeted Scott every day.

Men streamed in and out of the building, carrying various tools and materials, their shirts drenched with sweat. They were so focused on the job at hand that no one seemed to notice her. But then she realized, the men were probably used to female suits visiting the site, and the way Scott had run things, they'd probably all been warned against catcalls.

A high pitched *beep—beep—beep* pierced the steady hum of equipment. She turned to her right and saw a man on a forklift unloading drywall from a long-bed truck. Straight ahead, the mammoth tower crane hoisted windows to one of the upper floors. She raised her hand to her brow and shielded her eyes from the sun, watching the ascent of the glass. A crew waited high above, ready to receive the load.

She turned her attention back to ground level and scanned the sea of yellow hard hats searching for one in white, worn by those in management. She spotted a man she assumed was the lead superintendent off to the left, talking on a cell phone. She headed in his direction.

The air was heavy with dust from the naked soil. It swirled around her feet as she walked, leaving a light film on her emerald green pumps. As she approached, the man flipped off his cell phone and returned it to the clip on his belt.

"Are you Alvin Harney?" she asked.

"That's me." He took a rag from his pocket and dabbed at the sweat on the back of his neck. "What can I do for you?"

"My name is Toni Matthews. I was engaged to Scott Chadwick, and I was hoping I could have a few minutes of your time."

"Yes, I recognize you, and I'm really sorry about Mr. Chadwick. He was a good man."

"Thank you."

"You really shouldn't be out here in the open without a hard hat. We can talk in the office."

Alvin ushered her to the construction trailer. He unlocked the door and motioned for her to enter first. Once inside, she sat down at the same table she had sat at the day Scott died. She noticed the drawings of the hotel on the walls and the desk and filing cabinets on the left. Funny, she hadn't been aware of them on her last visit. On that day, almost everything around her had been a blur.

Alvin pulled out the chair across from her. As he sat down, he removed his hard hat and placed it on the edge of the table. Sweat had plastered his short salt-and-pepper hair flat to the sides of his head.

"Now, what did you want to talk to me about?" he asked.

"I was hoping you could tell me what happened here the morning Scott died."

"Well, I can tell you what I know, but it's not much."

"Please. Anything at all would be helpful."

"I got here a few minutes past five, and Scott arrived shortly after that. He didn't stop in the parking area; he drove his car right through the gate and around to the back side of the hotel. I had a few things I needed to check on before I met with him, so I came in here to my desk. I guess it was about fifteen or twenty minutes later when I went looking for him." Alvin paused and his eyes watered slightly. "I was the one who found him."

Toni felt the wound inside her opening again, and she fought back the rising tears. She couldn't let herself fall apart. "So you never actually spoke to Scott that morning?"

"No, I didn't."

"Are you sure he was alone?"

"Yeah, I'm sure. I couldn't have been more than five feet from his car when he passed through the gate, and there was no one with him."

"Is there any way someone could've been inside the hotel waiting for him?"

"I don't know how. When I arrived, the gate was locked. If somebody got in, they would've had to climb over the razor wire."

"You didn't see anyone else around the site?"

"The only other person here was Nico Williams, but he never went into the building. He was standing right outside my office the whole time."

"How do you know?"

"I could see him. The door was open, and he was out there talking on his cell phone."

Toni sighed in frustration. She was getting nowhere. "Could I speak to Mr. Williams? Maybe he saw something."

"It would be fine with me, if I knew where he was."

"What do you mean?"

"I haven't seen him since the day Scott died."

"He quit?"

Alvin shrugged. "It's fairly common in the construction business. Most of the workers here are family men with roots in the community, but there are also a lot who tend to move from place to place. It's not unusual for a man to come in and work a few days, collect a paycheck, and then you never see him again."

"How long did Mr. Williams work here?"

"He had just started. Last Monday was his first day."

"You don't have any idea where I could reach him?"

"No. Your best bet is to try the personnel department. They should have an address on file."

"Right." Toni chewed her lip. There had to be something she was missing. "Is there any way at all that somebody could've slipped into the hotel while you were at your desk?"

"I guess anything is possible. But if they did, Nico Williams would've seen them come through the gate."

"Did you talk to him about what happened?"

"No. I called 911 from my cell phone and then I waited there with the—with Mr. Chadwick until the police arrived. They were here within minutes. I don't remember speaking to Nico after that, but I know the police took a statement from him."

"Were you the one who called Clint?"

"I called him on his mobile phone, but I couldn't get an answer. I didn't know his home number, and it's not listed. Someone from the police department finally reached him."

"What about Brian?"

"Who?"

"Scott's brother. Brian Chadwick."

"To tell you the truth, until the funeral, I didn't know he had a brother. I knew you and Scott were getting married, so I wanted to call you. But seeing him lying there . . . I was just trying to comprehend how this had happened, and my brain went into a stall. I couldn't remember your name. When the police asked me who they should contact, the only person I could think of was Clint Shore."

Toni sighed again and then stood up. "I appreciate your taking the time to answer my questions. I know you must think it's odd."

"Not at all. I'd be doing the same thing if I were you. I never would've believed it if I hadn't been here myself."

Toni nodded. "I'll let you get back to work now."

His hat in his hand, Alvin started to open the trailer door, then paused. "Miss Matthews, I understand what you're going through. I lost my own wife a few years back. She was in a car accident, and I'm still not completely over it. I probably won't ever be. I try to concentrate on the good times we had together. They were the happiest times of my life. And even though it hurts now, I wouldn't trade one minute with her for all the money in the world. Knowing her was the greatest gift I ever received. I remind myself of that every time I start to miss her. Instead of dwelling on what I've lost, I think about how lucky I am to have had her in my life."

"Scott always spoke very highly of you, and not just professionally. Now I can see why."

The water was returning to Alvin's eyes. "Thank you. I thought the world of him. Still do."

They shook hands and Toni left the construction trailer. She kept her head down as she walked. She didn't want anyone to see the tears rolling down her cheeks.

Toni unlocked her car and slid behind the wheel. She leaned back against the headrest and sat there for a moment taking deep breaths. She retrieved a box of tissue from the back seat, pulled down her sun visor, and stared in the mirror.

Her face appeared to have aged ten years in the last few days. She wiped her cheeks with a tissue and then fished around in her purse for her compact. The powder covered her tear stains, but the haunted look in her eyes remained. That was something no makeup could fix.

Toni put away her compact and flipped up her sun visor. She had reached a roadblock. Alvin Harney hadn't seen anything. And who knew where Nico Williams was? What if Alvin was right? What if Nico was one of the transient workers? He could be out of state by now.

And there was still the matter of tracking down Gloria Keith. Toni wished she could just cut through all the bull and confront Brian directly—tell him she knew what he had done. She didn't have all the pieces yet, but she knew he murdered Scott. What would Brian say to that?

There was one way to find out.

Toni slipped off her shoes and cleaned them with a tissue. Then she started her car, pulled out of the parking area, and drove back down the access road. Was she crazy? Maybe. But even if she changed her mind and decided not to accuse Brian of murder just yet, she still needed to talk with him. She wanted to find out what he was doing at the hotel the morning Scott died. She could also ask him point-blank why he was contesting the will and tell him she knew about the judgment against him.

Brian was staying at the Renaissance Nashville Hotel located downtown near Chadwick & Shore. Toni pulled up to the porte cochere, handed her car over to the parking valet, and went inside. The lobby, decorated in apple green and warm red, was a mass of confusion. What appeared to be about one hundred senior citizens, all decked out in cowboy hats and boots, were trying to arrange themselves in groups for a tour, though without much success. Toni squeezed through the crowd and stepped up to the concierge desk. The pretty blonde behind the counter wore a smile painted on with bright melon lipstick. Etched into the badge on her lapel was the name *Sarah.*

"Hi," Toni said. "I'm here to see one of your guests, Brian Chadwick. He gave me his room number, but I seem to have lost it. I was wondering if you could look it up for me."

"I'm sorry. I'm not allowed to give out that information, but I can ring his room and let him know you're here."

"That would be great. Thanks."

Sarah browsed through the computer records and then picked up the house phone. Toni glanced at the keypad as she dialed. 2-1-2-4. After a few seconds, Sarah shook her head and put down the receiver. "There's no answer. Would you like to leave a message?"

"No, that's okay. I'll just call him later." Toni cut back through the herd of seniors and ambled toward the door.

Then she stopped.

Maybe this was the break she'd been hoping for. Her one chance to get some hard evidence against Brian. It was risky. She had no idea how long he would be away from his room. What if he was still somewhere in the hotel? He could be in the bar or one of the restaurants.

She circled back around the lobby. Sarah had a clear view of the elevators. Toni edged between two of the groups and peeked at the concierge desk. Sarah was too busy helping a Johnny Cash look-alike to notice her. Common sense was telling Toni to leave. Go home. Seek answers elsewhere. But her heart was crying out, *Go for it!*

The elevator was filling fast. Toni glanced back at Sarah. She seemed to be wrapping up her conversation with Mr. Cash. It was now or never.

Toni made a dash for the elevator and managed to slip in just before the doors closed.

Crowded between a man carrying multiple shopping bags and a rather large woman in a pale pink pantsuit, Toni glanced at the elevator keypad. The light for the twenty-first floor was unlit. She pushed the button. At least she didn't have to worry about any of the other riders getting off on her floor.

Toni watched the digital readout above the keypad as it counted upward. *5, 6, 7.* The elevator chimed at the eighth floor. When the doors opened, the woman in the pink suit pushed past her. She reminded Toni of a giant ball of cotton candy. They made stops at five other floors, emptying all the passengers except for Toni and a young couple whispering and holding hands. She guessed that they were probably on their honeymoon. It hurt her to see them—one more reminder of what she'd lost.

When they reached the twenty-first floor, Toni stepped out of the elevator. Black lettering on the wall indicated that rooms 2100 through 2129 were to the left. She turned and headed for 2124. When she reached Brian's room, she stood staring at the door.

Okay, she thought. *Now what?*

She decided to knock. He might be back in his room by now, or he could have been in the shower when Sarah called. Toni tapped on the door. She waited a few seconds and tapped again. Still no answer. So far, so good. But how was she supposed to get in?

Toni spotted a cart laden with towels and toiletries at the end of the hallway. As she approached the cart, a middle-aged Hispanic woman in a blue housekeeping uniform came out of one of the rooms. Toni read her name tag—*Rosa.*

"Excuse me, Rosa." Toni said. "I'm Mrs. Chadwick from room 2124. I was on my way to meet my husband—we're going on a tour—and I accidentally locked my camera and my key card inside the room. I was wondering if you could open the door for me."

Rosa put her hands on her hips and gave Toni a look of exasperation. "What you say your name is?"

"Mrs. Brian Chadwick, room 2124. If I don't hurry, I'll miss my tour."

Rosa looked Toni over and then laughed and shook her head. "You need to slow down, be more careful."

Toni followed Rosa to the room. With a quick swipe of the housekeeping card, the door was open.

"Thank you so much," Toni said. She handed the housekeeper a tip. Rosa shook her head again and tucked the money into her pocket. Toni pushed the door closed behind her.

The suite was larger than she'd expected, decorated in shades of beige and green with floral drapes, a beige sofa, and two matching chairs. A flat-screen television rested on a marble-topped credenza, and the day's newspaper lay neatly folded on the coffee table.

Floor-to-ceiling windows revealed a spectacular view of the city. She could see the Bridgestone Arena and the historic Ryman Auditorium, former home of the Grand Ole Opry, down below.

Toni entered the bedroom. The white comforter on the bed was pulled back, and the pillows were rumpled, but as in the sitting area, she didn't see anything interesting. Brian had left none of his personal items lying about. She dropped her purse on the bed, crossed the room, and slid open the closet door. Three suits hung inside along with several shirts, a couple of pairs of khaki pants, and a pair of jeans. An empty suitcase and a garment bag lay on the floor. She rifled through the pockets of Brian's clothes, but found only some change and a parking receipt from the hotel.

She moved to the dresser on the opposite wall and pulled open the top drawer. Nothing but underwear. Boxer briefs. Ralph Lauren. The drawer below held several pairs of socks. She poked through them, running her hand underneath. Her fingers touched something that felt like a small magazine. She pulled it out. It was an envelope—the kind you get at a one-hour photo shop.

Toni opened the envelope and took out the prints. Her breath caught in her throat, and she started to tremble. She sank down on the corner of the bed.

The face in the photos was her own.

• • •

Brian drove into the parking lot of his hotel, bypassing the valet. He found an empty space and slid the gearshift into park, leaving the convertible top down. Small white clouds billowed across the turquoise sky. The mercury had risen to an unseasonable seventy-five degrees, the promise of summer in the air. The day was far too beautiful to waste in an attorney's office, which was where he had spent the past two hours.

He had learned that Toni now had a new attorney in her employ. Mark Ross had brought in a probate specialist, famous for settling some of the largest estates in the south. Whenever millions were on the line, family battles usually ensued—only in this case, Toni was hardly family.

Brian's best chance at claiming the estate was to find out if Scott had any previous wills. There was a good possibility Brian had been named as the heir before Scott's engagement. Since Toni had never become a Chadwick, the judge might be convinced to revert to a prior will. After breaking into Toni's house, Brian had searched Scott's study and computer but couldn't find anything, not even a copy of the newest will.

Brian switched off the ignition and scooped the case containing his laptop computer off the passenger seat. He wondered where Toni was now. He had tried to locate her earlier in the morning using the tracking Web site, but the server had been down. He would try again when he got back to his room.

With shaky hands, Toni thumbed through the prints. Brian had shot the film the day of the funeral. Several of the pictures featured Toni alone, standing in her front doorway. Others included Mark holding a grocery bag. The photos that disturbed her the most were close-ups of her face. Brian had been watching her. But why? Was he planning to kill her too?

Toni heard the door to the suite swing open.

He was back.

She jumped up, grabbed her purse, and ran into the bathroom, the photos still clutched in her hand. She was trapped. She had to hide, and fast. She hopped into the tub and pulled the shower curtain closed.

Beads of perspiration popped out on her forehead and upper lip. If Brian decided to take a shower, there would be no way out. If he found her, he would probably kill her right here. Toni heard movement in the bedroom. She had forgotten to close the sock drawer. He would know someone had been in his room. He would discover the pictures were missing.

She heard footsteps on the tile floor of the bathroom. Toni had the sudden urge to scream, but she held her breath and willed herself to remain still and quiet. She could hear glass tinkling, as if Brian was moving things around by the sink.

More footsteps, and then silence. She could feel him standing on the other side of the curtain. She could almost hear him breathing. Her heart pounded in her chest, and the acid taste of bile rose in her throat.

Without warning, the curtain ripped open, and Toni screamed.

11

It was awful, Mr. Ross." Nina, the private-duty nurse, shook her head, her pudgy cheeks flushed. "Really bad. The worst spell I've seen."

Mark sat close to the bed, holding his mother's hand. Nina had sedated her, but she remained semiconscious, mumbling incoherently. In her other hand, she clutched a rag doll with yellow yarn pigtails and a blue gingham dress.

"She was screaming and pulling at her hair," Nina continued. "She threw her water glass at me and nearly hit me in the head." Nina smoothed her own blonde hair and tucked in the strands that had slipped from her tight bun. "She just kept on crying, and then she said I was trying to kill her. That's when I phoned you."

"Thank you, Nina," Mark said. "You did the right thing."

He let go of his mother's hand and pulled the covers up around her. At fifty-one, Arlene Ross had the appearance of a woman in her late sixties. Her once lustrous chestnut hair was now dull and almost completely gray. Countless lines etched the face men had not so long ago described as beautiful. Her skin had grown sallow and her frame thin. The disease that ravaged her brain was destroying the rest of her body as well.

The doctors all said the same thing. Her dementia was the result of a head injury she had sustained eighteen years earlier while working for the Chadwicks. She had accepted the position of housekeeper and nanny when Mark was only seven. The job included room and board, and Mark and his mother had moved into a small cottage on the Chadwick property. There was only one bedroom, so Mark slept on a pullout sofa bed in the living room.

The arrangement was fine for a boy of seven, but became awkward as Mark reached puberty. When his discomfort became apparent, his mother had spoken to Mr. Chadwick. Shortly after, the Chadwicks cleaned out the storage room above their garage and converted it into a bedroom. They had the walls painted, installed plush carpeting over the worn hardwood, and purchased new furniture and drapes.

When the renovations were complete, Mark moved into the main house. He remembered lying awake that first night in his new room, pretending that he too was a Chadwick son, not the illegitimate child of a housekeeper. The Chadwicks had made him feel like family, and for a while there, he believed he was.

The morning after his first night in the house, he came downstairs intending to join his mother for breakfast in the cottage, only to find a place set for him at the Chadwicks' table. For the first time, he actually felt as though he belonged, that he wasn't just part of the hired help. The line that divided him from Scott had begun to blur, and his mother felt it too.

"Make sure you stay on your best behavior," Arlene said to him. "Mind your manners, and don't cause any trouble. They've accepted you now, so don't do anything to make them regret it."

He had taken his mother's advice and done everything he could think of to remain in their good graces. He and Scott grew as close as blood brothers, sharing everything. But his newfound kinship was not destined to last. Just before he turned sixteen, Arlene had her accident, and things began to change again.

It was a Monday morning in July, the week after the Fourth. At nine o'clock, the air was already thick with humidity. Mark, Scott, and Brian found solace from the heat in the backyard pool. They were in the middle of a belly-flop contest when they heard Caitlin screaming from inside the house. At first, they thought she was just playing, but then they realized something was terribly wrong.

Scott was first inside the house with the other two boys close behind. What they found would forever alter the course of Mark's life. On the floor at the bottom of the staircase, Arlene lay in a pool of blood, a deep gash at her temple. Mrs. Chadwick knelt beside her, the phone clutched in her hand, begging for help from the 911 operator.

Arlene was in a coma for three days. When she awoke, Mark assumed things would return to normal. The doctors released her from the hospital, and after a few days of rest, she resumed her duties at the Chadwick home. But something was different.

The symptoms were mild at first. She would misplace things or forget to do the grocery shopping. But as the months stretched on, Arlene's memory grew worse. One day she went to pick Caitlin up from ballet class and couldn't remember how to get home. That night Mr. Chadwick told Mark to move back into the cottage. He needed to keep an eye on his mother and make sure she didn't accidentally harm herself. And although they let Arlene stay on, a new housekeeper moved into Mark's room in the main house a few days later. The Chadwicks' trust in Arlene had been broken, the line dividing family and hired hand redrawn.

"She should be out for a least another hour," Nina said. "Can I get you something to drink?"

"Iced tea would be nice."

"I'll be right back."

Nina left the room, and Mark rose and walked to the window. He peered through the blinds at the parking lot below. He watched a young mother strap her child into his car seat and slam the rear door before taking her place behind the wheel of her Toyota.

Mark had purchased the two-bedroom condo for his mother several years earlier. It was only a few miles from his own home in Blanton Hills—close enough in case of an emergency, but far enough away to allow him to forget her constant agony when he so chose.

He had hired three private-duty nurses, each working eight-hour shifts during the week, and one nurse who lived in on the weekends. He also employed two women who alternately cleaned and prepared his mother's meals each day. They all took excellent care of Arlene—much better than the care she had received in the nursing home. And he had set up a trust that would continue that care if anything ever happened to him.

The door to the bedroom opened, and Nina entered with a glass of iced tea and a plate covered with a thick slab of coffee cake.

"I thought you might be hungry," she said.

"Thank you. I am a little." Mark glanced at his watch. "You've had more than your share of drama for the day. Why don't you go ahead and take off? I can stay here until Helen arrives for her shift."

Nina placed the food on a table next to the window. "Are you sure?"

"You said yourself she should be out at least an hour. There's less than two left on your shift. Go on home. You deserve it."

"Well, I do have some shopping to take care of. But if something else happens and you need me, my cell number is on the refrigerator."

"Don't worry. We'll be fine."

Mark picked up the tea glass and returned to the window. He heard Nina leave through the front door. Sipping his tea, he watched her get into her Honda and pull out of the parking lot. He wondered if she had baked the coffee cake herself. Nina was a wonderful nurse, but her skills fell short in the cooking department. However, she didn't seem to be aware of that fact. She regularly brought in desserts of one kind or another. She had made some cookies once that were hard enough to scrape ice off his windshield.

Arlene moaned, startling him. Mark left his glass on the table and sat down in the chair next to the bed. His mother tossed her head and mouthed words only she could understand. Then she began to whine. A helpless cry like that of a lost child.

Mark stroked her cheek. "Shhh, everything's okay," he said. "I'm right here."

But he knew his words were meaningless. She had no idea who Mark was. She didn't even know she had a son. The disease had robbed her of her memories. Had stolen her intellect. A mind that had once delighted in the poetry of Emily Dickinson now could not even comprehend the simplest rhymes. She had trouble feeding herself and had no control over her bowels. Living had become a form of torture. There was no joy, only pain and confusion.

Spittle slid down the corner of Arlene's mouth. Mark grabbed a tissue from the box on the nightstand and wiped her chin. She seemed to be settling back down, the demons in her head receding.

He tossed the tissue in the wastebasket and ran his fingers over her forehead, brushing the hair off her face. Then he slipped his hand underneath her head and removed one of her pillows. Filled with down, the pillow weighed little more than a pound, but it would be enough.

Enough to quiet her sobs, to end her suffering, to bring her peace at last.

Toni's scream echoed through the room, but she wasn't the only one who had screamed. Rosa stood before her trembling, the color drained from her face.

The housekeeper collapsed back against the sink and put her hand to her heart. *"Ay Dios mío!"*

Toni couldn't help but laugh, but as relief washed over her, her legs turned to rubber. She had to grab on to the side of the tub to keep from falling. "I'm so sorry," she said. "I didn't realize you were in here, and you really scared me."

"I scare you? Why you in the shower?"

Toni shook her head and laughed again, trying to think of an excuse. "Well, I was just—checking the soap. I wanted to make sure we had enough. My husband—Brian—he has this strange quirk. He likes to have a brand-new bar every time he takes a shower."

Toni knew the explanation sounded ridiculous, but she was too rattled to come up with anything remotely plausible. "So if you could just leave a few extras, we'd really appreciate it."

Rosa nodded, an expression of bewilderment on her face. "*Sí.*"

"Well, I really have go now, or I'm going to miss the tour bus."

Toni stepped out of the tub and rushed past Rosa into the bedroom.

She stuffed the photo envelope back into the drawer under Brian's socks and then took a second to study the room. Satisfied she had left things as she found them, Toni hurried out of the suite and ran down the hallway toward the elevator.

Brian dodged the towel cart and stepped through the open door to his suite. As he dropped his computer case on the sofa, a housekeeper walked out of the bedroom muttering to herself in Spanish. When she glanced up and saw Brian, she stopped and shook her head.

"Your wife, she already gone," Rosa told him.

"What?"

"She scare me half to death. I open the shower curtain, there she is. She scream, I scream. Enough to wake the dead."

"My wife?"

"*Sí.* She hurry out. Said you're late for your tour." Rosa gestured toward the door. "You should go, catch her."

"Right, I will."

It had to be Toni. But what was she doing in his room? And, more important, how much did she know? "My wife—she's about five feet six with dark red hair?"

A look of confusion crossed Rosa's face. "*Sí.*"

"How long ago did she leave?"

"Five minutes. Maybe less."

12

Mark turned the pillow over in his hands.

It would be so easy. All he had to do was cover her face. The drugs in her system would prevent any struggle, and she wouldn't experience any pain. Just the slightest amount of pressure, and Arlene would be set free. Free from the shell that imprisoned her in this world.

There would be no questions asked. The doctors had not expected her to live this long. And who could blame him anyway? Who would want such an existence? Days spent in torment, surrounded by strangers. Your own identity a mystery. Your only comfort found in the companionship of an aging rag doll.

If he ever succumbed to a similar fate, he hoped someone would have the courage to take mercy on him and release him from his bonds. Mark had debated the matter a hundred times. Had asked himself the same questions, and he always reached the same conclusion: she would be much better off when her life here ended. Still, he had never been able to go through with it. Something always held him back.

It was the same today—still holding him back. And it would continue to hold him back, right up until the day Arlene's body decided to surrender to death on its own.

He gently lifted his mother's head and slipped the pillow back beneath her. She slept peacefully now, her breathing a steady rhythm. The sedative had worked its magic yet again. Her face was relaxed, her lips curved almost into a smile. He hadn't seen her smile in such a long time.

Even when he brought her gifts, she would stare at them blankly. The only time she showed any emotion was during one of her spells.

And then it was usually fear or anger, or both. Like today. The times his mother was most alive were when she was in the throes of despair. In her own private hell. He longed for the day when it would all be over, when she could escape the anguish.

Mark leaned down, kissed Arlene's cheek, and then returned to the window.

Toni worked her way through the house closing all the slats on the plantation shutters and checking the doors and windows, making sure they were locked. Although the sun was still bright, she turned on all the lights, inside and out. When she was done, she went back downstairs and double-checked the security system.

Brian was out there somewhere. He could be watching her at this very moment. He might even be standing on the other side of the kitchen window, his face against the glass, peering through the minute cracks between the slats. She could almost feel his eyes on her, sense him studying her every move. The thought made the tiny hairs along the back of her neck bristle.

Stop it. This is crazy.

What she needed was something to steady her nerves. She pulled a bottle of merlot from the wine rack and removed the cork. Although the kitchen was pleasantly warm, her hands were like ice. They trembled as she poured the wine. It splashed over the rim of her glass onto the granite counter top.

Calm down. You're safe. Everything will be fine.

She grabbed a paper towel, wiped up the wine, and then carried her glass into the family room. She sat down on the sofa, curled her legs up under her, and took a long swallow of the wine. The liquid seeped through her body, spreading a comforting warmth. After a few more sips, she began to relax.

Her thoughts returned to Brian's hotel room. Why had he taken her picture? She wished she'd had the time to search the remaining drawers. She might have found the answer. From what she had uncovered so far, it didn't really make sense. If he believed she was an obstacle and could keep him from gaining control of Scott's money, why didn't he just go ahead and kill her? He knew what she looked like. He didn't need a photo. And then the realization hit.

The pictures were for someone else. For someone he had hired to kill her.

She remembered the article Brian had written about the CIA assassin. Although that former agent was still in prison, Brian could have other contacts like him. Professional killers. By hiring someone else to commit the murder, he would be free to establish an alibi for himself.

Brian probably knew she had been to see Detective Lewis. He might even know that she suspected him of Scott's murder. This way he could cover his tracks. Someone with CIA training would likely be able to kill her and never get caught. With a solid alibi and no amateur trigger man to rat him out, Brian could walk away a free man.

Free and a multimillionaire.

Despite the warming effects of the wine, a cold chill rushed through her. If she was right and Brian had hired a contract killer, it meant that she would have to watch every move she made. The hit man could disguise himself as anyone in order to get close to her. He could get hired at her office. Pretend to be another agent. He could be a waiter at a restaurant or a clerk at the grocery store. He might pose as a deliveryman or even a police officer. At least with Brian, she knew who the enemy was. Now she wasn't sure who to be afraid of.

For the first time in her life, Toni wished she owned a gun. Her father had kept a shotgun around the house when she was growing up. As far as she knew, he never did any hunting with it. The gun stayed locked in a cabinet in the basement and he had taken it out only a few times that she could remember. Even then, he used it only to shoot soda cans off a fence at his friend's farm.

He had let her fire it once when she was around ten years old. She still remembered the recoil and the bruise it left on her arm, the echo of the blast, and the burnt, sweet scent of the gunpowder. She hadn't even come close to hitting one of the cans. After her father died, she sold the gun along with several of his other belongings, most of his furniture, and the house where she grew up. Besides the shotgun, she'd had no other contact with a firearm.

Still, she felt as though she needed some sort of protection—something small that she could carry with her. She could purchase a handgun, but she knew there would be a waiting period for a carry permit. It could take several days, maybe even weeks, for it to be issued. She could be dead by then.

She had a can of pepper spray in her purse, but she didn't think it would do much good. Then she remembered something. She thought she'd glimpsed a hunting knife in one of the boxes Scott had brought over from his condo. She drained the last of the wine from her glass and went into the study.

Several cardboard boxes were still stacked in one corner of the room. During the two weeks they had lived in the house, Scott had been busy with work and the wedding. He planned to finish unpacking when they returned from their honeymoon. Now the task was hers. Toni opened the box on top. Inside, she found several books and some old copies of *Architectural Digest*.

As Toni slid the box off the stack, she lost her balance and bumped into a table that stood next to a leather wing chair. The table rocked and out of the corner of her eye, she glimpsed a black statue falling over the edge. She reached out and grabbed the statue, catching it before it crashed on the hardwood floor.

Carved from onyx, the image was of a rearing stallion. She had purchased the statue in Cozumel, in the small town of San Miguel, at a shop on the waterfront near the Plaza del Sol. The onyx felt cool against her skin. She sat cross-legged on the floor and traced the lines of the carving with her index finger. Scenes of the previous summer flashed through her mind like slides in a projector. She and Scott, hand in hand, strolling down El Malecon, exploring the various shops along the way, and then stopping for lunch at a sidewalk restaurant. Sweet memories she would treasure for the rest of her life.

Alvin Harney was right: she was the luckiest woman on earth. Scott had given her his love, and she would feel it in this house for as long as she lived. It was a love that transcended death.

Toni got up from the floor and placed the statue back on the table. She pushed the box of books out of the way and pulled open the box that had been underneath. Just more books. But the one on top seemed unusual. Thick and leather bound, it appeared to be a photo album. She lifted the book out and took it to the wing chair. She sat down and opened the cover expecting to see pictures of Scott and his family, but it wasn't a photo album. It was a scrapbook.

She flipped through the pages one by one, scanning every item. Brian's entire career fanned out before her, starting with the first article he had ever published—a puff piece for a newspaper in Virginia. All the articles she had found on the Internet were there as well. There were clippings documenting the various awards he had won, including a John Hancock Award and a George Polk Award for achievement in journalism.

Not being familiar with journalism, she had no real idea of the significance of the awards. But there was one name she did recognize—Pulitzer. She was surprised to read that Brian had been a finalist for the prize the prior year.

The last item in the book was an article he had written just a few weeks before Scott's death.

There was no mention of the lawsuit against Brian or the resulting judgment.

Toni closed the scrapbook. Scott had kept tabs on Brian all those years, saving every article he could find chronicling his brother's achievements. Just like parents would preserve their child's report cards. Scott was proud of Brian. Had loved him dearly despite their differences.

If only Brian had known. It might have softened his heart. If he needed money, he could have asked for a loan, and Scott might still be alive.

She had a sudden urge to destroy the book. Burn its contents. Obliterate everything pertaining to Brian. But what good would it do? Scott had obviously cherished the clippings. The old adage was true: love could be blind. Scott had no inkling of the monster Brian had become.

Toni placed the scrapbook on the corner of Scott's desk and began to rummage through the remaining boxes. By the time she got to the next-to-last box, she was beginning to think she'd imagined the knife. She ripped off the packing tape and lifted out a dartboard. She found what she was searching for underneath, but something was wrong. Now that she could see the weapon up close, she realized what it actually was: a fake knife with a rubber blade. Scott had probably bought it for Halloween or for some kind of silly prank.

Now what? A feeling of defenselessness washed over her. She felt like a sitting target. She went to the window and peeked out the shutters at the front lawn, surprised to see that it was already dark outside. Going through the boxes had taken longer than she realized.

The phone rang, and Toni jumped.

She glanced at the caller ID on Scott's desk phone and saw that it was Jill. She decided to let it go to voice mail, but apparently Jill didn't take the time to leave a message because Toni's cell phone chimed a moment later with a text alert.

She checked the message:

> Want 2 come over 4 dinner?
> Steaks on the grill.
> Luv, J :)

Maybe she should go. It would give her a chance to question Clint about his statement to the police. And if he pressed her to sell him Scott's share of the company, she would tell him that she couldn't do anything until she settled the lawsuit with Brian.

But was she really ready to face them? It had been hard enough at lunch listening to Jill recount her version of the events of the past few days. If they both ganged up on her, trying to convince her that Scott wasn't the man she'd always believed him to be, would she be able to handle it?

She wished she could tell Jill about the photos she'd found in Brian's hotel room, but when she thought about what she'd done, breaking into his room, going through his things, she realized how crazy it made her look. However deep down, she knew it wasn't crazy. She knew she was right.

Toni replied to the text, keying in that she already had plans for the evening. She hoped the lie wouldn't be questioned and that Jill wouldn't show up on her doorstep.

She set up her laptop computer on the breakfast table and then went to the restocked refrigerator and took out a plastic container filled with fresh chicken salad. She carried her sandwich and a Coke back to the table along with a pad of paper and a pencil.

Nico Williams still seemed to be her best lead to finding out what had really happened to Scott. If anyone else had entered the construction site that morning, it was very likely he had seen them. Even if his phone call had distracted him and someone had managed to slip by, it was still possible he possessed some valuable information.

Information he might not even be aware of.

Toni clicked open her Internet browser and started a phone directory search. Although Williams is a common name, she was nevertheless surprised at the number of entries in the area that were a possible match. No Nico Williams was listed, but there were four entries for Nicolas and close to a dozen more with the initial N.

She took a bite of her sandwich and dialed the first number. It was no longer in service. She hoped that wasn't a portent of things to come. She mentally crossed off the entry and dialed Nicolas number two. An elderly woman answered on the third ring.

"May I speak with Nico Williams?" Toni asked.

"Who?"

"Nicolas Williams."

"Honey, he's been dead for more than four years now."

"I'm sorry, I didn't know. He's obviously not the Mr. Williams I'm looking for, but maybe you can still help me. Do you know if he has a relative who goes by the name of Nico?"

There was a moment's hesitation and then, "Who is this?"

There was something strange in the woman's tone of voice. Something more than just the normal annoyance you'd expect to hear when asking such a benign question. Did she know Nico? Toni had a feeling she did. She had to come up with an explanation that would put the woman at ease.

"My name is Toni Matthews, and I'm with Chadwick & Shore Construction. I'm trying to locate the Nico Williams who did some subcontracting work for us. Our records show that we owe him a paycheck, but somehow we got his address mixed up and we don't know where to send it."

"I see. Well, I'm sorry, but I can't help you. I don't know any Nico."

So much for gut feelings. Toni had thought for sure the woman was a relative. "Thanks anyway. I'm sorry I bothered you." She hung up the phone and twisted off the cap of her Coke. There were still several more listings left to try. Surely one of them would be the right man.

Almost an hour later, Toni dialed the last possible listing in the bunch. N. V. Williams, who turned out to be Natalie. She was no closer to finding Nico than she had been when she started. Either he had an unlisted number, or the phone was in someone else's name. Or maybe he had only a cell phone. There was no way she could think of to find that number.

After doing a regular search on Nico's name and finding no hits that matched, Toni realized she had only one final chance of locating him tonight: tax records. Part of her monthly real estate dues paid for a subscription to the state's database. She could search all the tax records online. If Nico owned a home, she would find him.

Keeping the tab with the phone directory list open, she cross-checked all the properties in the neighboring counties owned by anyone with the name Nicolas or the single initial N with the numbers she'd already called. Some of the property owners who were a potential match had mailing addresses in other areas of the state. She ran another directory search for their phone numbers. It took over an hour to call all the owners on the list, and not one admitted to knowing Nico.

She shut the laptop computer and rubbed her eyes. The first thing in the morning she would go to Chadwick & Shore and get his record from the personnel department. She wished she had thought to do it earlier when she was there.

Toni rinsed off her plate, put it in the dishwasher, and then tossed the plastic soda bottle in the trash. Leaving all the lights on, she went upstairs to bed.

13

Toni lay awake in bed watching the clock and listening to every creak and pop her new home uttered as it settled. She could hear the wind pushing against the glass of the windows and the fan from the central heating and air unit cutting off and on. The empty house generated more noise than she ever thought was possible, feeding her fears and stoking her imagination.

The lamp on her bedside table illuminated the room and hindered her sleep, but she kept it switched on. She knew she was being paranoid, but she couldn't help it. Every time she closed her eyes, she saw Brian's face.

If only she hadn't butted in and engineered the reunion between the two brothers. It was her fault Scott was dead. If she'd minded her own business, he would be alive, and they would be married now. What a terrible mistake she'd made.

Please forgive me, she thought.

After finally getting a few restless hours of sleep, she got up Tuesday at dawn, showered, and dressed in charcoal gray slacks and a matching jacket. Not exactly a spring color, but dull and somber matched her mood.

Downstairs, she ate a quick breakfast of buttered toast and orange juice. With all the lights still on, she set the security system and then left the house and drove to Chadwick & Shore.

She pulled into the parking garage at 7:35 and nudged her car up to the guard station. The man inside immediately drew her attention. He didn't look right. He was hunched down in the booth, and she could see something small and black in his hand. Could it be a gun?

A sudden jolt of fear ran through her. Was he the regular parking attendant? There was the slightest hint of familiarity, but that might just be from his uniform. She couldn't be sure. He had his cap pulled down, hiding his eyes. Could he be the one?

The attendant looked up, meeting her gaze. Her face grew warm, and she could hear the sound of her own heart pounding in her ears. Then the security arm started to rise, and the attendant turned away. Now she could clearly see the paperback novel open in his hand. He had been reading.

The pounding in her ears subsided. This had to stop. It was one thing to be cautious, but she couldn't let her imagination run wild. Otherwise she was going to drive herself nuts. Besides, Brian wasn't stupid enough to have someone shoot her in broad daylight. He wouldn't want anyone to realize her death was a murder. He'd find a way to disguise it, as he had with Scott.

Toni drove through the gate to the Chadwick & Shore parking area. The office didn't officially open until eight o'clock, and she noticed that neither Clint's nor Jill's car was in the garage. One less thing to worry about. She wanted to get into the office and get the information on Nico without running into either of them. She didn't want to have to explain her reasons for being there.

Instead of parking in Scott's space, she circled around and pulled into a space two rows away. Wedged between an SUV and a minivan, no one would notice her car. Hoping that Clint and Jill wouldn't arrive until she was inside, she hurried across the parking garage and got into the elevator.

When she reached the office lobby, she walked past the empty reception desk and read the directory posted near the elevator. The human resources department was located on the same floor. She turned left and then right, following the arrows to an office near the end of the hallway. She tried the door, but it was locked.

She checked her watch. Fifteen minutes before eight. She had hoped the personnel employees would arrive early. The clerical staff at her own office usually did, giving themselves time to make coffee, have a doughnut or muffin, and chat a little before settling in for the day. She would just have to wait.

She had noticed a ladies' room a few doors back. If she hung out there, she might be able to lower the chances of someone seeing her. She could call her office and check on her listings while she waited. As she headed for the restroom, a young woman with chestnut hair pulled up in a ponytail walked down the hall past her. The girl looked barely old enough to be out of high school. Toni turned and watched as the girl unlocked the door to the human resources office and went inside. It seemed her wait was over.

She followed the girl into the office and stopped at the reception counter. The personnel employee was a few yards away on the other side, her back to Toni. The girl's ponytail bobbed up and down as she fidgeted with something on her desk.

"Good morning," Toni said.

"If you're here to fill out an application," the girl said without turning around, "they're on the table in the corner. Just help yourself."

"I don't need an application, just some information."

The girl turned and saw Toni, a look of recognition filling her eyes. She walked up to the counter. "Miss Matthews, I'm so sorry about Mr. Chadwick."

"Thank you." Toni searched her memory, but she had no recollection of the young woman. "Have we met?"

"No, we haven't, but I've seen your picture in all the real estate magazines, and I saw you at the funeral. I'm Marcie."

"It's nice to meet you, Marcie."

"The same here." The smile Marcie flashed revealed her obvious love of teeth whitener. "Is selling houses hard work?"

"At times it can be. It really all depends on the property."

"I always thought it would be fun to be a real estate agent, and I've even been thinking about getting my license, but I just don't know whether I'd be good at it. You said you needed some kind of information?"

"I need the personnel file for a subcontractor named Nico Williams."

Marcie's smile faded. "I'm sorry, but I can't give it to you."

"Why not?"

"Our human resources manager, Mrs. Duvall, is the only one who can let you see the personnel records."

"Okay, then, I'll just wait for her. When will she be in?"

"She has a doctor's appointment this morning, so I don't expect her for at least a few hours. Maybe you could come back later?"

"No. No, I can't. I'm too pushed for time today, and it's really important that I get his address and phone number. Do you know where the files are kept?"

"Well," she hesitated. "Yes, but I still can't help you. Mrs. Duvall has very strict rules about who's allowed in the files. She's the one you need to talk to."

Toni was losing her patience. She realized that Marcie wasn't being difficult on purpose; she was just trying to do her job. Toni smiled and forced a pleasant tone into her voice. "Did you know that I own half of Chadwick & Shore now?"

"No, I didn't."

"It's true, and I'm going to be working here," she lied. "Chadwick & Shore has wanted to break into the residential market for quite a while now, so I'll be heading up a new department—developing subdivisions. I'm moving into Scott's old office, and I'm going to need a really good personal assistant to help me. Preferably somebody from inside the company."

She saw a light come on in Marcie's eyes. Toni hated resorting to deception, but under the circumstances, she didn't really have a choice. She had to find Nico whatever it took.

"Well, since I do know where the files are and since you actually own part of the company now, maybe it wouldn't hurt just to let you have a quick look at it. So long as you didn't take it out of the office."

"That would be great. I really appreciate it."

"What was the subcontractor's name?"

"Nico Williams. It might be listed under Nicolas."

"I'll be right back."

Marcie smiled again and then disappeared down a hallway. Only a few more minutes and Toni would know how to contact Nico. She hoped he would be free to meet with her today. Whatever information he might have, she didn't want to discuss over the phone. She wanted to meet him face-to-face. Explain just how important his memories of that morning could be. But Nico wasn't the only person she needed to speak with.

Toni leaned across the counter and picked up a pen and a sticky note. She wrote down Gloria Keith's name. She might as well have Marcie check for a file on her while she was at it.

A few minutes later, Marcie returned, the file in her hand. "There's not much in it," she said. "He wasn't really a subcontractor per se. He was hired by the drywall company, so he was actually an employee of that subcontractor, if that makes any sense."

"Well, it sort of does, I guess."

"I had to search the computer to find out who he was. We file all the information under the main subcontractors' names. When we contract subs to do a job, they have their own people who do the work. We pay the subcontractors, and then they pay their crew. If the company we hire has its own workers' comp policy, then we have no idea who its employees are. If it doesn't have its own policy, then we have to cover its employees under ours. Luckily, that's the case with Mr. Williams. Otherwise we wouldn't have a file on him at all." She handed the folder to Toni.

Marcie was right; there were only two sheets of paper inside. All the information Toni needed was on the first. She was disappointed to find that Nico had listed his address as a post office box. She went ahead and jotted it down anyway, along with his phone number. As an afterthought, she copied down his driver's license and social security numbers as well. You never knew what you might need.

Toni closed the file and gave it back to Marcie. "Oh, and if you don't mind, there's one more person I need to check."

Marcie took the sticky note. "Gloria Keith. Is she a subcontractor too?"

"No, I think she would be one of the clerical staff. Maybe even a temp."

Marcie left the note on the counter and walked over to her desk. "Do you just need her address and phone number, or do you need to see her file?"

"Just address and phone number would be fine."

"I can pull that information up on the computer." Marcie sat down at her desk and began typing on the keyboard. She waited a second, and then her nose wrinkled into a frown. She began typing again. A few seconds later, she shook her head. "No, there's no record of her. She's not clerical, not a temp, and not a sub."

So much for that idea. "Thanks anyway for trying. I wasn't really sure if she worked here."

"I'm sorry I couldn't help."

"But you did help. You got me the information on Nico Williams, and that's something I won't forget."

Marcie's perfect, overly whitened smile returned.

Jill stepped off the elevator, crossed the lobby, and headed down the hallway toward the accounting department. Clint was running late again, so she had agreed to pick up some cost reports for him. He'd been up most of the night studying the specs for the projects Scott had been working on. It was a lot to digest. The project managers were all looking to him for guidance, asking questions he didn't know the answers to. Until now he hadn't realized the magnitude of the load Scott had carried.

And then this morning, he had gotten a call regarding an apartment complex in Antioch that was nearing completion. Somehow they had installed the wrong cabinets in forty of the units—cabinets that were double the price of those originally quoted. The supplier refused to accept the blame, claiming to have shipped the right order.

They could pull the cabinets out, send them back, and reorder, but that would extend the completion date by at least four weeks, and there would be additional labor costs. Or they could just keep the higher-priced cabinets. Either way, Chadwick & Shore would lose money. They needed to figure out which option would be the less expensive one in order to make a decision.

Jill pushed open the door to accounting, walked past the desks belonging to the various clerks, and headed down the hallway to the senior accountant's office. She knocked once and then went in without waiting for a reply.

Mitchell Phillips sat at his desk, a coffee cup in his hand. The rising steam clouded the glasses perched on the end of his nose. "Hello, Jill," he said. "Can I get you some coffee?"

"Who has the time?"

Obviously perplexed by the answer, Mitchell put down his cup. "What can I do for you this morning?"

"We have a small crisis at the apartments in Antioch. I need to get copies of the detailed cost reports to date, as well as the original cost estimates."

"No problem." Mitchell leaned across his desk and pushed a button on the intercom. A female voice answered. "Bring me the files on the Wind Song Terrace Apartments," he said.

In a matter of moments, a woman appeared with the files. Mitchell rifled through the contents pulling out several of the documents. He handed them to the clerk. "Make copies of all these, please."

Jill took a seat next to Mitchell's desk and forced herself to engage in small talk while they waited. When the clerk returned with the copies, Mitchell checked to make sure they were all there before placing them inside a file folder. He handed the file to Jill. "I think you'll find everything you need here."

Jill stood, dropping her purse on the chair. She thumbed through the reports. Satisfied, she closed the file. "This should do it."

"Let me know if you need anything else."

Jill left Mitchell's office, nodded at the clerks as she passed their desks, and pulled open the accounting department door. Across the hallway, one door down, she spotted Toni leaving human resources. She started to call out to her, but stopped when she heard someone calling her own name. She turned around. Mitchell was walking toward her.

"You forgot your purse," he said.

Jill let go of the door, letting it close. She took her purse from Mitchell. "I'm glad you caught me before I left. I don't think I could have gotten very far without it."

"Call me if you need more information on the apartments."

"I will."

Jill opened the door again and walked out into the hallway. Toni had disappeared. What had she wanted from the human resources department? Jill decided to find out. She went inside and walked up to the reception counter.

"Marcie, was that Toni Matthews I just saw leaving?" she asked.

"Yes."

"Why was she here?"

Marcie picked a file up off the counter. "Um, real estate. My mother has decided to sell her house, and Miss Matthews is going to put it on the market for her. She was just picking up the key."

"I see."

Jill glanced down. She saw a sticky note on the other side of the counter with the name Gloria Keith in Toni's handwriting. So that was it. Toni was trying to find the mysterious Gloria, and she had told Marcie not to mention it to anyone.

Jill wished Toni could just forget about the circumstances surrounding Scott's death. The longer she tried to make sense of it, the longer she put off mourning. Maybe that was the whole idea. Jill knew all too well how difficult it was to lose the love of your life. She had been down that road once herself.

She had been seventeen when she met Richard. He was tall and handsome with huge brown eyes. A private in the army, stationed at Fort Campbell, Kentucky. He promised to give her a better life and take her out of the squalor she had known.

As a benefit of being in the military, they would travel the world. Far away from her mother who drank too much. And more important, away from her mother's steady parade of boyfriends, each one slimier than the one before.

Finally, she had someone who really cared about her. Not someone who just wanted to use her for sex. Against her mother's protests, Jill quit high school and married Richard in a little chapel in Clarksville. They moved into married housing on the base, and for nearly a year, her life was like a fairy tale. But then it all ended.

Richard was killed during a training exercise. For a long while, she thought she would die too. After Richard's funeral, she refused to return to her mother's house. Seventeen years of that hell had been enough. She took Richard's death benefits, moved to Nashville, and got her GED and then her real estate license.

Things had changed a lot since then. She had changed. All that was a part of her old life—the life she kept buried and shared with no one. The life she tried to forget. Still, losing Richard was one pain she would always remember.

14

Toni got into her car and pulled her cell phone out of her purse. She punched in the number listed in Nico's personnel file and waited for the call to connect. She recognized the exchange issued by a local cellular company. Her own number began with the same three digits.

After one ring, a mechanical voice answered. "The number you have reached is no longer in service."

"Dammit!" She banged her palm against the steering wheel.

Great. Now what? Nico had most likely moved, and she would probably never find him. She crumpled up the sticky note and tossed it into the trash bag hanging on the rear of the passenger seat. She had been so sure he had seen something. Had some sliver of information, the missing puzzle piece that would tie Brian to Scott's death. Now it looked as if she would never know.

There had to be something else she could do. Something she hadn't thought of. She just couldn't give up on Nico yet; she had to figure out a way to locate him. She climbed between the two front seats and fished through the trash until she found the sticky note. As she was returning to her seat, she glanced through the windshield and saw Jill walking across the parking garage.

Toni ducked. She watched Jill get into her car and speed away. Clint's car was still missing, and she needed to leave before he arrived. She didn't want to pass him on the way out.

Toni drove out of the garage and headed toward Interstate 65. She picked up her phone again and dialed her office. Janet answered.

"Hi, it's me," Toni said. "I need you to do something for me."

"Sure, what's up?"

"Based on the number of sales I've had the last two quarters, I was thinking of hiring some help for you and Cheryl. I know you could use it."

"Really? We have been spread pretty thin lately—not that I'm complaining or anything."

"I know. Anyway there's a girl named Marcie who works in the human resources department at Chadwick & Shore. I need you to call her and ask her to bring her résumé by the office. Have her fill out an application while she's there, and make sure she understands she'll have to take classes and get her real estate license."

"I'll do it as soon as we hang up. Anything else?"

"That's it. How are things on your end? Have you run into any problems?"

"Not so far."

"I'll knock on wood."

"Oh, before you go, you do have a message here. Townsend Mortgage called. They approved the loan on Rachel Court, and they set the closing for two o'clock tomorrow. Do you still want me to cover it for you?"

"Yes, if you don't mind. I'm not really up to it yet."

"Don't worry. I'll hold the sellers' hands for you, and they won't even realize you're not there."

"Thanks."

Toni hung up the phone. She was glad to hear the mortgage company had approved the loan. It was touch-and-go there for a while. A few problems had surfaced regarding the buyer's recent divorce. His ex-wife had failed to make payments on a car still in his name. Luckily, he had managed to clear things up.

That was it!

Why didn't she think of it sooner? She had all the required information. She dialed the number for the loan officer at Townsend.

"Helen Dove."

"Helen, it's Toni."

"How are you, sweetie?"

"I'm holding up."

"I'm glad to hear it. I've been thinking about you all week, and saying a few prayers for you too."

"Thanks. I need all the prayers I can get."

"Did Janet tell you about Rachel Court?"

"Yes she did, but that's not why I'm calling. I have a buyer I need you to prequalify."

"Okay, go ahead."

"He recently did some work for Chadwick & Shore, and I think he'll be a good prospect, but I'm not real sure about his credit history. He was a little sketchy with the details. I'd like to get a credit report pulled before I spend a lot of time showing him houses."

"Smart girl. What's his name?"

"Nico Williams."

"Address?"

"Umm, well, I didn't realize it until now, but he has it listed as a post office box. Is that a problem?"

"No. It won't matter. His physical address will come back on the report."

"That's what I thought." Toni gave Helen Nico's social security and driver's license numbers.

"I've got back-to-back closings today, but as soon as I get a minute, I'll pull the report."

"Thanks. Oh, and Helen, could you give me his correct address when it comes back? I like to have my files complete."

"Will do."

"Great. One more thing: I don't know when I'll be back in the office, so phone me either on my cell or at home with the information."

"You got it. Take care, sweetie."

Toni smiled as she ended the call. Maybe she would be able to find

Nico after all. Even if he had moved, it was possible that he had left a forwarding address with his neighbors. Or they might know his relatives or a girlfriend—something that could help her track him down.

Now if she could only get a lead on Gloria Keith. Who was she? What was her connection to Scott? Toni drummed her fingers on the steering wheel. If she were Detective Lewis and she wanted to find out about someone who had died, who would she talk to? Who would she take a statement from? The obvious choices were the deceased's close friends, relatives, and coworkers.

Where did Gloria fit in? She had to be a business associate. That would be the only way to explain why Toni had never heard of her. Maybe she had met with Scott the day before he died. Maybe that's why Lewis decided to question her.

Toni tried to recall anything Scott might have said about his schedule that day. The only thing she could remember him talking about was the hotel. But if Gloria had been involved with the project, Jill would have known her. Then Toni realized something: she had spent the previous night scouring phone listings for Nico's number, but she had never once thought to look for Gloria's.

Toni glanced at her phone on the passenger's seat and fought the temptation to run a search while she drove. Another agent at her office had ended up in intensive care from trying to text while she was on the interstate. Instead, she'd take the next exit—it was less than half a mile down the road.

She looked at the SUV traveling beside her and then checked her rearview mirror. A steady line of cars filled the right-hand lane. Toni stomped on the gas and swerved over, inciting a storm of honking horns. She waved in apology and pulled off the interstate. She drove into a gas station near the exit.

Toni parked her car and ran a phone directory search for Gloria. Two listings were possible matches: G. A. Keith and G. S. Keith. Toni dialed the first number and a man answered. "May I speak to Gloria?" Toni asked.

"You've got the wrong number." The man slammed down the phone.

Strike one, Toni thought. She punched in the second number. After four rings, the phone switched to voice mail.

"Hi, this is Gloria. You know what to do."

Toni hung up the phone. It had to be her. How many Gloria Keiths could there be in the Nashville area? She wrote down the address and then pulled up the map on her car's navigation system. Gloria lived on a small street off West End Avenue, near Vanderbilt University.

Toni checked her watch. It was only 8:45. How long before Gloria would be home? Did she come home for lunch? Or would it be after five before she returned? Finding her address had been easy. Waiting was the hard part.

Toni pulled out of the gas station and drove along a side street, lost in thought. What information did Gloria have? Did she know Brian? Toni ran through several different scenarios in her mind, driving on autopilot. The next thing she knew, she was at the cemetery. And like the day of the funeral when she had driven to the hotel, she couldn't remember exactly how she had gotten there. The feeling was even stranger today—as if an unseen force had called silently to her, drawing her to the place where she had said her last good-bye to Scott.

She rolled through the gates and stopped near the same spot she and Mark had parked for the funeral. Dozens of other cars were lining the lane up ahead, and she could see a memorial service in progress down the slope. The same funeral home that conducted Scott's service, the same green awning.

Toni switched off the ignition and got out. She scanned the cemetery, looking for anyone who seemed out of place. Seeing no one of interest, she locked her car door and headed up the slope to Scott's grave.

It's funny, she thought, when you're in love and you're happy, you think you have all the time in the world. You dream and you make plans and you believe you'll grow old together. You never once stop to think about your own mortality, or that of the person you love. It's so easy to get caught up in everyday matters, to become complacent, to take time for granted.

Now she wished she had done more to savor the moments she'd shared with Scott. She wished she'd spent less time working, less time worrying about things that weren't important, and more time letting him know just how much she loved him. She wished they'd eloped right after the proposal instead of waiting so she could have the perfect wedding.

What a fool she'd been.

There was no going back now. She could only go forward. But she would give her life to have just one more day with him.

Toni knelt next to Scott's grave and picked the wilted flowers up off the mound of earth. The headstone hadn't been set yet, and she wondered how many more days it would be until it arrived. It was still impossible to believe he was gone.

There'd been several times when she had thought she'd seen him—at the grocery store, the gas station. She'd even imagined hearing his voice and turned around, only to find a stranger standing next to her. How long would his image haunt her? How long before she'd stop expecting to find him next to her when she woke up? When would she stop expecting to see him walk through the door at the end of the day?

More than once, she'd seen something on television or read an item in the newspaper and thought, *I have to tell Scott*—only to realize she couldn't tell him. When would her heart be able to accept what her mind knew to be true?

How am I ever going to let him go?

Brian parked the Mustang just outside the gates of the cemetery and watched Toni through his binoculars. He half-believed she was on to him. Why else would she have conned her way into his hotel room? And today she had been overly cautious—almost as if she knew he was following her.

He had noticed her constantly checking her rearview mirror, and then she had made the sudden exit from the interstate. Now the trip to the cemetery. Although he didn't think she had actually spotted him, he knew she was suspicious.

At least one thing was certain. She hadn't yet found the tap he'd put on her home phone line when he'd broken in. Just last night, he'd camped outside her house hidden in the clump of evergreens, listening to her make call after call, desperately trying to locate Nico Williams.

He guessed that was the reason she had driven to Chadwick & Shore first thing this morning. He considered following her inside just to make sure, but decided against it. He wondered where she would go next. It didn't really matter. With the tracking system installed, she wouldn't be able to lose him. He would stay out of sight and make her feel at ease.

But wherever she went, whatever she did, he would be right behind her.

15

Toni knocked on the door of apartment G-101. It was only eleven thirty, but she hoped that by some chance, Gloria might be home. When there was no answer, she knocked again. She leaned toward the door and listened for any sounds coming from inside the apartment. Not able to hear anything, she decided to leave. She had already started to walk away when the door swung open.

A woman with short honey-colored hair and the body of a centerfold model stood in the doorway. She looked to be in her early twenties and was wearing a turquoise tank top and low-rise jeans. A pair of oversized gold hoops dangled from her ears.

"Hi, I'm looking for Gloria Keith."

"That's me."

"My name is Toni Matthews. I was hoping—"

"I know who you are, I've been expecting you. Come on in."

Gloria led her into the small living room that was stuffed with large antiques. "Have a seat," she said.

Toni sat down on a Victorian sofa in mint condition. She glanced around the room. A matching side table held pictures of Gloria and a man in his mid-thirties, along with pictures of a thin older woman. The facial resemblance to Gloria led Toni to believe it was probably her mother. Most of the other furnishings were from the same period, each as perfectly preserved as the sofa. Whoever Gloria was, she had expensive tastes.

Gloria sat next to Toni. "I see you like the furniture."

Although Toni had never been fond of the Victorian style, she smiled. "You have some very nice pieces."

"They belonged to my grandmother. She died a few months ago, and I just couldn't bring myself to sell them."

"Oh, I'm sorry to hear that."

"It happens. But that's something you know all about, don't you?"

Surprised by Gloria's rudeness, Toni hesitated, and then nodded. "Yes, I do."

"Which is why you're here, right?"

Toni wondered why a woman she had only just met would regard her with such veiled hostility. "I wanted to talk to you about my fiancé, Scott Chadwick. After he died, you gave a statement to the police—"

"And you want to know why."

"Yes."

Gloria smiled and shook her head. "You haven't figured it out yet?"

"Figured what out?"

"They say the wife is always the last to know, and I guess it's true." Gloria smiled again. "Scott and I were lovers."

Toni felt as if someone had just punched her in the stomach. That was the last thing she was expecting to hear. "What do you mean, you were lovers? You mean before I met him?"

"Not only *before* you met him. We were lovers right up until the very end."

Toni felt her intestines knot. "I don't believe you."

"I have no reason to lie."

Toni just sat there staring at her. It couldn't be true. "Why are you doing this?"

Gloria grinned as if she'd just won a prize. "It's time you faced the facts. Scott needed something more than you could ever give him. He wasn't satisfied sharing his bed with a boring, uptight businesswoman."

Toni slapped Gloria hard across the face.

"You bitch!" Gloria jumped up from the sofa. "You have no right to come into my house and think you can knock me around."

"You're right, I don't. Just like you don't have the right to lie about your relationship with Scott."

"I'm not lying." Gloria rubbed her left cheek. "We met a few years ago when he guest-lectured for my design class at Vandy, and we never stopped seeing each other. The day before he died, he was right here in this apartment, and he made love to me right here on this rug."

"No. No, that didn't happen."

"Believe what you want."

Toni scooted to the edge of the sofa. "Did you tell Detective Lewis that Scott wanted to commit suicide?"

"So you don't believe that either, huh?"

"What did you tell the police?"

"I told them the truth about Scott, about how he told me he'd rather die than lose his money and his business, because he knew if he lost them, he'd lose you too."

"That's insane. His money never mattered to me."

"He didn't believe that, and he said he couldn't start a new business because the banks would never lend to him once he filed for bankruptcy. Scott felt that his life was already over so all he wanted to do was get out before things blew up."

"You're wrong. Scott knew how much I loved him, and he knew I never would have left him just because his business was gone."

"Are you sure?"

"Of course, I'm sure."

"I hate to break this to you, but you didn't know Scott as well as you think you did."

Toni felt the urge to slap Gloria again. "I knew him better than anyone else."

"Really? I don't think so."

"You expect me to believe that you knew him better?"

"Yeah, I did. He told me everything."

"So I guess he filled you in on all his family history, told you about his fight with Brian, and gave you details about what his sister went through."

"Are you talking about Caitlin's abortion?"

Pain sliced through Toni's chest, and for a second, she thought she would vomit. "Somebody else told you about Caitlin. Who was it?"

"Like I said. Scott."

Toni locked eyes with Gloria. "Look—I don't know why you're lying, but I know you are."

Unable to hold her gaze, Gloria looked away. "If you'll excuse me, I'm going to get some ice for my face." She started toward the kitchen.

Even though she didn't believe a word of what Gloria had said, Toni still felt nauseous. "Do you mind if I use your bathroom?"

"It's at the end of the hall."

Toni let the cold water run over her hands and then splashed some on her face. How could this be happening? Why would Gloria make up such a crazy story? What did she have to gain?

Toni opened the medicine cabinet. She found all the usual things a woman would keep in her bathroom. She noticed there was only one toothbrush, and there weren't any men's toiletries at all. Inside the vanity, Gloria had stowed several rolls of toilet paper and some cleaning products. Toni checked the tub. Shampoo, conditioner, and some lavender bubble bath. There was nothing in the room to indicate that Scott, or any other man for that matter, had ever showered there.

Toni eased open the bathroom door and glanced down the hallway. She could hear Gloria still in the kitchen. Leaving the bathroom light on, she pushed the door closed and then slipped into one of the bedrooms.

An elegantly carved bed stood against one wall. A chest of drawers, a dresser, and an armoire crowded the remainder of the room. Several photos on display featured the same three subjects as those in the living room.

Toni closed her eyes and tried to sense Scott's presence, to smell a hint of his cologne. Anything that would lead her to believe he had been there. She felt nothing.

She slid open the door to the closet. The trendiest of women's fashions hung inside, along with several designer gowns and a full-length sable coat. Toni wondered what Gloria did for a living. Her wardrobe was worth a fortune. Maybe Grandma had left her the money to pay for the clothes, not to mention her silicone boobs.

Toni checked the hallway again and then stole out of the first bedroom and into the second. The decor came as a shock. A child's painted white furniture and a canopy bed filled the room. A menagerie of stuffed animals covered the ruffled pink bedspread, and framed prints of horses lined the walls.

Did Gloria have a daughter? Toni hadn't seen any pictures of a little girl anywhere in the apartment. She realized there were no pictures of Scott either.

She opened one of the chest drawers. It was empty. So was the dresser. Something was off here.

Way off.

She hurried out of the bedroom and back to the bathroom. After flushing the toilet, she turned off the light and returned to the living room. Gloria sat on the sofa holding an ice pack against her face.

"I'm sorry I took so long," Toni said. "I needed some time to regain my composure."

Gloria shrugged. "Whatever."

Toni didn't bother sitting down. "I shouldn't have hit you, and I'm sorry for that. But you shouldn't have provoked me either."

"I'm just telling it like it is."

"No, you're not. It may be true that you had a fling with Scott at one time and you may have even remained friends, but there's one thing I know for sure: there's no way he slept with you after he starting seeing me."

"Is that so?"

"Yes. Scott may have been having problems at the office, and it's possible he mentioned them to you. And for some reason, maybe for the attention or maybe to get back at him for dumping you, you decided to make up a story about him wanting to commit suicide. You even went to the police. But there's one thing I know that you don't."

"Really? What's that?"

"Scott wasn't alone at the hotel that morning. He was pushed off that balcony—murdered. I know who killed him, and in a few days, I'll have all the evidence I need to prove it."

Gloria stared at her, dumbfounded. She opened her mouth as if she was about to say something, but then closed it again. It didn't matter. Toni had heard enough.

She turned her back and walked out of the apartment, slamming the door behind her.

16

Toni reread the first handwritten condition listed on the sales contract and again failed to comprehend the words. She had been staring at the document for twenty minutes and still had no idea what it said. Her mind was stuck on Gloria Keith, and it refused to budge.

She dropped the contract on top of her desk and cradled her head in her hands. She closed her eyes and massaged her temples. Was it possible? Could Scott have had a lover on the side? The very nature of his job kept him out of the office most of the day, and he had no one to account to for his time. The opportunity had definitely been there. But none of the signs were.

Wouldn't she have known if he had been seeing someone else? Wouldn't she have sensed it? During all the time they were together, she had never once suspected Scott of being unfaithful. He was too straightforward and too loyal. Cheating wasn't in his personality; he just wasn't the type. She knew him inside and out, didn't she?

Then why didn't she know about Caitlin?

Scott had kept a large portion of his life hidden from her. He'd claimed that part of his past wasn't important, but he should have shared it with her anyway. Was it that painful to discuss? If so, then why did he tell Gloria?

Toni had the urge to shove everything off of her desk—the papers, the computer, everything. She closed her eyes, took a deep breath, and counted to ten.

No matter how bad things looked, there had to be an explanation. A missing puzzle piece that would complete the picture and make sense out of the whole mess. She would keep digging until she found it. She had to prove to herself that Scott was indeed the man she'd believed him to be. A good and honest man, a man who loved her with all his heart.

She picked up the contract again and tried to concentrate.

The intercom buzzed.

"Yes?"

It was Janet. "You have a call on line 1," she said. "The man says that he's ready to make an offer on your listing in Leiper's Fork and he'll speak only to you."

"I'll take it, thanks."

Built by a country music star, the horse farm southwest of Nashville was her highest-priced listing. It was currently on the market at $5.5 million. She picked up the phone. "Toni Matthews."

"Miss Matthews, my name is Davis Michener. You may have heard of me; I own the chain of Michener's restaurants."

She recognized the name. His family-style restaurants were located throughout the southeastern part of the country. "Yes, I have. How can I help you, Mr. Michener?"

"You have a piece of property out in Leiper's Fork that's exactly what my wife and I have been looking for."

"I'm glad to hear it."

"We saw the grounds and the stables this morning. When we drove by the gate, we noticed it was open, so we took the liberty of going up to the house. I hope that was okay."

Another agent must have left it open. She had written strict instructions in the showing information that the owners wanted the gate kept closed at all times. She would have to check the list and find out who showed the property last.

"Yes, that's fine," Toni said. "I'm glad you were able to get in."

"From what we've seen so far, we love the place. We just need to see inside the home, and then we'll be ready to sign a contract. We'd like to do it tonight."

"That's sounds wonderful. I just need you to come by the office first, and then I'll take you out to the house."

"No, that's not possible. You see, we're down in Columbia right now, and I have a business meeting late this afternoon, but we can meet you at the house after that. Say, around seven thirty?"

Toni had a policy never to meet a buyer without having them come into the office first. That way she could prequalify them, get a copy of their driver's license and some background information. Make sure they were for real. She had heard too many stories of agents being robbed, or sometimes worse. The property at Leiper's Fork was vacant, and it would be dark by seven thirty.

"I'd love to meet you there," Toni said. "But our company's managing broker insists that we meet all customers here at the office."

"I can understand that, but we just don't have the time. We have to be at the airport before ten o'clock, and my wife will be heartbroken if we don't get to see it first. Your assistant told me the asking price, and it's a lot less than we figured. We're prepared to pay cash. Of course, I guess we could have another agent show it to us."

Toni knew that any other agent would jump at the chance. Why should she give up the sales side of the commission when it was right here in her hand? Maybe it would be okay to break her policy just this once. After all, Mr. Michener was a well-known businessman, and she could always ask another agent to go with her and pay that person a percentage for his or her trouble. "Since you're on such a tight schedule, I'll be happy to meet you at the property."

"You're sure? We don't want to get you into any trouble with your boss."

"I'm sure. It'll be fine. Just let me get a phone number in case I need to contact you before then."

Toni wrote down Mr. Michener's cell phone number. She still felt a little uneasy about breaking her cardinal rule, but if she made the sale, it would be worth it. "Thank you, Mr. Michener. I'll see you at seven thirty."

She slid her laptop computer across the desk and did a search for Michener's restaurants. On the company's Web site, she found a picture of Mr. Michener and his wife, Celia. The voice she'd heard seemed to be the right age to fit the photo. She dialed the number for the restaurant home office.

"Thank you for calling Michener's. How may I help you?"

"Toni Matthews for Davis Michener, please."

"I'm sorry, Mr. Michener is out of the office this week. May I take a message?"

"No, no message. Thank you."

Toni punched in the sequence of digits that would block her caller ID information from being sent and then keyed in the number Mr. Michener had given her. He answered on the second ring.

"Davis Michener."

"Hi, Mr. Michener, it's Toni Matthews again. I forgot to ask you earlier how you found out about the Leiper's Fork listing."

"Oh, we saw it in that real estate magazine, *Homes & Land*."

The advertisement for Leiper's Fork was indeed running in the current issue. "Great, thank you. I'll see you tonight."

Satisfied that Davis Michener was who he claimed to be, Toni phoned Dana Dawson. "How would you like to go on a showing with me?" she asked.

Dana agreed to attend the showing without hesitation. Toni hung up the phone and went back to her contract. She forced herself to focus on the terms of the offer. The buyers wanted the sellers to leave all the window treatments and to pay for a home warranty. They also wanted the playground equipment in the back yard. That last item might prove to be a deal breaker. She knew the sellers had already arranged to move it to their new home.

She buzzed Janet on the intercom. "Can you call the Wilsons and let them know that I have an offer?"

"Uh, I already did, remember? You asked me to call them half an hour ago."

"Oh, right. What did they say?"

"They'll be home the rest of the afternoon."

It took Toni nearly two hours to get the Wilsons to come to an agreement on a counteroffer. As she had suspected, Mr. Wilson was dead set against leaving his son's playground equipment, and Mrs. Wilson had no intention of leaving any of the window treatments. On top of all that, even after seeing a market analysis, they both felt that the sales price on the offer was too low. By the time Toni left their house, it was almost five o'clock.

Instead of returning to her office, she drove to the office of the agent who had written the offer. After getting a copy for her files, she gave the original to the sales agent. The two sides were so far apart that it would be a miracle if the contract was ever worked out.

As Toni walked back to her car, she scanned the parking lot, looking for anyone suspicious. Seeing no one, she let her mind drift back to Gloria. Although she didn't believe that Scott had cheated, the encounter still bothered her. She wondered how long it had been since their breakup. Scott had asked Toni to marry him ten months ago, and she was pretty sure that he had dated her exclusively for at least a year prior.

Gloria's attitude definitely fit that of a woman scorned, even after all that time. But if she still carried feelings for Scott, why were there no mementos of him in her apartment? Maybe because she had a new boyfriend. The man Toni had seen in the photographs. But if she did have a new love, why would she tell the police that she was still seeing Scott? Wouldn't that jeopardize her new relationship? None of it really made any sense.

Toni got into her car and fastened her safety belt. Mark's office was just down the street. If Scott had dated Gloria, he would know about it. Maybe she could get some straight answers for a change. She picked up her cell phone and dialed Mark's number.

"Hi, it's Toni."

"Hey. I was just thinking about calling you. What are you up to?"

"I'm just getting a little bit of work done. I'm down the street at a real estate office, and I was wondering if I could swing by. There's something I need to talk to you about."

"Sure. Come on over."

Toni was at Mark's office in a matter of minutes. His secretary showed her in and then asked to leave for the day. Mark agreed and closed the door behind her. Instead of sitting at his desk, he took a seat in a chair next to Toni.

"What's on your mind?" he asked.

"Well, I'm going to ask you something, and I want you to tell me the truth. I don't want it sugarcoated, and I don't want you to try to protect me. No matter how you think I might react, I need you to be honest."

"Do you want my opinion on whether Brian will get the house?"

"No. No, that's not it."

"Then what? What could be so important?"

"Promise me first."

"I promise. I'll be honest with you."

Toni took a deep breath. She wanted to know the truth, but at the same time, she dreaded hearing it. "Tell me about Gloria Keith."

Mark's face froze. He dropped his head, stared at the floor a moment, then got up from his chair and walked to the window. He stood there, saying nothing.

Toni's heart felt as if it had stopped. It refused to beat again until she heard his reply.

Finally, Mark turned from the window. "How do you know about Gloria Keith?"

Toni's throat tightened. Why was he asking questions? Why didn't he just come out and say it. Why couldn't he just tell her and get it over with? "Does it matter?"

Mark dropped his gaze to the floor again and shook his head. He returned to his chair and sat on the edge, his elbows on his knees. "I had no idea he was seeing her. Not until after . . ."

"After Scott died?"

Mark nodded. "She was at the police station. Detective Lewis called me in for an interview. She was leaving as I was going in. She stopped me, and we talked. I swear, I didn't know until then."

"Scott never told you about her?"

"No. I don't really think she was the kind of girl worth mentioning. She's not like you. She seems more like the type that's just for fun."

"Even so, don't you think it's strange that he never talked about her at all? I thought men liked to brag about their conquests."

"Scott dated a lot of different women before he met you. It's possible that he said something about her back then and I just don't remember it."

"So aside from what Gloria told you at the station, you have no real evidence that Scott was still seeing her. Is that right?"

"I feel like I'm being cross-examined."

"But I'm right, aren't I? The only thing you have is her word."

"That's true. It's all hearsay."

"Don't make fun of me."

"I'm sorry. I'm just not sure what you're going for here."

"Then I'll tell you—I don't believe her. I think Scott broke up with her a long time ago, and I think she made up the story she told to Detective Lewis."

Mark didn't answer. He just looked at her.

"What?" she asked. "Tell me what you're thinking."

"Nothing."

"You promised."

Mark took her hand in his. "I think you're in a lot of pain. I think you need someone to direct your anger toward."

"And you think Gloria Keith is my target?"

"If you take your anger out on her, then you can avoid being angry at Scott."

In that instant, she realized Mark was right. She desperately needed someone to blame, someone other than the man she loved. "Okay, so I'm mad—I'm mad as hell." She fought back the tears welling in her eyes.

"Why did he keep so many secrets from me? And how could he have let this happen? How could he leave me?"

Mark reached out and tried to pull her to him, but she pushed him away.

"Don't," she said. "I can't do this right now. I just can't."

She got up from her chair, but Mark blocked her way to the door. "Where are you going?"

"I just need to be alone. Please just let me go; just give me some time to think."

17

Dana Dawson leaned her hip against Janet's empty desk and waited for Cheryl to get off the phone. The client on the line seemed to be giving the poor assistant the third degree. Although his words weren't clear, his rant could be heard across the room. Dana made a face and then stuck out her tongue, trying to coax a smile from Cheryl.

Cheryl shook her head and then rolled her eyes. "Yes, I'll be sure to tell Toni," she said into the receiver. "I'll go ahead and put in the ad change myself." She hung up the phone.

"What was his problem?"

"The newspaper listed his house as three baths instead of three and a half."

"Oh no, it'll never sell now." Dana laughed. She'd dealt with a few clients who had the same kind of attitude.

"The way he was yelling, you'd think the world was about to come to an end." Cheryl closed the file on her desk. "So what can I do for you?"

"I need to get a copy of the termite inspection for Coldwater Court."

Cheryl pulled the file from the filing cabinet and flipped through the contents. When she found the termite inspection, she placed it on the copier and hit the start button. The machine hummed as the light began to pass across the document. Halfway through, it stopped.

"It's jammed again," Cheryl said. "This stupid copier's been acting up all day." She opened the front of the machine and tried to dislodge the paper. "It's no use; I'll have to call the repairman."

Dana felt sorry that Cheryl was having such a rough day. "That's okay, just give me the inspection, and I'll run downstairs and make a copy."

"No, you stay here. I'll do it."

"Are you sure?"

"It'll give me a chance to walk off some of my frustration."

After leaving Mark's office, Toni had driven down the highway, no destination in mind. Although she was convinced Gloria had lied, she couldn't get the woman out of her head. Why would she go to the police and tell them Scott wanted to kill himself? Why would she announce to the world that he was having an affair when he had been scheduled to be married that same week? Had her breakup with Scott been so bitter that she wanted to ruin his reputation?

Even if Scott had been sleeping with Gloria, Toni doubted his business associates would care. The only person that lie could hurt was Toni herself. But the lie about the suicide had done some real damage.

Because of her, Detective Lewis refused to consider the possibility that Scott's death was a homicide. Gloria had single-handedly prevented a murder investigation. Thanks to her, Brian might go free.

Toni couldn't let that happen.

She glanced out the passenger window and then realized where she was. She had driven north on Interstate 65 all the way to Goodlettsville; the exit for Rivergate Mall was just up ahead. She checked the clock on the dashboard. It was already six forty-five. She had promised to meet Mr. and Mrs. Michener in Leiper's Fork at seven thirty. There was no way she could make it on time.

She would have to apologize and see if they would be willing to reschedule. If they were really serious about the property, they would be back. But more than likely, they would find another agent.

That would be okay. Handling both sides of a sale that large could be overly time-consuming. Each party would require a lot of hand-holding, and she wasn't ready to devote herself to that yet. Not until after she had collected enough evidence to prove what Brian had done. She wanted to make sure he was locked away for a long, long time.

Toni pulled off the interstate and drove into the mall parking lot. She rummaged through her briefcase for the Micheners' phone number. Then she remembered: she had left it on her desk. She would have to call the office. Cheryl would still be there since it was her night to work late.

Dana sat in Janet's chair and opened spider solitaire on her computer. She couldn't help noticing the papers on the desk. Toni had a new listing that she hadn't made public yet. All the forms were postdated, and there were instructions not to enter it into the multiple listing service or allow it to be shown.

Dana wondered if it was a pocket listing—a property so hot that Toni wanted to keep it from hitting the market just long enough to find her own buyer. Dana quickly dismissed the idea. Although other agents used that trick all the time, she knew Toni would never even consider it. There must be another explanation.

From the very first day Dana began working at McKay-Wynn Properties, Toni had been an inspiration to her. She recalled how nervous she'd been right before her first listing appointment, almost to the point of wanting to cancel. Toni had realized she was a wreck and offered to go with her. Just having the experienced agent there for support infused her with a sense of confidence and helped her win the listing.

Her father had wanted her to become a doctor like himself and her older brother, but Dana couldn't handle the thought of dealing with sickness and death on a daily basis. Instead, she preferred a career where most of the people she worked with were happy and excited to be moving on to a new phase in their lives, not worried that they might not be around to see tomorrow.

She remembered the day she broke the news to her parents that she wouldn't be attending medical school. She'd avoided telling them for months, afraid they'd be angry. When she finally managed to sit them down and speak the words, she thought her father would have a stroke. Although his face had reddened, he'd kept his emotions under control. He listened quietly as she explained all the reasons medicine was the wrong field for her. When she was finished, he sat still, staring at the floor, not speaking. Her mother had just smiled and said, "I knew it all along."

After a few moments, her father rose from his chair, pulled her into his arms, and told her all he wanted was for her to be happy. And now she was.

The phone rang.

"Toni Matthews' office."

"Dana?"

"Hi, Toni."

"Are you trying to steal Cheryl's job?"

Dana laughed. "No, she just had to run downstairs for a minute."

"Well, I'm glad you're there because I can't make the showing tonight. I'm stuck in Goodlettsville."

"That's okay. I can still go."

"Are you sure? Remember, I've never actually met these buyers and the house is empty."

"Toni, I've been showing houses for almost a year now. I think I can handle it."

Toni hesitated. Since she'd already checked out Mr. Michener's story, Dana should be fine. "If you're absolutely positive you want to go, I'll split the commission fifty-fifty."

"You don't have to do that, a referral fee will be plenty."

"It's fifty-fifty or nothing, and if you decide not to go, their phone number is on my desk."

Gloria lay on her back on the white bed and stared up at the ruffled pink canopy. She was in her childhood dream room—the room she had fantasized about nearly every night while she was growing up.

She remembered those nights long ago, trying to fall asleep on the tattered sofa bed with a broken spring poking her ribs. She would close her eyes and pretend her sister, Sylvia, wasn't really lying beside her and that her brother was not sleeping next to them on the living room floor.

She would shut out the noises from the trailers next door and from the bedroom down the hall. She would imagine herself in this room. All by herself. A room of her own. One fit for a princess.

The first time she had seen the room of her dreams, she was six years old. It was Amanda Peterson's birthday. Amanda's mother had invited all the girls in her class over for a party. After playing games and eating cake, they had all gone into Amanda's room.

Gloria had never seen anything so beautiful. Everything had been pink and white. There were dolls and stuffed animals everywhere. She remembered standing in the middle of the room afraid to touch anything.

When she got home, she pulled out an old JCPenney catalog that Miss Pauline, the trailer park manager, had given her to make paper dolls. Inside she found a room similar to Amanda's. She tore out the picture and put it up on the refrigerator, and she made a vow: someday, somehow, she would have that room. And two years ago, right after she turned twenty, that day had arrived.

Although she was too old to really enjoy it now, she bought the furniture anyway before purchasing any of the antiques. She wanted to fulfill the promise she had made to herself. And in a few years, she would find a little girl to adopt—one nobody else wanted. A little girl who would love the room as much as she had.

Gloria pushed away her memories and sat up. She had a lot of packing to do. All the white furniture, including the bed, was going into storage. She was moving to a smaller apartment over a hundred miles away. But the move was only temporary. Just until things blew over. After that, she would live in her own house. A brand new two-story just west of Nashville, with three bedrooms and a big backyard.

She might even get a dog.

With fifteen minutes to spare, Dana pulled her car up to the front gates of the horse farm. She was glad to see that the Micheners hadn't arrived yet. She wanted to go through the house and turn on all the lights and put some soft music on the stereo system. She liked to set the right mood for the buyers. Make them feel at home.

This was her first time showing a property valued over $1 million, and the excitement made her stomach flutter. She imagined herself at the closing table, chatting with the buyers and congratulating them on the good deal they'd managed to get. If she did her best, worked hard, and earned their trust, the Micheners would be sure to recommend her to their friends. If that happened, she'd be well on her way to becoming a top producer.

Thank you for giving me this opportunity, Toni.

She lowered her window and punched in the security code. When the gates swung open, she drove up the long winding drive and parked her red Mercedes beneath the darkened porte cochere. Why were all the outside lights off? It wasn't as if the sellers couldn't afford the electric bill.

Leaving her headlights on, Dana got out of her car and walked up to the front door. A steady cadence of crickets and tree frogs echoed through the hills. Their songs soothed her and made her wish she lived in the country instead of sharing a condo with her brother downtown. She fumbled with the lockbox hanging from the doorknob. After a few seconds, it opened, and she took out the key.

Once the door was unlocked, she returned to her car and switched off her headlights. The last thing she wanted was to get stuck out in the boonies with a dead battery. She hoped to show the house and get the contract written up by nine o'clock. That way, she could get to bed at a decent hour.

She had an early breakfast date in the morning with a young doctor from Vanderbilt hospital who was nearing completion of his residency program. They'd been seeing each other for over six months, and if things worked out as she hoped, they might be engaged by the end of the year.

Because she was part of such a closely knit family, Dana viewed her parents' approval as extremely important. To her delight, they'd fallen in love with Kyle just as easily as she had. He was everything she'd ever dreamed of in a husband—handsome, intelligent, and loving. He encouraged her in everything she did, and, one of the most important things of all, he knew how to make her laugh.

Dana grabbed her briefcase from the passenger seat and walked back to the front door. She wore her lucky suit—a three-button blazer and skirt in Mediterranean blue, her favorite color. It was the same suit she'd worn on her first listing appointment.

As she turned the knob, she thought she heard a noise coming from inside the house. She knew the owners had moved out before putting their home on the market.

She paused and listened.

All she could hear was the band of night creatures still playing on. It had probably just been the house settling or the wind blowing a tree branch across one of the windows.

She pushed the door open and stepped into the foyer. The house was dark and still. Dana ran her hand along the wall next to the door searching for the light switch and found a bank of three. She flipped the first switch. Nothing happened. She flipped the other two. Still no lights came on.

This is just great, she thought.

There must be a blown fuse or a tripped breaker. That would also explain why the outside lights were off. Now she would have to go back out to her car, rummage through her trunk for a flashlight, and then stumble around the house looking for the breaker box.

She hoped she could get the lights on before the Micheners arrived. They had a plane to catch, and she didn't want to hold them up or make them think she was incompetent. Blowing the sale for Toni was another of her concerns. Out of all the agents in the office, Toni had trusted her to show the highest-priced listing held by the company, and she didn't want to let her friend down.

She leaned over and placed her briefcase on the floor. When she stood back up, she noticed a bright red dot on the lapel of her jacket.

"What the—"

A searing pain shot through Dana's chest as the bullet pierced her heart.

18

Toni pulled into her driveway and pushed the remote button for the garage door. It felt strange coming home to a house that was all lit up. It looked so cheery and welcoming, almost as if a party was going on inside. She wished that were the case. How many competent twenty-nine-year-olds were afraid to turn their lights off at night? But then again, how many thought they had a killer watching them?

She drove into the garage, shut the door, and then looked around before getting out of her car. The idea of someone being in her garage seemed unlikely. But she had once read an article in a real estate magazine about thieves who were able to clone garage door remotes. If her suspicions were correct and Brian had hired someone to kill her—someone with specialized training—that person would probably know how to do it.

She went inside the house and immediately reset the security system. After dropping her purse on the kitchen counter, she noticed the green alert light on her cell phone was blinking. She hadn't even heard it ring. She wondered if the Micheners had called. It was more likely to be Cheryl telling her that they had decided to use another agent.

She woke the phone and saw the voice mail icon in the upper left corner. Instead of Cheryl or the Micheners, she heard Mark's voice.

"Toni, I'm sorry about this afternoon. Please call me when you get this. I don't care how late it is."

She erased the message. She didn't feel like talking to Mark—not now anyway. He meant well, but he agreed with Jill and Clint. Why was she the only one who still believed in Scott? Sure, she was angry with him, but she thought she had a right to be. Just like every other person in her life she'd loved, he'd left her. His death wasn't his fault, but she felt abandoned nonetheless.

The secrets angered her far more. A broken family was one of the things she'd had in common with Scott. They'd talked for hours about her mother leaving and her father's battle with cancer. And Scott had opened up about the loss of his parents, or so she'd thought at the time.

The fact that there had been an omission between them tore at her heart. And although she tried hard not to think about it, she couldn't help but wonder whether there were more secrets she hadn't yet discovered.

Her stomach growled, and she realized she hadn't eaten since breakfast. She opened her refrigerator and scanned the contents. She didn't really feel like cooking. She could order a pizza, but then she would have to unlock the door for the delivery person. It seemed ridiculous, but she didn't want to take that risk. She decided to polish off the rest of the chicken salad.

Grabbing a plate, two slices of bread, the chicken salad, a Coke, and a bag of chips, she took them all into the family room. She piled the food onto the coffee table, pulled off her jacket, and kicked off her shoes. She found a rerun of *Friends* on television, then opened the container of chicken salad and spread it across the bread while Joey and Ross tried to find a way off the roof of the apartment building.

As the characters started down the fire escape, Toni heard a noise outside. She put down her sandwich. A dog was barking. It was close—somewhere in her backyard. She peeked through the slats in the plantation shutters and searched the lawn. She couldn't see anything. It sounded as if the barking was coming from the end of the house that had no windows.

Her neighbors to the left had a dog. A chocolate Lab with an Energizer in its tail. She had seen it in their yard a few times, but had never heard it bark before. Maybe it had never had a reason—until now.

Could Brian be outside?

Toni muted the volume on the television. She stood next to the french doors listening for any other sounds in the yard. The barking was too loud to make out anything else.

This is stupid, she thought.

She was being paranoid again. Dogs barked. It didn't necessarily mean that anything was wrong. Trying to convince herself that the dog was chasing a rabbit or opossum or maybe even a raccoon, Toni went back to her sandwich. She reasoned with herself. If the person after her was in her yard, wouldn't he shut the dog up? Kill it before it could warn her? That made sense. She had nothing to worry about. If the dog yelped in pain, then she would worry.

After finishing her dinner, she curled up on the sofa. With the TV volume low, she tried to concentrate on an old western in black and white. It was no use. She kept thinking about Brian. He had made Scott's death look like a suicide. What did he have planned for her?

A thought crossed her mind, and she sat up. What if Brian, or someone he'd hired, was taunting the dog, deliberately trying to make it bark? Could someone be using the animal as a means to lure her out of the house?

It happened in horror movies all the time. First, there would be a noise outside. Then a scantily clad teenage babysitter, or some other beautiful but stupid character, would go out to investigate. The next thing you knew, the killer would be slashing her to pieces. Only this wasn't a movie, and she had no intention of going out into the dark.

The dog continued barking throughout the night, fueling her imagination and making it impossible for her to let go of her fear. It was after dawn on Wednesday morning when she finally drifted off to sleep. Later that afternoon, Toni awoke on the sofa with a kink in her neck.

She stretched and rolled her shoulders moving her head from side to side. As she glanced at the television, still on from the night before, she saw Dana Dawson's picture on the screen. Then the camera switched to a female reporter standing outside the gates of the horse farm in Leiper's Fork.

Toni grabbed the remote and turned up the volume.

"—killed last night by a single gunshot wound to the heart," the reporter was saying. "A groundskeeper found her body early this morning. The police are telling us robbery was the apparent motive. The victim's purse and jewelry are missing as well as her car. But the police are not yet sure how many items are missing from the home."

Dana was dead. Shot last night.

The Micheners.

Toni picked up the phone. Her hands shaking, she dialed the office. Janet answered.

"Have you heard about Dana?" Toni asked.

"Yes, we got the news about an hour ago, and we were going to call you but—"

"It was supposed to be me."

"What?"

"Remember the man who called yesterday, the one who said his name was Davis Michener? I was supposed to meet him at Leiper's Fork last night, but Dana went in my place. Look on my desk, and get me his phone number, please."

Across town, another phone rang.

"Yeah?"

"You idiot, how could you have killed the wrong person?"

"It was dark. They look a lot alike, and I couldn't tell, not until after it was over."

"Well, now she knows for sure. What if she goes to the police again?"

"She won't. I'll take care of it."

"You better, and no screwups this time. I want her dead."

Janet came back on the line.

"I've looked all over your desk, and I can't find any number for the Micheners."

Dana must have taken it. The police probably wouldn't be able to trace the number anyway. More than likely, the cell phone was either stolen or a cheap throwaway. And Toni knew that the person she had talked to the day before was definitely not Davis Michener. She hung up the phone and dialed the number for the police station.

"Detective Lewis, please," Toni said.

"He's not in. Can I take a message?"

"No, no message. I'll call back later."

Would it really do any good? Detective Lewis probably wouldn't believe her anyway. The police saw Dana's death as a robbery. To them, money had been the object. After all, the house was worth over $5 million. Any thief would assume valuable items were inside.

She knew what the police were thinking. After Dana had let the thief into the house, she became a liability, so he got rid of her. But Toni knew better. Whoever shot Dana had missed his target. He hadn't been aiming for Dana. He had been aiming for Toni.

An icy knot formed in her chest. Dana was dead, and it was all her fault. She should have known better. She should never have let Dana go to that showing. Now another family was suffering the same grief and pain she'd felt since losing Scott. Only this time, it could have been prevented. This time, Toni should have been the one who died.

She thought about calling Dana's parents, but what would she say? How could she explain that she was the one to blame for their only daughter's death? How could they ever forgive her? Toni remembered the last lunch she'd shared with Dana, filled with girl talk. Dana had giggled in that way young women do when asked about the man they're dating—the man she hoped to one day marry.

There were so many things that Dana had wanted to do—go mountain climbing, take a vacation to Australia, run in the Blanton Hills 5K Race for the Cure in the fall, and follow in Toni's footsteps to become a top-selling agent. Her life had held so much promise, and now it was over.

Toni went upstairs to the master bathroom and pulled off her clothes. Turning on the water as hot as she could stand it, she stepped into the shower. She stood under the steaming spray trying to knock the chill out of her body.

Why had she ever agreed to meet the fake Micheners at the house in the first place? Damn Brian! She wished he'd been the one who had died, not Caitlin. By now, he had to know the killer made a mistake. How long did she have before he tried again?

When the water turned tepid, Toni got out of the shower. After drying her hair, she dressed in a thick cable-knit sweater and a pair of jeans. As long as she stayed locked in the house, she felt relatively safe. But she didn't really want to be alone.

She tried to reach Jill, but found out she had meetings scheduled all afternoon. Toni phoned Mark as well, but he was in court, and his secretary didn't expect him back until late.

She wandered through the house, unsure what to do. As she entered the study, she heard the rumble of thunder in the distance. She parted the shutters and looked out the window. Dark clouds rolled across the sky, a storm moving in from the west.

She ran her fingers along the edge of Scott's desk and then sat down in his chair. She wished she could travel back in time. Turn the clock back to the days when she and Scott were together. Happy. Looking forward to their future. She never could have imagined the way things would end. So much had changed in one week.

She leaned back in the chair and watched the pictures flash by on the computer screen saver. Scott owned a digital camera, but he seldom used it. He preferred his old Canon EOS 35 mm. After getting the film developed, he had taken the time to scan every photo from their trip to Cozumel onto his computer's hard drive.

Shots of them on the beach morphed into scenes of their day spent with Clint and Jill aboard a sailboat. There were pictures of the four of them at the park at Chankanaab Lagoon and on a side trip to the ruins at Tulum. The slide show ended with a photo of Scott and Toni dining at an alfresco restaurant on the waterfront.

As the last picture began to dissolve, Toni's heart nearly stopped.

It couldn't be. Her eyes must be playing tricks on her. She pulled the photo album from the bookshelf next to Scott's desk and opened it near the back. She flipped through the pictures of their trip. On the last page, she found the one she was looking for. Taken as a favor by another American tourist, the photo showed Scott and Toni sitting at an umbrella table smiling, his arm around her, his head tilted toward hers.

And in the background, at a table to the right, sat Gloria Keith.

19

Toni couldn't believe it: Gloria had been in Mexico. Why? Was she telling the truth about her relationship with Scott after all? Did he bring her there? No, it didn't make sense. He couldn't have; he had spent all his time with Toni. They were together the whole trip. And yet it seemed too odd to be a coincidence.

Toni studied the photo. It was definitely Gloria. Wearing a purple sundress and holding a margarita, she had her face turned directly toward the camera as if she were posing too. Had she followed them to Cozumel in a fit of jealousy? Or was it just a weird coincidence? One of fate's little jokes that put them in the same place at the same time?

Maybe she had been there with her new boyfriend. The table where she sat was at the edge of the picture, the right side cut off. It was impossible to tell whether someone else had been sitting with her.

Considering the amount of joy Gloria had received from telling Toni she'd slept with Scott, it was surprising she hadn't come over and introduced herself. She seemed like the type who would try to make Toni jealous. But Gloria had never spoken to Scott that day. Why?

It would have been perfectly natural for her to say hello—and was actually strange that she didn't. Toni recalled they had been at the restaurant for at least an hour. Gloria had to have seen them, and Scott must have been aware of her. How could anyone sit that close to a former lover for that length of time and not realize it?

Their tables had been near enough to overhear each other's conversations. But Scott had never acknowledged Gloria. Even if they had parted on bad terms and he had pretended not to see her, he should have had some kind of reaction. There should have been a change in his body language. Toni should have sensed something was going on. Shouldn't she?

Toni searched through Scott's desk until she found his magnifying glass. She flipped back in the album to the first page of pictures from their trip. One by one, she examined every photo. Gloria didn't appear in any of the other shots, but that didn't mean that she hadn't been lurking close by.

Something just wasn't right. Toni could feel it in the pit of her stomach. She put the magnifying glass down and tried to remember everything Gloria had said at her apartment the day before. It wasn't much, only that she and Scott had been lovers and that they'd been together right before he died. Of course she'd claimed Scott told her he wanted to take his own life, which, like everything else, was just another lie.

Then Toni realized what she had said to Gloria. The words echoed in her mind.

I know who killed Scott, and soon I'll have the evidence to prove it.

A few hours later, someone had called Toni's office pretending to be Davis Michener. That someone had killed Dana.

Gloria was the only person who knew that Toni was collecting evidence against Brian. What if they were working together? They could have been planning Scott's murder for months. Watching him, waiting for the right opportunity. Going as far as following him to Mexico.

Even if they didn't plan to kill him there, Gloria's plane ticket would show she had been in Cozumel on the same date as Scott. It could serve as proof they were having an affair. That would make her story seem even more credible to the police.

Then another idea hit Toni: maybe the reason Scott hadn't reacted to Gloria at the restaurant was that he had never seen her before. If Gloria and Brian were partners, he could have told her about Caitlin. Her knowing about the abortion was the one thing that had spawned a seed of doubt in Toni's mind. Now it seemed possible there was a plausible explanation for everything Gloria had said.

Neither Mark nor Jill knew Gloria. If Scott had really dated her, they should have met her at least once. And Gloria was definitely not someone anyone would forget meeting.

Toni closed the photo album. She had to find out exactly what was going on before it was too late. What if she confronted Gloria? Pretended to have proof that Brian murdered Scott with Gloria's help? Maybe Toni could get her to confess and convince her to talk to the police. She could point out the fact that if Gloria turned herself in, she could arrange some type of plea bargain.

Mark could go with her and explain all of the legal ramifications. Of course, she would first have to convince him she wasn't crazy.

A clap of thunder reverberated through the house, and the computer screen went blank. Shadows invaded the room that had been brightly lit a moment before. The power was out. A shiver danced down the back of Toni's neck. Although the security system had a battery backup, the darkness filled her with an overwhelming sense of vulnerability.

What if it hadn't been the storm that knocked out the electricity? What if someone had cut the power line? What if they had somehow disarmed the security system?

Come on, get a grip. You're being stupid again.

She picked up the phone to see if it was still working and was relieved to hear a dial tone. She punched in the number for Mark's cell phone. After a few rings, his voice mail answered. She decided to leave another message. "Hi Mark, it's Toni. I really need to talk to you. Please call me as soon as you can."

With the power off, she no longer felt safe. She told herself she was being silly, that it was nothing a few candles wouldn't fix. But her fear continued to grow along with the shadows. She felt an overpowering urge to get out of the house.

Jill would probably be finished with her meetings before Mark got out of court. Toni could drive over to Chadwick & Shore and wait in Jill's office. Once Jill was through with her work for the day, they could pick up Mark, and the three of them could go to Gloria's apartment together.

Even if they didn't believe Toni at first, she felt certain her friends would go along with the plan just to humor her.

Toni fished around in Scott's desk until she found his mini voice recorder. She checked to make sure the batteries were still good. Whatever Gloria told them, Toni wanted it recorded.

After slipping on a lightweight jacket, she grabbed an umbrella and headed out to the garage. Despite the four windows facing the front lawn, the gloom here was even denser. She tossed her belongings onto the passenger seat and then walked to the rear of her car. With the electricity out, she would have to raise the garage door by hand. As she opened the door, a gust of wind caught her jacket. It billowed out behind her like a ship's sail.

Pulling the jacket tight around her, she scanned the lawn. Satisfied that no one was lurking outside, she got into her car. Cascades of rain pummeled her windshield as she drove onto the street. Lightning split the sky ahead, followed by jarring thunder. The storm showed no signs of letting up soon.

As she reached the end of her street and turned right, Toni tried to think of a way to persuade Gloria to open up to her. She would have to be careful of what she said. She had to make Gloria believe that there was plenty of evidence against her. But she couldn't say too much, or Gloria would know she was lying. Maybe Jill and Mark would have some ideas.

Toni's head jerked as the car behind her rammed into her back bumper. Steadying the wheel with both hands, she checked her rearview mirror. She saw a green sedan with four silver circles intertwined on the hood: an Audi. The windows were tinted enough that she couldn't tell who was driving. Considering the careless way the sedan was traveling on the wet pavement, it was probably some idiot trying to send a text message. It seemed a little early in the day for the driver to be drunk.

Leaves and small branches, ripped from the trees by the storm, littered the narrow road that wound through the rolling hills. To her left lay fenced pasture, to her right, a thick grove of cedars and oaks. Toni put on her blinker and started looking for a safe place to pull over. As she slowed, the car slammed into her again.

This was no accident.

Toni stomped on the gas, accelerating as fast as she dared on the slick winding road. The Audi matched her speed, clinging tight to her tail. The rain continued to hammer her windshield, blurring the way ahead.

She was scared to drive any faster in this weather, but what choice did she have? If she slowed down, the Audi would run her off the road. She could pull into the next driveway, but then she would risk getting shot like Dana. And if she stopped at a house, she might end up putting someone else's life in danger as well.

She thought about calling 911 on her cell phone, but it was in her purse on the passenger's seat. At the speed she was driving, she was afraid to take her eyes off the road long enough to find the phone, let alone dial the number. She only had one option.

At the bottom of the next hill, the road curved sharply to the left before crossing over the Cherokee River. A few miles past the bridge, the road connected with a busy four-lane highway. If she could reach the highway, she might be able to lose the Audi in traffic, and then she could drive straight to the police station.

She glanced in her rearview mirror. The sedan was mere inches from her bumper. Any closer, and they would be touching. As she mounted the hill, Toni pushed the accelerator to the floor, trying to put distance between her car and the Audi. She needed to shake the sedan from her tail before she reached the top. Once there, she knew she would have to let off the gas and reduce her speed enough to round the tight curve before the bridge.

As if reading her mind, the Audi barreled ahead, closing the gap. Her hands clammy, Toni tightened her grip on the steering wheel while keeping her foot nailed to the floor. As she crested the hill, she eased off the gas. The sedan lurched forward and butted her bumper. Once, then twice. Her reflexes told her to speed up, but that was impossible. She had to slow down or she would never make the curve. Toni pressed on the brake.

The Audi struck her again, this time retaining contact with her car, pushing her down the hill. The sedan obviously planned to shove her off the road and into the river. She continued to ride the brake, but with the sedan bearing on her, she realized she was still going too fast.

As they neared the bottom of the hill, the Audi swerved into the oncoming lane and plowed into Toni's side. Her car careened out of control, skidding across the wet pavement. She fought to stay on the road. Through the pelting rain, she saw the curve and the bridge in front of her. Even as she braked, she knew it was too late.

Toni's car tore through the guardrail, and the air bag exploded in her face.

20

The Audi stopped halfway across the bridge. With the engine idling, the driver waited and watched Toni's car sink into the murky waters of the river. The Audi's dashboard clock counted off the minutes, one, two, and then three, as the BMW floated downstream, spun around, and descended nose first. By the time six minutes had elapsed, even the faint glow from the car's headlights had disappeared.

For the driver, there was no thrill in the killing. But like the others that came before, no sadness either. Motivated by self-preservation, the task was simply one that had to be completed.

The driver glanced back at the street. The headlights of an oncoming car flashed through the trees lining the next curve. Shifting the sedan into gear, the driver rolled across the bridge. There was no need to risk drawing attention to the Audi or to the damaged guardrail. And continuing to watch the BMW was unnecessary: if Toni hadn't escaped by now, there was no way she could survive.

Mark swiveled around in his chair and stared out the rain-streaked window. From his vantage point on the fourth floor, he had a clear view across the street, crowded with rush-hour traffic, of the historic church on the corner. The high winds from the storm had shattered several of the church's upper stained-glass windows. A group of men on scaffolding worked in the cold drizzle covering the area of missing panes with plastic sheeting. Above their heads, the steeple stretched upward against the gunmetal sky.

Mark rotated toward his desk and picked up the phone message from Toni. His secretary had scribbled the note, marked urgent, three hours earlier. Since the time he returned to his office, Mark had made several attempts to reach Toni. All he got was her voice mail.

He dialed her cell number one more time. After hearing the familiar greeting, he decided to leave another message. "Hi, it's me again. I'm working late tonight, so call me at the office. Or if you're free, you can swing by, and we can order some takeout. Talk to you later."

He put down the phone, folded the message in half, and tapped it against his desk. He hoped Toni wasn't still upset with him. He remembered the fire that had flashed in her eyes right before she stomped out of his office the previous day.

All he wanted to do was help her, but she would be forever loyal to Scott's memory, and she expected everyone else to be too. At least she was finally able to admit that she was angry with him for leaving her. That was a step in the right direction. It was difficult for her to be objective now, but eventually she would realize that although Scott had been a good man, he was far from perfect.

Mark turned back to the window. With the plastic sheeting in place, the workers across the street had begun to tear down their scaffolding. In a few weeks, they would install new stained glass, and the church where Toni had planned to marry Scott would be as beautiful as it had always been.

Mark knew Toni had her own storm to weather. But once it was over, she would emerge stronger than before. She would be able to move on and open up her heart again. But as anxious as he was for that day to come, he had to be careful not to push her. Cultivating a deeper relationship would take time and patience. No doubt several months would pass before she would allow herself to consider anything beyond friendship. It might even take a year or more. It didn't matter.

Whenever she was ready, he intended to be there.

By the time Toni came to, water had flooded the car up to her waist. Although it was spring, the river felt as cold as ice. The surge cut through her jeans chilling her to the core. But as her mind cleared, it was the realization of what had happened and exactly where she was that caused her to tremble. Her BMW had soared off the road and plunged into the river. The silty haze outside the windshield told her the front end of the car was fully submerged.

Everything around her was in silhouette, framed by shadows as dense and murky as the river itself. Even the bright white fabric of the deflated air bag now appeared dingy gray. Trying to remain calm, she unlatched her seat belt and reached for the window control. She pressed the button. Nothing happened. She tried again, jabbing all the buttons. Then she slammed her fist against the controls.

"Dammit, roll down!"

It was no use. The windows remained closed. She remembered watching part of an accident survival program a few weeks earlier on the Discovery Channel. The show had included instructions on how to escape from a vehicle that was trapped underwater, but she had been only half listening, and now the details were foggy. One thing she did recall was that the water pressure outside the vehicle needed to be equal to that inside before the doors would open.

Although the car had not yet filled with water, she whispered a silent prayer and tried to unlock the door. She struggled with the latch, but the door remained locked. Toni realized the electrical system had shorted out. There was no way to get the doors open now.

The water continued to rise, rushing in with the sound and force of jets in a whirlpool tub. The deluge brought with it a dank scent that reminded Toni of rotting leaves. Of death and decay. The river would bury her alive.

She fought the panic that was growing inside her. *I will not die here. Not like this.*

With the water level now at her chest, Toni braced herself against the driver's seat and steering wheel and then kicked the passenger's side window as hard as she could. The soles of her loafers made a dull thud as they contacted with the glass. The window refused to budge. She kicked the window a second and then a third time, but the glass held firm.

Frustrated, she shed her jacket and crawled between the seats into the rear of the car. The water seemed to be rising faster now. It lapped at her chin, threatening to invade her mouth and nostrils. She pressed her lips together, but still managed to taste the bitter swill. She swallowed, then pushed her tongue against her teeth and fought the urge to vomit. It wasn't so much the taste of the dirty river that sickened her. It was the thought of the water forcing its way into her lungs, stealing the life from her body.

Toni shook the image from her mind, and grabbed the passenger's seat headrest. Pressing her back against the driver's seat for leverage, she took a deep breath. Trying unsuccessfully to keep her nose above water, she kicked repeatedly at the rear passenger window. The water resistance weakened the thrust of the blows, making her efforts useless.

Tears crept into her eyes. There was no way out. The water had almost completely filled the interior of the car. Finding an air pocket in the rear corner of the passenger's side, Toni pushed her face against the roof.

Memories of her childhood streamed through her mind. A Christmas morning before her mother left. Her parents sitting next to her by the tree singing "Jingle Bells." The smell of her mother's perfume—vanilla with a hint of spice. The time she got lost in the department store when she was five. The agony of feeling all alone and then the relief that swept through her when at last she ran into her mother's waiting arms.

There was her first kiss from Bobby Holland. Her sixteenth birthday party and her first prom. Her high school graduation. Her father's death. And meeting Scott. Finding a love stronger than any she had ever known, but then losing him as well.

Scott's face drifted before her.

Was it the same for him when he died? Did he think of her in those last few seconds? Or was his fall to the ground too fast for memories? Did he feel pain? Or was he overcome with numbness the way she was now? Did he curse his killer? Or did he whisper his forgiveness?

Unlike Scott, she had not seen the person responsible for her death. Had Brian been the one driving the car? Or was it someone else? Would she ever know? Did the afterlife allow the comfort of that knowledge? And here, in this earthly life, would that person go free?

There was no one left to question the reasons for her death. No one who would believe it was anything more than an accident on a rain-slicked road. And with Toni gone, there would be no one to bring Scott's killer to justice. Brian would live out the rest of his life as if nothing had happened, using Scott's money instead of earning his own. He might even end up hurting someone else if they got in his way.

Toni couldn't let that happen. She couldn't just wait here to die; she had to fight. She would kick the window again with all her strength and keep kicking until there was no air left. If only she had worn different shoes. A high-heeled pump might have been able to crack the glass.

Then it dawned on her: *she could use her umbrella.*

The end of the small folding umbrella had a metal tip similar to a center punch. Leaving the sanctuary of the air pocket, Toni dove beneath the water. Not wanting to open her eyes, she felt her way between the seats and into the front compartment of the car. The crash had hurled her belongings from the passenger seat. She found the contents of her purse scattered across the floorboard.

She touched the various objects, identifying them in her mind. Her cell phone—useless now. Her wallet and checkbook, a hairbrush. Where was the umbrella? She knew it had been beside her purse before the accident.

A rush of fear shot through her: if she couldn't find the umbrella, she had no hope of escape. When she finally stretched her arm under the seat, her fingers closed around the handle.

Her lungs burning, Toni returned to the rear of the car. The air pocket had grown smaller now; the river was squeezing out the remaining bits of life. She knew this would be it—her last chance.

Taking a final breath from the pocket, Toni plunged back into the water. Holding the umbrella with both hands, she rammed the point against the rear passenger window. The sharp clack of the blow reverberated through the car, but the glass remained intact. Firming her grip on the umbrella, she struck again, putting the force of her entire body weight into the blow.

The window cracked in a pattern that reminded her of a spider's web. After knocking out all of the shards, Toni swam through the opening.

She was free.

21

With her lungs threatening to explode, Toni broke the surface of the river. She gulped the fresh air and struggled to keep her head above water as the current pushed her downstream. Where was the driver of the Audi? Was he watching from the riverbank, waiting to finish the job he had started?

Something clawed at her leg.

She kicked hard and spun around, expecting to see a man in a wetsuit ready to clamp his hands around her arms and drag her under, but no one was there. As the river carried her backward around a bend, she looked up toward the bridge. The road appeared deserted.

Fighting the current, she swam toward the shore. The river drained her strength; she could feel her body growing weaker by the second. She kept her eyes focused on the bank, praying she would make it.

After several agonizing minutes, her foot struck bottom. The water was no longer over her head. She tried to stand, but the current was too swift. As the river continued to shove her further downstream, she inched closer to the bank.

Out of the corner of her eye, she spotted a tree branch hanging low over the water. She thrust forward, stretched out her arms, and grabbed the limb. As the rough bark bit into her wet palms, pain shot through her hands, but she didn't dare let go.

Toni clung to the branch for several minutes. The current pounded against her and threatened to knock her loose. She took long, deep breaths and tried to summon the strength to pull herself onto the shore, but her arms felt limp and useless.

You can do this. You've come this far. Don't give up now.

She closed her eyes and pictured Linda Hamilton's sculpted biceps in the second *Terminator* movie. Then she imagined her own arms as being twice as muscular and twice as strong.

Loosening her grip on the limb, she moved her left hand across her right and began to travel up the branch toward the bank. She continued placing one hand above the other until her knees scraped the rocky river bottom. Her palms bloody, she crawled onto the shore.

The rain had weakened to a drizzle by now, and the winds had calmed. Toni lay on her stomach, listening for the driver of the Audi, although if she were to hear him searching for her, she wasn't sure she'd be able to run. But for now, the only sounds around her were the warble of a mockingbird and the faint staccato of a dog barking in the distance.

She rolled over and sat up. Her jeans were torn, her knees skinned and bleeding. Somewhere along the way, she had lost her shoes. The soaked sweater clung to her, cold and heavy, and for the first time, she realized she was shivering.

Her skin looked pale and shriveled, and her hands burned. She was freezing and exhausted. But she was alive. Toni pulled off her sweater and wrung out the water as best she could. As she slipped it back over her head, she heard a voice in the distance. A woman's voice calling to someone.

Toni crawled behind an oak tree and then stood up. Through the grove of hardwoods, she saw the back side of a house. A woman was standing in the driveway scanning the tree line. She called out again, and Toni saw a small white dog run across the yard and jump into the woman's arms.

Toni peered through the woods trying to detect any other signs of movement, any indication that the driver of the Audi was near. No one else was around. She moved out from behind the tree and started toward the house. The woman there could help her. She could phone the police.

But after a few steps, Toni stopped.

Brian, or whoever it was who ran her off the road, probably thought he had succeeded in killing her. Maybe it would be better if she played dead for a while. With the house still in sight, she dropped to a crouch.

She waited until the woman and dog were back inside, and then headed through the woods toward her own home.

It would have been far easier and faster to walk back along the road, but she didn't want to risk someone seeing her. She picked her way through the thick underbrush. Briars snagged her clothing, and her wet feet grew numb with cold. Although the rain had stopped, the trees continued to shower her with water stored on their leaves.

By the time Toni reached the edge of her property two hours later, the sun hung low in the sky. She leaned against the mesh fence surrounding the tennis court and pulled pine needles out of her socks, then massaged her toes trying to regain some feeling. Her feet would probably be sore for days. She gazed across the lawn at the back of her house. The electricity was back on; every window glowed with light, a warm beacon calling her to safety.

She left the tennis court and walked to the pool area. Scott had hidden a spare key in a magnetic box underneath one of the pieces of wrought iron furniture, but she didn't know which one. Once she found it, she let herself in through the breakfast room door and stripped in the laundry room.

Knowing the wet clothing might be found and give her away, she grabbed a trash bag, stuffed her jeans and sweater inside, and then went upstairs to shower.

How long would it be before Brian realized she was still alive? She was fairly confident her car wouldn't be found before morning. Even in daylight, it might not be visible from the bridge.

She knew her friends would start to worry when they didn't hear from her. They would probably form their own search party. Still, it could be days before they fished her BMW out of the water. Would she have time to find Nico? After nearly drowning, confronting Gloria didn't sound like such a good idea.

One thing was for certain. She couldn't stay at home. She would have to disappear. Toni dried off from her shower and then rubbed an antibiotic ointment onto her knees and palms. She dressed in jeans and a sweatshirt, and pulled her hair up into a ponytail.

In her closet, she stuffed an overnight bag with clothing for a few days and slipped on a denim cap embroidered with the words *Hard Rock Café, Jamaica*. As she turned to leave, she glanced at the column of shelves near the door and realized she had a problem.

Her purse was still inside her car at the bottom of the river. She had no money, no credit cards, and no identification. Without cash, she wouldn't be able to get very far. She grabbed an empty handbag from one of the shelves and headed downstairs.

In the study, she pulled out the paper sack that held Scott's belongings. She dumped the contents on top of the desk and then looked inside his wallet. There was a little over a hundred dollars, not enough for what she had planned. His ATM card for their joint checking and savings accounts was there as well, but she knew any withdrawals she made could be traced.

Was Brian that good? Did he have that capability? Even if he didn't, once her friends reported her missing, the police might check the accounts. If she used the card, they would see the activity and know she was still alive.

She stared at the built-in bookcase next to the fireplace. What about Scott's safe? He had given her the combination the day after they moved in. She wondered if it was still empty. She slid her hand along the top of the bookcase and pushed the hidden latch. The bookcase swung forward, revealing the safe.

Inside she found Scott's passport, some computer backup disks, and ten thousand dollars in cash. How much would she actually need? She had no idea how long she would be gone or what problems she might run into. To be on the safe side, she counted out three thousand and put the rest back.

After closing the bookcase, she put the money inside Scott's wallet and slipped it into the handbag she had taken from the closet. Now that she had the funds, all she needed was a place to stay. A hotel was a bad idea. Too many people would be coming and going; she was almost certain to be spotted.

Thankfully, she had left her briefcase at home. She snapped it open and took out the key to Josh Martin's house. When the authorities recovered her car with no body inside, Brian would probably check out her vacant listings, but he would never know to look for her at Josh's house. It wasn't scheduled to hit the market for another two weeks.

Toni returned to the laundry room, grabbed the trash bag containing her muddy clothes, and then double-checked the contents of her overnight bag. When she was sure she hadn't forgotten anything, she retrieved Scott's keys from the kitchen drawer.

Time to play dead.

22

The saleswoman squinted her false-lashed eyes and pointed a silver fingernail. "Don't I know you from somewhere?"

Toni had purposely driven thirty miles east of Nashville down Interstate 40 to the small town of Lebanon. Although she had seen the various shops in the large outlet mall advertised many times, she had never been here before. She didn't know anyone who lived in the town and had felt fairly confident she wouldn't run into anyone who would recognize her, especially with her hair pulled up under her cap.

The clerk probably just remembered her face from a real estate magazine. She only hoped the woman would forget exactly which day Toni had been in the shop. Once her friends realized she was missing, they would more than likely have her picture plastered all across middle Tennessee. Posters asking *Have you seen this woman*?

"No, I don't think so," Toni said.

She turned away from the display case and walked toward the rear of the store. After browsing a few minutes, she picked up a foam head topped with a blonde wig in a short layered style.

"That's the Lexy in buttercream," the saleswoman told her. "It's the last one we have in stock, and she's on sale for 25 percent off. Do you want to try it on?"

"No, that's okay."

"You should. That color would look really good on you, with your blue eyes and all. It's one of our best brands too." She touched her own platinum locks. "Mine's an Eva Gabor."

"It's very nice."

"You think so? I was torn between this one and a Raquel Welch. The Raquel is a little bit straighter and longer in the back. It reminds me of that woman who used to be on *Charlie's Angels*—not the movie, the TV show. You know, the one who had the poster? I'll probably end up buying it too, not that I really expect to look like her, even though my husband, Wayne, said he sees a little resemblance. I asked my sister, but she didn't see it. Wayne told me not to pay her any mind. He thinks she's just jealous. She always was kind of plain, and the clothes she wears—collars buttoned all the way up to her chin, skirts down below her knees. I swear, she looks like she should be holed up in some library instead of behind the checkout counter at Walmart. Heaven knows, she didn't get that from me! Anyway, I guess that's what happens when you work here with these beautiful pieces. You end up wanting to wear them all."

Okay, one nut short of a fruitcake here, Toni thought.

Just listening to the woman made her exhausted. At least if the clerk did remember waiting on Toni and phoned in a tip to the police, they probably wouldn't take her seriously.

Toni held out the wig. "Luckily, I only need one, and I think this is it."

"Now I know who you are!"

Oh, no. Please don't let her remember my name.

"You're that country singer—the one that wears those red leather pants. I've seen your music video a hundred times."

Relieved, Toni put her finger to her lips in a shushing gesture and played along. "I don't want anyone to know. I don't want to draw a crowd."

"I understand. If you sign one autograph, you'll have to sign a hundred, and then you could be stuck here all night. I bet that's why you're wearing that cap, so nobody will know it's you."

Toni nodded. "That's right."

"It must be hard being a celebrity—everybody wants a piece of you. That was Elvis's problem. They say he couldn't even go outside his house in the daytime because the fans wouldn't leave him alone. He could only go out at night after everything closed. I heard they used to open up the stores in Memphis in the wee hours of the morning so he could do his shopping. I don't think I'd want that kind of fame. No offense."

She took the wig from Toni and headed toward the cash register. Halfway there, she stopped. "You know, you can wear this out if you want to. With the Lexy on, nobody will ever guess who you are."

Toni was tempted. If she wore the disguise now, the urge to keep looking over her shoulder wouldn't be so strong. But then the clerk would probably want to help her put it on. If she took her cap off, the woman might realize that she wasn't the singer after all.

"No, I'm kind of in a hurry, so I think I'll take my chances."

After adding a wig cap liner and a few accessories the saleswoman assured her she could not live without, Toni paid for her purchase.

She hit two more shops—one that sold cosmetics, the other eyeglasses. She was about to head back to her car when she spotted a sporting goods store. A teenaged clerk greeted her as she walked through the door.

"Can I help you find something?" he asked.

"I'm looking for a hunting knife."

The teen directed her to a section in the rear of the store. Looking through the glass display case at the collection of knives proved a bit overwhelming. She'd never imagined there were so many different kinds. The man behind the counter finished his discussion with another customer and ambled over to help her.

"Can I show you something?" he asked. With his long gray hair and full beard, he reminded her of Jeff Bridges in *True Grit.*

"Um . . . I don't know."

"Looking for a gift?"

Toni knew the clerk would never believe that she was a hunter. "Yes, it's for my boyfriend."

"Big game or small?"

"Excuse me?"

"What kind of hunting does he do? Does he go after big game, like deer, or is he more of a bird and rabbit man?"

An image of Brian popped into Toni's head. He definitely didn't remind her of a bunny. "He likes to hunt deer—big deer."

"Okay, then. I'd suggest a fixed-blade knife with a drop point like this one." He removed a black-handled knife from the case.

The weapon had a metal butt and guard and a four-inch stainless-steel blade that reflected the overhead lighting like a mirror. It also came with a black leather sheath designed to be worn on a belt. Although a knife was better than no defense at all, there was a distinct disadvantage of having a knife instead of a gun: whoever planned to kill her would have to get really close before she could use it.

The thought of stabbing someone made Toni's stomach churn, but if faced with death, she would do whatever was necessary to survive.

"I'll take it," she said.

Before getting back onto the interstate to head to Josh's house, Toni pulled into a Hardee's drive-through and ordered a double cheeseburger and a Coke. It was only eight thirty, but she was so exhausted, it felt more like four in the morning.

She wondered what Brian was doing. Was he celebrating? And what would he do once he figured out she had escaped? She had to find proof of his role in Scott's death before that happened—which led her back to Nico.

At this point, the construction worker seemed to be her only hope.

Josh Martin lived in Brentwood in a well-established neighborhood with large wooded lots. Toni killed her lights before pulling up the winding drive, rounding the curves by memory. It was possible that Josh's neighbors knew he was out of town, and she didn't want some busybody to notice her arrival and come snooping around.

Or, worse, call the police.

She parked next to the garage and went around behind the house to the back door. Josh had left lights on in the den and the kitchen. She made her way through the house and into the garage. She was surprised to see his SUV parked inside; a friend must have taken him to the airport. She only hoped he hadn't asked anyone to come by and check on the house.

After opening the garage door, she pulled Scott's X5 into the empty bay. Maybe she should track Josh down and tell him what was going on. Make sure it was okay to hide out at his place. But in all honesty, he tended to be the smothering type, one of the major reasons their romantic relationship had ended. If she called him, he would probably insist on coming home to help her.

The idea of bringing in reinforcements was appealing but impossible. It was enough her own life was in danger. She was already responsible for getting Dana killed, and she couldn't risk putting Josh in harm's way.

Toni went inside, curled up on the sofa in the den, and flipped on the television. The local news would be on at ten, and she wanted to see if there were any new developments regarding Dana.

There was one encouraging thing in all this. Detective Lewis wouldn't be handling the case. He worked for the Blanton Hills Police Department, so Leiper's Fork was out of his jurisdiction. Maybe she'd get lucky and the sheriff's department would assign someone a little more competent. Or at least someone willing to listen. Lewis was so close-minded, he couldn't begin to see what was happening.

The cuts on Toni's knees and hands still burned, and her left shoulder was sore. She felt as though she hadn't slept in years. More than once, she caught herself drifting off and had to shake herself awake. After seeing a teaser ad declaring Dana's murder the top news story, she forced herself to sit up and keep her eyes open.

As promised, at ten o'clock, after a brief comment regarding the weather and a short lead-in, the news began with a reporter stationed at the gates of the horse farm. She stood next to the For Sale sign bearing Toni's name.

"We now know the house was vacant except for a few furnishings," the reporter said. "However, it was completely ransacked. The thieves were apparently looking for anything of value, possibly even prescription medicines that may have been left behind. Earlier today, I spoke with the chief deputy of the Williamson County Sheriff's Department. Here's what he had to say."

The station cut to the tape.

"Chief, what can you tell us concerning the investigation?"

"It's well under way. We have a forensic unit on the scene now, and they're combing the house for evidence."

"When did the crime occur?"

"The time of death has not been released yet, but we do believe it happened sometime between seven and ten o'clock last night."

"We've seen pictures of the real estate agent, Dana Dawson. She was a beautiful young woman. Do you know if she was sexually assaulted?"

"We've found no evidence to suggest that she was."

"Does it appear Ms. Dawson put up a struggle?"

"At this time, everything indicates the deceased was taken by surprise. We believe she was showing the home to someone posing as a buyer. No one outside the real estate agency knew the house was unoccupied, and with a home of this size, in this price range, the perpetrators probably thought there were a lot of valuables inside."

"Do you have any leads so far?"

"We're following up on several tips we've received, and we're confident the person or persons responsible will be apprehended."

The story shifted to an interview with Toni's managing broker, Henry McKay. He spoke about Dana's exceptional sales record and stated what a fine person she had been. He then assured all concerned homeowners that this was an isolated incident and they shouldn't worry about having their houses up for sale.

The camera switched back to a live shot of the reporter.

"We'll continue to follow the case and keep you updated on any further developments. In the meantime, the victim's family is offering a $100,000 reward for information resulting in a conviction. If any of our viewers has any knowledge of this crime, we urge you to call the police."

So they still had no clue. The police believed it had been a simple robbery. Toni wondered whether Janet had spoken to them about the scheduled showing with the fake Micheners. Not that it would do any good. The police would just think the killers were looking for someone—anyone—to get them inside the house.

Toni switched off the TV and dragged herself to the guest room. She was too tired to think. In the morning, when her head was clear, she'd plan her next move.

23

At nine o'clock Thursday morning, Brian stood in the empty garage and stared at the spot normally occupied by his brother's silver BMW.

Toni was gone.

It was his fault. He had let her get away. He kicked the plastic trash can near the door, knocking it over and spilling garbage across the floor. He should have known to install a tracking device on Scott's car. Now she could be anywhere.

He knew she wouldn't turn to Detective Lewis again. Reports of her coworker's murder were all over the news, and she was sure to have seen them. There was no way she would trust the police to protect her. This time she would run. She'd find a place to hide.

He went back inside the house and began searching for clues as to where she could have gone. In the study, he rummaged through the desk and then checked both Scott's desktop computer and Toni's laptop computer for e-mail, but found nothing of interest. A review of the Internet browser history proved just as fruitless.

He flipped through a stack of bills and examined Toni's credit card statement. Nothing stood out—nothing that would help him find her. Toni's briefcase lay on a chair in the corner, and he popped it open. Inside was a printout detailing each of her listings, some marked vacant. It was a starting point, although he doubted she'd risk hiding out in such an obvious location.

Upstairs, he combed the master bedroom and bath. In the closet, he found a matching set of luggage stacked in a corner. All the pieces you would expect to find seemed to be there. Chances were she hadn't gone very far. Either that, or she'd left in a rush and planned to purchase clothing and whatever other essentials she might need later.

In the kitchen, he noticed a small memo pad next to the phone. Finding a pencil in a drawer, he rubbed the lead across the sheet of paper on top, revealing the indentions from Toni's last note. All he uncovered was a grocery list. He was about to press redial on the telephone when it rang. He waited for the call to transfer to voice mail.

After a minute had passed, he picked up the phone and punched in the access code Toni had written on a piece of notepaper and pinned to the corkboard hanging above.

"Hi, Toni; it's Helen. I've got that credit report on Nico Williams, and it's clean. His score's in the high sevens and he doesn't have any real debt to speak of, so it looks like he's a good prospect. Oh, and he lives in Franklin."

Brian wrote down Nico's address and then saved the voice-mail message as new, confident that his search was over. He was willing to bet that before the day was finished, Toni would call to check her messages. She'd head straight to Franklin.

And he would be there waiting.

Toni woke up around nine thirty and eased up out of bed. She felt as though she'd run the Boston Marathon and swum the English Channel all in one day. Every muscle in her body ached, and her legs felt as if they'd been carved from lead. Even her toes hurt. But she didn't mind the pain; she just thanked God she was alive.

Unlike Scott, she'd cheated death. And she would give anything to trade places with him. His impact on the world had been far greater than hers. Although they'd both worked together for Habitat for Humanity, Scott had done so much more. It wasn't just the large contributions to Miracle Flights for Kids and St. Jude Children's Research Hospital that had made a difference. It was the giving of his time.

No matter how busy he was, he regularly volunteered at the Blanton Hills Boys & Girls Club, and he had become a mentor to several of the children there. Because of Scott, many of those kids would go on to college, courtesy of the scholarships he had funded.

Being entombed in the submerged car had made her realize one thing: it doesn't matter how long your life is; it's how you live it that's important.

After showering and dressing, she stood in front of the bathroom mirror, slipped on her new blonde wig, and pinned it in place. Using a dark foundation, she contoured her face to make her nose look thinner and her cheekbones more pronounced. Next, she applied blue eye shadow—a color she never wore—to her lids and spread a pale pink gloss on her lips. Satisfied with the way her makeup had turned out, she donned her new glasses—the weakest readers she could find with slightly tinted lenses.

Toni studied her reflection: the transformation was amazing.

"Only Scott would know me now," she said to the woman in the mirror. "And it might even take him a few minutes." She smiled in satisfaction and returned the makeup to its case. Phase 1 of her disappearing act was going better than expected.

Her next task involved the hunting knife she had purchased the night before. Still a little intimidated by the weapon, she pulled it from the sheath and examined the blade. It was hard to believe the turn her life had taken.

A little more than a week ago, she was dreaming of an over-water bungalow at the Four Seasons Resort in Bora Bora, carefree days spent lounging on white sand, and sweet nights spent in Scott's arms. Now she was contemplating taking the life of another human being. She hoped it never came to that. Prayed that she could defend herself without having to go that far.

She ran her belt through the loop on the back of the sheath and checked the mirror. The light cotton sweater she wore was just the right length to hide the knife. No one would ever know she carried it.

Toni wondered if anyone was looking for her yet. Maybe she should at least call Jill and Mark and tell them what had happened. Let them know she was okay. She was sure they would keep her secret.

She was also anxious to check her voice mail, but using Josh's phone was out of the question. Everyone she knew had caller ID, and if she did speak with Jill and Mark, she didn't want them to know where she was staying.

They'd rush right over and try to drag her back to one of their places. Even if she called them from a pay phone, they'd probably beg to come and get her. Both were cherished friends, and she hated to worry them, but she had to do this alone.

Her stomach grumbled; she was starving. Downstairs, she looked in Josh's refrigerator. It was empty except for a bottle of ketchup and a six-pack of Samuel Adams. No surprise there. She'd have to remember to pick up some groceries while she was out. Grabbing her purse, she headed to the garage. She opened the door of Josh's SUV and slipped the garage remote off the sun visor. Circling behind the vehicle, she walked toward Scott's BMW, and then stopped. She had another problem: the vanity plate.

The plate read CHADWCK. She might as well paint *kill me now* on her forehead.

For a split second, she considered taking Josh's car. Then she thought about how easily the Audi had run her off the road. She wasn't about to risk totaling someone else's SUV. Besides, there was an easier solution.

Toni opened the back of Scott's X5. She took a screwdriver from the tool kit inside, removed the BMW's license plate, and replaced it with the plate from Josh's SUV. The number of silver X5 Bimmers in the Nashville area was too high to count. Now she could get lost in that sea. She'd just have to watch her speed and try not to get pulled over.

She drove south from Brentwood to the CoolSprings Galleria and found an empty parking spot near the main mall entrance. She scanned the lot, searching for any familiar faces. Seeing none, she opened the door and got out. Time to show off the new look.

As she walked toward the entrance, she kept her gaze focused straight ahead and tried not to seem nervous. Once inside, she joined the steady stream of shoppers flowing along the corridor. She kept her head down and avoided all eye contact with those walking toward her. Around the corner to the right, she saw the small kiosk she had passed countless times. Luckily, there were no other customers.

"What do I need to get a prepaid cell phone?" she asked.

The bored-looking clerk stared at her as though it was a trick question. "Uh, money?"

"I know that. What I meant was, do you need to see some ID—a driver's license or something?"

"Nope."

"Would I have to give you a credit card?'

"You can write a check, but you'd need ID for that."

"How about cash?"

Toni picked out a base model phone and waited while the clerk activated her minutes. With that done, she went to the food court. She was standing in line at a sandwich counter when she heard a familiar voice. She looked up to see three agents from her office—Lydia, Meg, and Penny—ordering burgers from the next food vendor.

Why did they have to be at CoolSprings today of all days? She was about to turn her head when Meg looked straight at her.

Toni froze.

Did the agent know? Could she tell? But then without so much as a smile, Meg swung her eyes back toward the menu board and stepped up to give her order. The encounter gave Toni a boost of confidence. If someone she saw daily didn't recognize her, Brian surely wouldn't.

Toni paid for her food and carried her tray to the table next to the three agents. She sat with her back to them and listened as they discussed Dana's murder. Each had her own theory regarding the events of that night, but all agreed on one thing: they were terrified that whoever had killed Dana might be looking for more victims. Instead of showing properties alone, they had decided to work in pairs for the next few weeks.

Toni's ears perked up when she heard her own name.

"I heard the police are looking for her," Lydia said.

"Toni? Why?" Penny asked.

"Well, it seems she had an appointment to show the farm the very same night."

"That's not all," Meg chimed in. "Whoever Dana met there contacted Toni first, and for some reason, Toni decided not to go."

"Thank goodness for her," Penny said.

"I just wish Dana had cancelled too," Lydia added.

"We've all heard stories about agents being robbed," Meg reminded them, "but I never thought something like this would actually happen to somebody we know. From now on, I'm going to double-check everything customers tell me before I take them to see anything."

"I'm seriously thinking about giving up working with buyers completely and just being a listing agent," Penny told them.

"I've thought about that too," Lydia said.

The table was silent for a moment.

"Where is Toni anyway?" Penny asked.

"She's gone out of town for a while, I think," Meg replied.

"With all she's been through lately, she needs to get away," Lydia said. "I just hope she doesn't blame herself for what happened to Dana."

"Or Scott," Meg added.

When the topic changed to Penny's new listing, Toni decided to leave. She ate the last bite of her sandwich and tossed her wrapper and empty Coke cup in the trash. Evidently Janet had told the police about the call from the fake Mr. Michener. Now they wanted a statement. But contacting them would do more harm than good. Without any proof, there was no way they'd believe her story. And she still needed everyone, including the police, to think she was dead—or at least missing.

Toni wondered who else had been trying to reach her. After leaving the food court, she hurried back to her car and turned on her new cell phone. The battery needed charging, but there seemed to be enough juice to make a couple of quick calls. She dialed her voice mail. She heard messages from Mark and Jill and several from her office. The last one was from Helen Dove of Townsend Mortgage.

A rush of adrenaline swept through Toni: Helen had located Nico.

Finally, things were looking up.

Toni listened to the message twice to make sure she had written the address down correctly. She entered the house number and street name into her navigation system and began humming to herself.

Nico's place was just a few minutes away.

24

A stone fence, heavily landscaped in front with evergreen shrubs and pansies in a myriad of colors and backed by a row of pines, encircled the subdivision of lavish homes built not more than two years ago. Toni remembered driving through this development once before when the houses were being built. Almost all had been custom presales, so she had never shown them. However, she had admired the various exterior designs—all unique, but retaining a certain southern flair.

She checked the scribbled address, verifying the street name, and then turned into the main entrance. It was not exactly the neighborhood she had pictured for Nico. Not that she was an elitist—far from it. But she had imagined the construction worker living in a more modest environment.

None of the houses were likely to be rental properties. However, in her phone message, Helen hadn't mentioned a mortgage. If Nico had one, it would have shown up on his credit report.

She wondered what line of work he had been in before hanging drywall for Chadwick & Shore. To afford one of the mammoth homes, he had to be doing well financially. Maybe he came from a wealthy family or had married into money. It was also possible he was staying with relatives.

Toni reached the end of the street and then turned left. She noted the house numbers on the mailboxes. Nico's number was 5771. That would mean he lived several houses down, on the right. As she neared the end of the cul-de-sac, she spotted a two-story colonial with the correct address. She was about to pull into the driveway when an alarming thought struck her.

Did Brian know Nico had been at the construction site the morning of Scott's death? She had easily obtained the information. What would stop Brian from finding out? Was he also searching for the possible witness, determined to shut him up? And if she had managed to track Nico down, wouldn't Brian be able to do the same? Maybe he already had. Maybe that was the reason Nico hadn't shown up for work the next day.

Maybe he was dead.

No. She wouldn't allow herself to think that way. Nico had to be alive. He was her last resort, the only person who may have seen Brian at the hotel. Still, she felt a little uneasy about going up to the house. Instead of pulling into the drive, she circled the cul-de-sac and parked by the curb a few houses down.

She surveyed the street, but all seemed quiet. No children playing—school was still in session. No moms pushing baby strollers—the wind was too brisk for walks with little ones. There wasn't a single person outside at all that she could see.

Toni adjusted the hunting knife secured to her belt, and then got out of her car and crossed the street. The sweet scent of freshly mowed grass wafted through the air and reminded her of springs long gone. Of homemade lemonade and necklaces chained from dandelions. Of the years when her father was alive and life was simpler.

As she made her way up the sidewalk, a pair of robins burst from a Bradford pear tree, causing her to jump. When she reached the colonial, she turned around and checked the street and the adjacent lawns before heading up the drive. The house was impressive. She estimated it to be somewhere around six thousand square feet, with wide columns supporting a two-story porch spanning the home's width.

She mounted the steps and rang the bell next to the double mahogany doors. The chimes echoed inside and made the house seem even more cavernous than before. She stood there for a few seconds expecting to hear footsteps, but no one appeared. She rang again and then peeked through the sidelight.

The foyer was too dark to see anything. She stood and waited a little longer, realizing that either no one was home or those inside had made the decision not to answer.

The anticipation of seeing Nico was making her crazy. Toni had spent so much time looking for the construction worker that she wasn't about to leave without talking to him. Or at least speaking to someone who knew him—even if she had to sleep in her car tonight.

She walked the length of the porch, checking all the windows, hoping to glimpse someone inside, but all the blinds were closed. She went back down the steps and then rounded the corner of the house, following the drive to the backyard, past the closed garage to a screened porch.

When she tried the door, it swung open with a screech. A white wicker sofa, chaise, and several matching chairs, all with pillows in yellow and white, filled the porch. She noticed a yellow chenille throw and a paperback romance on the foot of the chaise. A vase of fresh daffodils graced the glass-topped table. The scene looked as though it had been plucked from the pages of *Better Homes & Gardens.*

She crossed the porch to a pair of french doors leading into the house and tested the knobs. Locked. She cupped her hands around her eyes and peered through the glass. A large family room lay off the porch. The television was turned off, and the room appeared deserted. The only thing left to do was to go back to her car and wait for someone to come home.

As she was leaving the screened porch, Toni glanced across the pool at the separate detached garage. She stopped so suddenly that she almost fell down the steps. The garage door was halfway up. Inside, she saw a dark green car with four intertwined silver circles on the trunk.

An Audi sedan.

She ran around the pool to the garage and raised the door all the way. From the rear, the car seemed identical to the one that had run her off the road. She rolled a bicycle out of her path and stepped around to the right side. The proof she saw made her heart pound. She stared at the front fender, dented and streaked with red paint.

Nico had tried to kill her.

He was the man Brian had hired.

Had Nico killed Scott? No, he couldn't have. Alvin Harney said Nico never entered the hotel that morning. Instead, he had stood outside the office talking on a cell phone. Maybe he had only pretended to be on the phone. He could have been acting as a lookout for Brian. Nico was the one person who could have made sure Brian got onto the construction site without Alvin seeing him.

Toni heard a car. She looked up to see a black Jaguar pulling into the driveway. Dropping to a crouch, she scooted around to the front of the Audi. From her vantage point, she watched the Jaguar come to a stop. The doors opened, and a large man with a blonde crew cut and a young girl around ten or eleven years old emerged. She could hear them talking about the girl's school assignments. The man, who she assumed was Nico, smiled and put his arm around the girl's shoulders. Then the grin faded.

He stopped and looked directly at Toni.

Toni froze. Her mind told her to duck, but her body would not respond. Terrified, she stared back.

Nico dropped his arm from the girl's shoulders and started walking toward the garage. "What did I tell you about that garage door?" he said.

"Not to leave it open," the girl answered.

The man was nearly all the way to the garage before Toni could make herself move. She got down behind the left front tire of the Audi and tucked herself into a ball. If he caught her, child or no child as a witness, it would be over.

"I don't mind you keeping your bike in here," Nico said. "But you have to remember to keep this door closed."

The door rumbled as it went down, and Toni heard the latch snap into place. After a few seconds, she opened her eyes. Shadows filled the garage. She had to get out of there, but what if Nico was still outside?

She sat on the cold concrete floor and stared at a glass jar filled with nuts and bolts in various sizes. Unexpectedly, the vase her mother had sent her as a wedding gift popped into her mind. She wondered what her mother was doing now. Had she heard about Scott? Would she even care?

Deep down, Toni believed her mom loved her on some level. At least she hoped so. But how could anyone discard her own flesh and blood so easily? Had she not realized that her leaving would cloud her only child's entire life?

Even Nico, a cold-blooded killer, seemed to have more parental concern than Toni's mother had ever possessed. Even wolves protect their young.

Toni glanced at her watch and realized ten minutes had passed. A shaft of light beamed through the window in the back door. It beckoned to her, calling her to come out. Still, she was afraid. Could she make it to her car without being spotted?

She got to her feet, pulled the hunting knife from the sheath on her side, and then inched the back door open. From here, she could see the pool and the house, but not the driveway. She stood still and listened. She didn't hear any voices.

Expecting to be seized at any moment, she crept along the side of the garage. As she neared the corner, the Jaguar came into view. Nico and the child were nowhere in sight. They must have gone inside.

Toni forced herself to take several deep breaths, and then, with the hunting knife in her right hand and her car keys in her left, she ran as fast as she could down the driveway. She didn't stop until she reached her car. As she was opening the door, someone grabbed her left arm. Panicked, she jerked and tried to pull away. The fingers clamped harder.

Brian's fingers.

His eyes drilled into hers.

"No!" she screamed, and tried to wrench her arm free.

"Toni, stop!"

Toni swung her right hand around and slashed Brian's arm with the hunting knife. The blade sliced through his lightweight jacket as if it were paper. He cried out in pain as he let her go. She jumped into her car and slammed the door. After activating the locks, she threw the knife on the passenger seat and put the key in the ignition.

Holding his left arm to his chest, Brian pounded his right fist on her window. "Open the door, dammit! Open it now!"

Toni started the car and put the gas pedal to the floor.

25

Mark took a swig from his soda can and browsed the candy machine.

He'd been stuck at the courthouse since the early morning, and now, at nearly three o'clock, his stomach was grumbling. He checked the slot for his favorite, a Snickers bar, but the space was empty. It always seemed that on the days he really wanted a Snickers, the machine was out. He settled on a Milky Way and pushed the appropriate buttons.

As he leaned down to retrieve the candy, he glanced at the newspaper box to his left. On the front page of *The Tennessean*, he glimpsed a familiar face. Then he read the headline: LOCAL REALTOR MURDERED.

Forgetting the candy bar, he purchased a paper.

He'd been so busy with work the past two days that he hadn't had time to turn on a TV or listen to any news reports. He unfolded the paper and skimmed the article. The bottom of the page featured a photo of the crime scene; prominent in the shot was Toni's real estate sign.

He remembered the message she had left on his voice mail the day before. There had been something unusual in her tone. At the time, he had chalked it up to stress. Now he wasn't so sure. He pulled the cell phone from his pocket and dialed her number. She didn't answer at home or on her cell phone. He called her office.

"This is Mark Ross. Is Toni in? She's been trying to reach me."

"She's not here," Cheryl said. "Has she tried to get in touch with you today?"

"No, it was yesterday."

"To be honest, we don't know where she is, and with everything that's happened, we're starting to get worried. Hold on a minute. Janet wants to speak with you."

He paced in front of the vending machines and waited for the assistant to come on the line.

"Mr. Ross?"

"Yes."

"We haven't heard from Toni since yesterday afternoon. She didn't show up for a closing she planned to be at this morning, and she even missed a listing appointment. We've been trying to reach her since the closing, and she hasn't returned any of our calls. Did she say anything to you about where she was going?"

"No, she just left me a message to call her."

There was silence for a second and then, "Did you know that one of the agents in our office was found murdered yesterday?"

"I just heard. But don't worry. I'll find Toni and have her call you."

Mark hung up the phone.

He didn't want to admit it to Janet, but he had an uneasy feeling as well. He checked his watch. If he hurried, he'd have just enough time to drive out to Toni's house and back before his next meeting.

Running on pure adrenaline, Toni made it to I-65 in record time. All the while, she kept checking her rearview mirror to make sure no one was following her. Instead of driving north, back to Brentwood, she headed south. Now that Brian knew she was alive and using Scott's car, she felt it best not to return to Josh's until after dark. Brian would probably be scouring all of Williamson County looking for her.

She took off the glasses and the wig and ran her hands through her hair. The disguise was worthless now. How had Brian known who she was anyway? She remembered the photos she found in his hotel room. Had he studied her that closely? Even if he did know her eyes, how had he recognized her at a distance? Maybe it had been her voice. But that was impossible. She hadn't screamed until after he grabbed her. It didn't make sense.

It was almost as if he knew she would be there.

She glanced at the knife on the passenger seat. The blade glistened in the sun, the edge smeared with dried blood: she had cut Brian's arm. There'd been no other choice. He should be grateful she hadn't aimed for his chest; he might be dead now. She probably should have killed him. She should have stabbed him again and again until all the anger and pain she felt over losing Scott drained from her soul.

Was that what she wanted? To kill Brian? Was that vengeance necessary in order for her to heal?

When she realized how close she had come to death herself, she started to shake. Afraid of causing a wreck, she pulled off the side of the interstate. She sat with the car idling, trying to calm down. What she needed was music. Soothing, relaxing music.

Toni reached in the back of the SUV and retrieved Scott's CD case. She picked out a collection of ballads she had burned herself—nothing too sappy, just slow and calming. After stowing the knife under the passenger seat so she wouldn't have to be reminded of what she'd just done, she stuck the CD in the player and eased back onto the road.

Forcing herself to take long, deep breaths, she waited for the music to start. Nothing happened. She ejected the CD and pushed it back in again. Still, it refused to play. She figured it was dirty or had gotten cracked or scratched. She took the disk out and replaced it with the *Eagles, Greatest Hits*.

She tried to concentrate on the lyrics pouring from the speakers, tried to lose herself in the rhythm. Three songs began and ended, but it was hopeless. Her mind kept forming images of Brian's hand wrapped around her arm. The heat from his touch was still there, as if he had branded her with a hot iron. And then she saw his eyes—those cold stone-gray eyes. She decided to take the next exit.

Fearing that somehow Brian might know she had gone south, she bypassed the fast food chains near the off-ramp and headed in the direction she felt the town would most likely be. She got behind a line of cars with local license plates, and when they turned right at the next light, she followed. This was foreign territory. All she knew was that she was somewhere in Maury County.

About a half-mile down the road, a small diner sat wedged between a car wash and a hair salon. The sign outside proclaimed the lunch special to be country fried steak, mashed potatoes, and fried okra. Nothing like good ole southern cooking.

The heavy smell of grease and strong coffee greeted her as she pushed open the door. Noticing the sign that read *Please be seated*, she slid into a booth upholstered in red vinyl. Only a handful of other patrons were in the diner. Three elderly men sat at the counter, and a middle-aged couple occupied a booth nearby. She guessed it was due to the time. Too late for lunch and too early for dinner.

A waitress in a powder-blue uniform, who seemed to be bordering on retirement age herself, brought Toni a menu and some silverware wrapped in a paper napkin. She confirmed the special was indeed country fried steak, then headed over to refill the elderly men's coffee cups. A few minutes later, she returned.

"What can I get you, honey?"

"I'll have a Coke." She handed the waitress the menu.

"Just a Coke?"

"I'd prefer something stronger, but I'm driving."

"Uh-huh. Man troubles."

"Is it that obvious?"

"When you've been working here as long as I have, seeing people come and go, you learn to read the signs." She put her hand on Toni's shoulder, her eyes soft with empathy. "I know just what you need. Barney, he's the cook around here, just took a fresh pecan pie out of the oven. Why don't you let me bring you a big slice with a couple scoops of ice cream—on the house?"

The woman's motherly warmth melted the tension surrounding Toni, and for the first time since Scott died, she felt a genuine smile touch her lips. "Okay, I'll have some, but put it on my bill."

As the waitress headed toward the kitchen, Toni rested her head on her palms and tried to assimilate what she had learned. She couldn't believe the irony. All this time, she had been searching for Nico, certain he would be her savior—the key to clearing Scott's name and setting things right. But in reality, Nico was as close as you could get to Satan incarnate.

When she first saw Nico get out of the Jaguar, she was surprised how harmless he looked—like a typical dad, his arm affectionately draped around his daughter's shoulder. But when his eyes locked on the garage, the facade fell away. She found herself staring straight into hell. She could actually feel the evil radiating from every pore of his body.

At the time, she had been too scared for it to register, but she knew that face—the one that was so adept at hiding its true nature. She had seen it before. The day she visited Gloria's apartment.

Nico was the man in Gloria's photographs.

After pounding on Toni's door for several minutes, Mark finally convinced himself she wasn't home. At first, he hadn't been sure. Visions of her in total meltdown, refusing to speak to anyone, accosted his mind. But clearing his thoughts of those just led to visions far worse.

Trying to shake off the helpless feeling plaguing him, he reached for his cell phone. Jill answered on the second ring. Mark didn't bother with the usual niceties. "Where's Toni?" he asked.

"Toni? She's probably either at home or her office. Why?"

"You haven't talked to her today?"

"No, not yet."

"Dana Dawson was murdered. At Toni's listing."

"I know, I heard about it just a few minutes ago, and I called Toni, but she hasn't called me back yet."

"You and the rest of the world."

"What?"

"Look, if you hear from her, tell her to call me—immediately."

"You're starting to scare me."

"Well, maybe we should be scared."

After hanging up, Mark phoned his office and told his secretary to cancel the rest of his meetings for the day and his first two the following morning. He didn't know how long it would take him to find Toni. It wasn't like her to disappear without a word to anyone.

Something bad had happened. He was sure of it.

As he drove back toward town, he ran through a list of Toni's friends in his mind. He had the phone numbers for some of them, but not all. He decided to go to her office. She probably kept the information on her computer. As he neared the bridge, he slowed to a crawl, allowing a large black dog to amble across the road. Then he stopped.

Not for the dog, but because of what he saw. He pulled over and got out of his car.

He prayed to God he was wrong.

26

"This will sting for a second," the pretty ER doctor warned just before injecting an anesthetic into Brian's forearm. "And I'm afraid you will have a scar."

"There goes my modeling career."

Ignoring his attempt at humor, the doctor tossed the hypodermic into the trash before disappearing behind the closed curtain. After several minutes, she returned accompanied by a short, rotund nurse whose name tag read *Peggy Lund.*

Peggy had tweezed her black-penciled eyebrows into sharp upside-down vees that mirrored the bright red pout of her mouth. The combination of her makeup, generous cheeks, close-cropped hair, and wide forehead reminded Brian of an overdone Kewpie doll.

He swallowed a laugh and instead smiled at the nurse. She nodded and returned his grin. The doctor, however, did not. Instead, she regarded him with cold eyes as she went about the task of stitching up the gash that stretched from his elbow nearly to his wrist.

It was obvious she didn't believe the story that he'd tripped and fallen against a saw blade. Why should she? He wouldn't. He was so pissed at having lost Toni again that he hadn't thought to make up anything on the way to the hospital. So he just said the first thing that popped into his mind.

Doctors were required to report gunshot wounds to the police. He didn't think it was mandatory to report stabbings, but that didn't mean they wouldn't. He hoped the doctor would keep her suspicions to herself. Talking to law enforcement was a hassle he didn't need.

Brian's cell phone rang.

"Don't even think about it," the doctor said.

The look she shot him said if he dared move even a millimeter, he might end up with the suture needle jabbed in his nuts.

Despite the warning, he was tempted to answer. Before Toni sped off, he had managed to memorize the license plate number on Scott's SUV. Although Toni had probably stolen the plate at random, he thought it was worth checking out. There was a slight chance he'd get lucky and it would belong to someone she knew.

At the very least, the address of the person she swiped it from might point him to the general area where she was hiding. As soon as he had arrived at the hospital, he'd left a voice message for a friend who could run the license number. Instinct told him that friend was now on the other end of his cell.

"How many nights will you be staying?" the clerk asked as he peered over the top of his wire-rimmed glasses.

After leaving the diner, Toni had driven farther into town and stopped at a small motel with a flashing sign advertising rooms for $79. The way the man behind the counter was staring led her to believe he didn't see many women traveling alone, especially without any luggage. He probably thought she was here for an afternoon rendezvous with her lover.

"Only one night."

He nodded. "I just need a credit card."

"I'll be paying cash."

A smirk appeared on his face. "If you can't give me a credit card, then I'll have to charge you for an additional night as a deposit. Just in case there's damage to the room."

She guessed he didn't get many visitors paying in cash either. "That's not a problem."

The clerk took her money and handed her a key. "Checkout is at 11 a.m."

Toni paused just inside the door of the motel office and surveyed the parking lot before heading to her room. She had parked Scott's SUV at the far end, on the other side of a van, and hoped it wouldn't be visible from the street. She checked her watch. A few hours remained before nightfall, before she would feel safe enough to leave.

Mark sat on an outcropping of rock at the edge of the riverbank, his head in his hands. He stared down at his muddy wing tips and cursed himself.

Why had he left Toni alone?

He should have insisted she stay with him for a few weeks. He could have kept a better eye on her. Made sure she didn't freak out over Gloria and helped her deal with her feelings. But in all reality, he knew she never would have agreed to it.

He glanced up toward the bridge. The lights from the patrol cars flashed an eerie ultramarine through the dusk. They had the road blocked. Clint had called him on his cell phone. He and Jill had tried to get down to the river, but the police weren't letting anyone through.

Mark could see a group of Blanton Hills police still examining the ripped guardrail with flashlights. Since the moment he had spotted the twisted metal marred with red paint, he had begun phoning Toni at fifteen-minute intervals, praying she would pick up. Praying he was wrong and she was safe.

The wrenching in his chest grew tighter with every unanswered call.

He turned his attention back toward the river just in time to see one of the divers motion to an officer on the shore.

They had found something.

Toni shook herself awake, the blaring sun from her dream extinguished by the darkness of the dingy motel room. But the shrill laughter did not fade as easily. She could still hear it. Could still see the faces of the demons taunting her.

In the dream, she stood rigid on the top floor of the hotel, her hands bound behind her back. At her throat, she could feel the cold steel of the hunting knife. He had wrestled it from her. Nico. And now she was too afraid to scream or even breathe. He loosened his arm from around her waist and smiled down at her. She watched as his teeth transformed into wolflike fangs.

He shoved her forward onto the balcony. Brian was there. And Gloria. Their backs were toward her, their gaze transfixed by a giant eagle on the ledge. Then the eagle turned and she could see his face, the sun shining behind him like a halo.

It wasn't a bird at all.

What she thought were wings were the arms of a man, bound together as hers were.

When he first saw her, he smiled—a smile that lifted her heart and made her feel as though she could fly. That they could fly off the balcony together and everything would be all right. A heartbeat later, his smile was gone, replaced by a look of fear.

Scott!

She tried to scream, but her voice was gone. As she struggled to free herself, Nico's arms wound around her like an iron vine. Then she saw something in Brian's hand. He raised it toward her, and she realized it was a gun.

"Shoot her!" Gloria yelled.

"No, leave her alone," Scott said. "She doesn't know anything."

Brian lowered the gun and turned back toward the ledge. "If you're wrong and she knows, she's dead."

Dead.

The word echoed through her brain.

But then she heard Scott's voice. He whispered her name, soft and sweet. His face no longer masked by fear, but rather intense concentration. His eyes held hers for what seemed like an eternity but she knew were only fleeting seconds.

"I'll always be with you," Scott whispered. "Remember. Now and always."

But as soon as the words escaped his lips, Brian lunged toward him.

With a single push, Scott was gone.

She screamed inside her head. A sound only she could hear. Nico released his grip, and she stumbled forward, dropping to her knees.

And then the laughter began.

Maddening, deafening laughter.

They circled around her, Brian, Gloria, and Nico, their faces twisted with glee.

Toni sat up, her face and neck covered by a thin layer of sweat. She had no idea how long she'd slept. The clock on the bedside table flashed twelve-zero-zero. The power had gone out.

She crawled off the bed and pulled open the musty curtains. A steady rain shimmered in the pale glow of the motel parking lot's solitary street lamp. She checked the time on her new cell phone: 10:23 p.m. She'd been out for a while. Was it safe to go back to Josh's now? Maybe. But then what?

She had pinned all her hopes of solving Scott's murder on Nico's cooperation. He had been her one chance. Now that Nico was the enemy instead of her ally, what did she have left? How could she get Detective Lewis to believe her? At this point, what could she prove?

Nico had tried to kill her.

The red paint on his Audi would match the paint from her car. That should be enough to get the police to question Nico. Except for one thing: Brian knew she had been at Nico's. There was no way in hell he'd risk letting anyone else see the Audi.

By now, the car had probably already been chopped into a million pieces.

A wave of nausea hit her. Brian and Nico had killed Scott. Now they were trying to kill her, and there wasn't a damn thing she could do about it.

Or was there?

What about Gloria? Toni sensed the woman was not nearly as strong as she pretended. Could she be convinced Nico was using her? Could she be the key to cracking this whole conspiracy?

Toni knew that going to see Gloria again might be akin to shooting herself. Still, what other choices did she have? She could either live the rest of her life on the run, hoping Nico and Brian never caught her, or she could remain on the offensive. Keep charging until she found a way to bring them down.

Toni went into the bathroom and rubbed a cold washcloth across her face. She stared at her reflection. Her bone structure, her ocean-blue eyes, and her thick auburn hair were all traits she shared with her mother.

Had she inherited another characteristic as well?

When her father died, she'd fled from the pain. Instead of working through her feelings, she tucked them away, out of sight, the same as she had the box of her father's photographs and letters. Just like her mother, she'd built a new life for herself far away from the memories. She'd let fear dictate the course of her life. But this time, she decided, things would be different.

Toni stood in front of the mirror and vowed to confront whatever lay ahead, no matter what the consequences. From this day forward, she'd never run away again.

Not from anything.

27

Toni parked two buildings down from Gloria's apartment, killed her headlights, and waited.

Being so close to Vanderbilt, the complex housed its share of students. Toni watched a group of them climb out of a Toyota, arms laden with beer and snacks. They trudged in a follow-the-leader line across the parking lot and then up the stairs to a corner apartment. Once they were inside, the lot appeared deserted except for Toni and a large calico cat sitting on the hood of the beat-up Ford Escort parked next to her.

After leaving the motel, Toni had stopped at a Walmart and purchased some dark gray sweats and a stocking cap. She twisted her hair into a knot on top of her head and pulled the cap down over her ears before getting out of the car. The calico jumped to the BMW's hood and meowed, begging to be petted. Toni obliged and stroked the cat.

"Shhh. You be quiet now."

With no one else in sight, Toni headed for building G. Gloria's apartment was adjacent to the laundry building, the most brightly lit area of the complex. Toni emerged from the shadows and knocked on Gloria's door.

The calico followed her and wound itself around Toni's ankles. She scratched the cat's head and knocked again.

No answer.

Gloria was probably with Nico and Brian. Toni pounded on the door one last time before giving up and walking back to her car. Should she wait for Gloria to return? What if Nico came back with her?

The calico stared at Toni through the windshield.

"What do you think, Callie?"

The cat cocked its head, seeming to ponder the situation.

From where she was parked, Toni had a clear view of Gloria's building. Anyone arriving would be easily recognizable under the street lamps. If she saw Nico or Brian, she would leave.

"Keep your toes crossed, Callie."

Jill was crying again.

Mark got up from his chair and paced the reception area. He could hear Clint whispering to Jill, trying to calm her. She'd been grating on Mark's nerves ever since they arrived at the police station. One minute she'd be calm, telling them she knew Toni was fine, that someone else had crashed into the river. The next minute, she'd erupt in tears, convinced Toni was gone. He wished she would just shut up so he could think.

Mark walked to the window and stared out at the cold night. Was Toni out there somewhere? Or had he lost her forever?

Once the divers began heading for the shore, one of the officers at the scene had escorted Mark from the river despite his protests. He had overheard one of the policemen say the divers had found a car, but no one would tell him anything. Instead he was being put through the torture of waiting.

"Mr. and Mrs. Shore, Mr. Ross, I'm sorry this has taken so long." Detective Lewis shook Mark's hand. "Why don't we go down the hall for some privacy?"

"No," Mark said. "Just tell us right here. Did you find Toni?"

The detective hesitated. "Let's have a seat."

Jill slumped back against Clint on the worn sofa as Detective Lewis perched on the edge of a corner chair. Mark remained standing, his hands balled into fists.

"We did find a car in the river," Detective Lewis said, his focus on Mark. "One of the divers was able to get the license plate number. We ran a check, and you were right: the car is registered to Toni Matthews."

"I knew it," Jill sobbed. "She's dead."

"No, I didn't say that. I just said that we know the car belongs to her."

"So what are you telling us?" Mark asked. "Someone else was driving Toni's car?"

"At this point," Lewis said, "we're not sure,"

"Dammit! Quit talking in circles." Mark fought the urge to shake the detective. "We've been waiting here for hours. You've met Toni more than once. You know exactly what she looks like. Just tell us. Is she alive or dead?"

"If I could give you that information, believe me, I would," Detective Lewis said. "Right now, we just don't know, but when the divers found the car, it was empty."

"So Toni got out?" Clint asked.

"No one was in the car," Detective Lewis said. "That's all we know for sure. One of the windows was broken, but we don't know whether that occurred due to the crash or if someone knocked it out on purpose."

"But Toni might still be alive?" Jill asked.

"It's possible. There's a chance she managed to get out before the car sank. However, it's also possible the current pulled her from the car."

"Toni's a strong swimmer," Mark said. "I bet she smashed the window and then swam to shore. Are your men still at the river? Are they looking for her?"

"We'll pull the car out first thing in the morning," Detective Lewis said. "The divers will search the river then."

"I'm talking about searching the shore," Mark said. "The current could have carried Toni miles down the river before she got out. She could be wandering around dazed. She could be hurt. We've got to find her—now."

The detective stood, leveling himself with Mark. "As soon as we realized no one was in the car, we had officers walk both sides of the riverbank. They didn't find anything. And you need to understand: even if she did manage to get out of the car, there's no guarantee she made it out of the water. I'm sorry. There's just nothing more we can do until daylight."

Mark had waited long enough.

"You might not be willing to do anything," he said. "But I sure as hell can."

• • •

Toni fished her cell phone from her purse and checked the time. It was after two in the morning, and there still was no sign of Gloria. Maybe she was spending the night at Nico's. Probably curled up in a big warm bed somewhere while the interior of Scott's X5 was growing colder by the minute.

Toni started the engine and switched on the heat. The calico didn't stir.

Bored, Toni scanned the radio stations. Finding nothing interesting, she decided to try playing her ballad CD again. She fumbled in the passenger seat but couldn't find it. Not wanting to turn on the interior lights, she pulled Scott's mini flashlight from the glove box. The CD had fallen onto the floor. She picked it up and opened the jewel case.

Stunned, she stared at the CD under the glow of the flashlight.

Toni always stuck clear labels on all the CDs she burned. This one had no label, only her name written in black marker.

Scott's handwriting.

Toni pushed the CD into the player. As she suspected, there was no music. It had to be a data CD.

Did Scott know something was going to happen to him? Had he left her a message? She needed to get to a computer.

Josh worked the same way as Toni did. He used a laptop computer instead of a desktop. She hadn't seen it around his house anywhere, so he must have taken it with him on his trip. With Brian still looking for her, Toni's home and office were both out of the question.

Then she remembered. A Kinko's was nearby, on West End Avenue, and she was pretty sure it stayed open 24/7.

28

Mark called in every outstanding favor he had. Contacted even the most remote of his acquaintances. Anyone whose name he knew, whose number he could find, he phoned. He didn't give a damn whom he woke up.

The current result was a team of fifty-two volunteers searching in the cold night for Toni. Several of Mark's friends and fellow attorneys, a van load of Realtors, the mayor of Blanton Hills, a couple of people from his office, most of the city council members, a few men from the rescue squad, a handful of first responders, a group from Blanton Hills Fire Department, and a half-dozen friends of friends all scoured the riverbanks in the darkness. Still more volunteers had promised to arrive at dawn.

Mark and Clint led the group, plowing through the mire that edged the river, seeking any clue, however small, that Toni had made it out of the water.

Mark needed to stay positive. He pictured her safe in one of the houses up the bank, wrapped in a blanket, sipping hot coffee, and relating her ordeal to a Good Samaritan. He couldn't bear to think of the alternative.

He thought about the first time they'd met. He had been looking for a condominium closer to his office and saw one of Toni's listings in a real estate magazine. She had captured his interest just as much as the property did. Thinking she might feel uncomfortable dating a customer, Mark planned to ask her out right after closing, but before he had the chance, she met Scott.

Mark knew the minute he saw them together that it was all over. Their chemistry electrified the room. When they announced their engagement, he hadn't been the least bit surprised.

He realized he could never replace Scott, but he hoped Toni would one day give him a chance to make her happy. A chance to build a solid relationship, one that would last a lifetime.

Toni had to be alive. She just had to be, and Mark was determined to find her.

Find her and never let her go.

Despite the late hour, customers streamed in and out of Kinko's as though it were the middle of the day. Toni stood in line, the blonde wig covering her hair once again. Although Brian had seen her in disguise, she still felt safer behind the facade.

When she finally reached the counter, a young man with a goatee and diamond stud earring explained the rental rates and went over a list of programs installed on the computers. Satisfied she understood the terms, he led Toni to a machine with a Windows operating system.

When goatee boy was gone, she popped in the disk. The directory came up and revealed a single file: *Toni*. From the familiar little icon and XLS extension, she could tell the file was an Excel Workbook. She held her breath and double-clicked.

The dreaded password box appeared on the screen.

Toni typed in three different passwords she knew Scott had used. None of them opened the file. Next, she tried his birthday, then her birthday. Both of their full names forward and backward. Every significant word she could come up with. Nothing worked.

Think.

If she had to leave Scott a message, one only he could open, how would she protect it? She would use a password that had no meaning to anyone else but them. Something no one else knew.

She typed in a date. The day she and Scott first said, "I love you."

The file opened.

The contents were not what she had expected. On the left, she saw a list of addresses. To the right, several columns of numbers. The headings were all abbreviations, and none of them made sense. Why would Scott leave her this?

She read through the addresses. The fifth one she recognized: Gloria's apartment complex. Why did everything always lead back to Gloria? Toni had developed a severe case of hatred for that girl.

Although she knew the Nashville area well, none of the other addresses meant anything to Toni. She decided to check the tax records. Maybe the properties had something in common. She logged onto the database and entered in the first address. Another apartment. Owned by an investment group, the name unfamiliar. Then she saw the name of the company that paid the taxes.

Chadwick & Shore Property Managements, LLC.

It was a normal practice for property management firms to pay taxes and other expenses on behalf of the owners and then collect for the bills along with their management fees. She checked the city and county tax amounts to see if they matched any of the numbers in the columns. Not even close. The land and building appraisals didn't fit either.

She typed in the remaining addresses. All the properties were apartments. All managed by Chadwick & Shore. She could find no other links. The owners' names were all different, and the property locations were scattered across Davidson and Williamson counties. Wanting to study them again later, she sent the tax records for all the properties to the printer.

How did the list of apartments relate to Scott's death? It had to mean something. Why else would he name the file "Toni," password-protect it, and stick it in a CD case where she was sure to find it?

Toni had convinced herself Brian killed Scott for the inheritance. Maybe there was something more. Could it be possible that Clint was somehow involved?

Scott and Clint were equal partners in Chadwick & Shore, including the property management division. Had Scott discovered something troubling going on with the management of the apartments? Maybe

Clint had embezzled some of the funds. But that theory didn't really seem plausible. Management fees were not exactly big bucks. Chadwick & Shore would have to pay the property owners all the rents collected every month, so there wouldn't be a large bank account to steal from.

And why would Clint need money anyway? The development and construction divisions of the company had always made a large profit. He didn't have any gambling or drug problems, and she knew he had made several successful investments. His finances seemed more than secure.

And how did Brian and Nico fit in with the apartments? Maybe they didn't. Maybe Scott was looking into irregularities in the property management division and left her the file in case Clint found out. Then Brian came back to town and killed Scott for his money. Killed him before Clint realized Scott was checking the rental properties.

It made sense in her mind, but not in her heart. In her gut, she knew that somehow everything was connected.

Toni wished she could get into Chadwick & Shore and search the computer in Scott's office. Access the property management files. She had the keys to the building and knew Scott's log-on password. But in order to get into his office, she would have to make it past Monty, the night security guard, and his not-so-friendly doberman. And security cameras looked down everywhere.

Although she was tempted, breaking in was just too risky. Clint paid Monty's salary. Even if Toni begged him to keep quiet about her visit, he wouldn't jeopardize his job. He would call Clint. If Clint was involved, he would summon Nico before she had time to sit down at Scott's desk.

Toni's head felt ready to explode. Far too many questions needed answers.

The dashboard clock glowed 4:52 a.m. Toni pulled into Josh's garage and gathered up her things. She had stopped by Gloria's again before coming back, but she still wasn't home.

Would Gloria be able to shed any light on the list of rental properties? After all, she did live in one of the apartments. Later in the morning, following a shower and a nap, Toni would return to Gloria's and interrogate her. Whatever it took, she would make the woman talk. Even if it meant she had to threaten her with the hunting knife. She would never actually use it, of course. But Gloria had no way of knowing that.

Toni flipped the light on in the kitchen and piled her stuff on the table.

A hand closed around her mouth and nose. Strong arms clinched tight around her body. She struggled, tried to scream.

Toni couldn't breathe. Dizziness overwhelmed her. She felt herself falling.

And then everything went black.

29

Toni opened her eyes and tried to focus. Her head ached, and her throat felt as though it had been packed with mothballs. She blinked and scanned the room, trying to get her bearings.

Josh's study.

Someone had tied her to his leather office chair. Duct tape covered her mouth.

"Nice to have you back." Brian stood in the doorway, his left arm wrapped with gauze. She regretted not killing him when she'd had the chance.

He crossed the room and sat on the edge of Josh's desk. "I know you're scared. I know you probably think I killed Scott, but you're wrong. I know he was murdered, but I didn't do it."

Toni studied his eyes.

How did he manage to seem so sincere? The mask of concern seemed almost real. Instead, she knew it was just another one of his many tricks.

"I'll take the tape off your mouth, but just realize that if you scream, the neighbors might hear you and call the police. If that happens, the people after you will find out you're still alive. Understand?"

She nodded.

"I'll do it quick so it won't hurt as bad."

Brian ripped the tape from her lips.

Toni's mouth stung like hell. She tried to speak, but coughed instead.

"Do you need some water?"

She cleared her throat. "Untie me."

"I will, but not yet. You need to listen to me first."

"Why should I?"

"Well, the way I see it, you don't have much of a choice."

She wanted to slap the stupid grin from his face. "Fine. Start talking."

"I want to get the person who killed Scott just as much as you do."

"Why should I believe you?"

"Because he was my brother. I loved him. I have no reason to want him dead."

"Really? I can think of several million reasons."

"I don't give a damn about Scott's money."

"That's a funny statement coming from a man who has a huge judgment against him. Not to mention court costs, attorneys' fees, and who knows what else."

"What are you talking about?"

"I've done a lot of research on you, and I know all about the meatpacking plant and the slander charges."

Brian laughed. "Is that so? Well, little Miss Investigator, you didn't dig deep enough. If you had, you would know another judge overturned that ruling. Aside from the mortgage on my town house, I don't owe anybody anything."

Toni didn't know what to think. "If you don't want Scott's money, then why contest his will?"

Brian took a deep breath, letting it out slowly. "I'm a reporter. By nature, I'm suspicious of everyone. I thought you killed Scott for his estate—you and Mark. I was convinced the two of you were having an affair."

"That's crazy."

"I know that now, and I have a confession to make. The night of the funeral, while you were asleep, I broke into your house. I bugged your telephones and installed a GPS tracking system on your car. After listening to all of your conversations, and following you for the past few days, I was pretty sure you were innocent. Of course, I wasn't completely convinced until your Realtor friend turned up dead."

"Dana Dawson."

"She was at your listing, meeting with your customer. I found out she had the same hair color as you and was roughly the same weight and height. At night, it would be hard to tell you apart. That's when I knew you were in serious trouble."

"Serious doesn't begin to describe it. Nico ran me off the road, and I almost drowned."

"Nico? The guy you tracked down in Franklin?"

"Yes, only I didn't know he was involved in Scott's death when I went looking for him. He was at the hotel that morning, pretending to be a construction worker, and I was stupid enough to think he could help me."

"I know about the crash. You made the ten o'clock news last night. The police found your car. When I realized Scott's SUV was missing, I figured you staged it so you could disappear."

"They found my car already? That's not good news. Now Nico will know I'm not dead and come looking for me."

"Doesn't matter. I won't let him, or anyone else, touch you."

For a split second, Toni caught a glimpse of Scott in Brian's eyes. Her stomach tightened, and she had to fight back a wave of tears.

Brian sensed her mood change. "What is it?"

"When are you going to untie me?"

He stood up. "Right now."

Once she was free, Toni followed Brian into the kitchen. He handed her a glass of water and apologized for drugging her and tying her to the chair. "I was afraid if you saw me, you'd slice me up again," he said.

"Oh yeah, I'm sorry about that, but you grabbed me, and I was terrified. What were you doing at Nico's house?"

"I was trying to find you and keep you out of trouble. I listened to the message with his address and figured you'd show up there sooner or later."

"The morning Scott died, why were you at the hotel?"

"Scott asked me to meet him there. He wanted to show me around, give me the grand tour, and then we planned to have lunch. Talk some things over."

Toni sat down at the kitchen table. She still wasn't sure she should believe Brian, but his answers did seem plausible. And he had passed up the perfect opportunity to kill her. "Who do you think murdered Scott?"

"Right now, I'm guessing Clint. Besides you, he has the most to gain. If you sell him Scott's half, he'll have total control of the company."

Toni thought about the spreadsheet. Could she trust Brian enough to show it to him? She studied his face. The look of sincerity was still there. If he didn't kill his brother, then he could help her figure out who did. And if he *was* responsible for Scott's death, he would end up killing her anyway whether he knew she had the spreadsheet or not. At this point, what more did she have to lose?

She pulled the computer disk from her purse. "What if there's another reason?"

After spreading the tax documents out on the table, she relayed the contents of the Excel file, making sure to tell Brian that Gloria's apartment complex was on the list. She also told him about Gloria being in Mexico and about visiting her apartment and seeing the pictures of her with Nico. "What do you think?"

"I'm not sure. I'd like to look at the numbers on the spreadsheet."

"I didn't print the spreadsheet, and there's no computer here to pull it up on."

"That's no problem. I've got a laptop back at my hotel."

Toni tapped her index finger on the water glass. "How did you figure out Scott was murdered when no one else did?"

"I felt it from the beginning. I was at the hotel and I saw the balcony. That detective tried to tell me that Scott was depressed over a business deal. But no matter how much time passes, a person's core personality doesn't change. I managed to get a copy of his medical records. Once I was sure he had never suffered from any kind of chemical imbalance, I knew their story was a crock. Scott would never kill himself."

"They told me the exact same thing, and I knew it couldn't be true. Jill said the company buying the hotel, water something . . . no, aqua something—wait a minute."

Toni shuffled through the tax documents. She held up one of the papers. "AlquilaCorp! That's the company buying the hotel. It owns one of the apartment buildings."

"Hmm. Never heard of it. You realize this could just be a coincidence? That's what investment firms do: buy properties."

"No, I don't think so. I think it means something. I think there's some kind of link between Scott's problems with the hotel and this list of apartments."

"Maybe. We'll never know unless we do some investigating into AlquilaCorp and the owners of the other properties. We can probably get a little information from a Web search. But for the real dirt, I've got a friend back in Washington with all kinds of connections. There's nothing he can't find out. Luckily, he owes me a lot of favors."

Toni gave Brian the computer disk and tax printouts to take back to his hotel. She hoped he would be able to make sense out of the columns of numbers. See something she had overlooked.

"I won't be long," Brian said. "I'll go ahead and check out of the hotel and bring my stuff back here. When I leave, lock the doors. Don't go outside for anything. I was able to find you. Nico could too."

After Brian left, Toni paced the house.

Despite being up all night, she was full of nervous energy. She felt certain she and Brian were finally on the verge of putting all the pieces together. She just wished she had been able to talk to Gloria. There was still a chance Toni could persuade her to cross over to the good side. She could mention AlquilaCorp. Pretend she knew more than she did.

The idea gnawed at her.

Although Brian told her not to leave, Toni felt compelled to go. Nico had not seen her wearing the wig and glasses. There was no way he could recognize her. If she hurried, she could get to Gloria's and back before Brian returned.

West End Avenue was at a standstill with Friday morning traffic. Cars packed bumper to bumper squeezed from one lane to another. Horns blared. Birds flew. Nashville drivers: they were enough to make you crazy.

After consciously hitting her turn signal far in advance, Toni turned onto the street that wound past Gloria's apartment. With most of the tenants off to work or classes, few cars remained in the lot. She parked at the far end of the complex and made sure Nico wasn't around before going up to Gloria's building.

Toni pounded on the door.

"She ain't home."

Toni turned to see a middle-aged woman standing in the breezeway. She wore a tattered pink housecoat, a lit cigarette in her hand.

"What?" Toni asked.

"Gloria. She ain't home."

"Do you know when she'll be back?"

"Ain't coming back. I saw the moving truck load up all her furniture. They got a new gal in the office now."

"The office?"

"You hard of hearing or something? The office. Where you pay your rent? They don't open 'til nine though."

"Right." *Gloria had worked at the apartment office.* "Did she tell you where she was going?"

"Nope." The woman took a draw from her cigarette. "Didn't know she was leaving 'til I saw the truck."

"Have you lived here long?"

"Going on three years." She gestured toward the apartment directly across from Gloria's.

"Did you know Gloria well?"

"Talked to her a couple times a week. She let me slide a few days on my rent every now and then. She was good that way."

Toni searched in her purse for Scott's wallet. She flipped it open to a small print of the photo she kept on her nightstand. Toni, Scott, Clint, and Jill in Mexico. "Have you ever seen either one of these men around here?"

The woman studied the photograph. "Can't say that I have."

Although Toni didn't expect the tenant to know Scott, she had hoped the woman could identify Clint. "You're sure? You've never seen the dark-haired man before?"

"Nope."

Toni sighed and slid the wallet back into her purse. "Thanks for talking to me."

"Yeah, sorry I don't know those men." The woman puffed the last of her cigarette, dropped the butt on the concrete, and ground it with her house shoe. "Her sister used to come around a lot, though."

"Her sister?"

"That blonde-haired woman in your picture. Name's Sylvia."

30

Sylvia?

Could it be true? Was Jill Gloria's sister? Could she have been living a double life all this time?

Before speaking with the woman at the apartments, Toni had thought Clint was the connection to Gloria. That he was the one having the affair with her. That could explain her being in Mexico.

Toni never would have guessed Gloria was actually related to Jill. That meant that the four of them—Clint, Jill, Gloria, and Nico—were probably all working together. And whatever criminal activity they were involved in must have something to do with the rental properties.

Toni pulled into Josh's garage and found Brian waiting for her. He sat on the steps leading up to the kitchen door, a less-than-happy look on his face.

"Where have you been?" Brian asked. "I distinctly told you to stay put."

"You're not going to believe what I found out." Toni related the information garnered from her visit to Gloria's apartment.

"I have to admit, that's a bombshell," Brian said. "But you should have waited for me."

"Nothing bad happened. I'm okay. And you're forgetting, I have managed to take care of myself these last few days."

"Just barely."

Toni tried to push past Brian into the kitchen.

"Wait," he said. "Give me your keys."

"What?"

"Your car keys. Hand them over."

"Are you kidding me?"

"No, I'm not. I don't want you running off by yourself again and getting killed."

"And I don't like being treated like a child."

Brian touched her shoulder. "Please. Just this once, humor me."

Toni realized he needed to feel that he was protecting her since he hadn't been able to protect Scott. "Fine."

She dropped the keys into Brian's palm. Once in the kitchen, she noticed two grocery bags on the table. "Did you look at the Excel file?"

"Yeah. The numbers don't make any sense to me either. I e-mailed it to Sam, my friend in Washington. As soon as he finds out anything on the investment firms, or the spreadsheet, he'll call."

Toni peeked into one of the grocery bags. "Jill oversees the entire property management division for Chadwick & Shore, and she put Gloria in charge of collecting the rents. What if they've been underreporting the funds they received?"

"That thought occurred to me too. Maybe Clint's not involved. Is it possible Jill's planning to divorce him and has been putting aside a little cash for herself? Do you know if they have a pre-nup?"

"Their marriage has always seemed pretty strong to me. I have no idea about a pre-nup, but I do know that Clint's not stupid. And the way he loves money, it wouldn't surprise me if he had a plan in place to cut her off if they ever divorced. It looks like if Jill wanted to kill somebody, it would be him."

"Then she'd be the prime suspect."

Toni nodded. "That's true, she would. It's just so hard for me to imagine Jill killing anybody. I've known her for two years now, and in all that time, I've never seen a bad side to her. But then again, I believed she was an only child."

"Maybe she never planned to kill Scott."

"You mean until he figured out what she was doing, and then she felt she had no choice."

"Either prison or murder."

Toni pulled a loaf of bread from one of the bags. "I know Scott thought he was protecting me, but I wish he had told me what was going on. If he had, he might still be alive." She felt the tears rising and forced them back down.

"There's some fried chicken from the deli in the fridge. I picked up a frozen pizza too."

"I'm sorry you weren't able to spend more time with him . . . that you didn't get to have that talk."

"Yeah, it sucks. But I can't let myself think about that. I need to focus on the here and now. So do you. Once we find out exactly what was going on—Jill, Nico, maybe Clint—whoever is responsible will pay."

They carried the fried chicken, a bag of chips, paper plates, and two sodas into the den. Brian put his laptop computer on the coffee table and opened it. "You know, Jill may have already been in prison. We have no idea who she really is," he said.

"Try doing a search on Sylvia Keith."

"Let me send an e-mail to Sam first. I'll ask him to dig into Jill's background. See if he can find out where Sylvia ends and Jill begins."

"I wonder if Clint knows Jill's real name and that she has a sister?"

"Until we find out different, I think we should consider Clint just as guilty as anyone else."

Toni watched as Brian typed out his e-mail and hit Send. "I hate having to wait on your friend to help us. Did you Google AlquilaCorp and the other apartment owners?"

"No, I wanted to hurry and get back. I figured we could do it here."

Brian keyed "Sylvia Keith" into the search engine. Several ancestry pages came up for a Sylvia who died in the 1800s. Another Sylvia owned show dogs, and, as expected, her picture didn't match. They waded through hundreds of hits, and none of them fit Jill.

Next, Brian tried to retrieve information on AlquilaCorp.

Your search did not match any documents.

"That's strange," he said. "You'd think there would be at least one or two entries. A business profile, a chamber of commerce listing, a phone book record, something."

One by one, he typed in the remaining property owners. A few pages came up for companies with similar names, but none matched exactly.

"I don't get it," Toni said. "Except for owning the apartments, it's like these companies don't even exist."

"Maybe they don't. Have you ever heard of a shell company?"

"That's like a fake company owned by another company?"

"Pretty much. Most of the time, they're used to hide someone's identity."

Toni cocked her head. "Do you think Jill owns all of these companies?"

"I don't think so. If she did, she sure wouldn't need Clint's money."

"Maybe Clint owns them, and he's just trying to keep them separate from Chadwick & Shore."

"Could be."

"Maybe the rents aren't involved at all. What if Clint was siphoning off Chadwick & Shore funds to buy the properties? Oh, and what if—"

"What if Nico shot JFK from the grassy knoll?"

"Very funny."

Brian picked up a chicken leg. "Look, there are lots of different scenarios we could come up with here. We're going to drive ourselves crazy if we don't stop this. Instead of speculating, going off on wild tangents, let's just wait and see what Sam uncovers."

"Fine." Toni dumped a mound of chips on her plate.

Brian chuckled. "You can't do it, can you?"

"What?"

"It's all over your face. Your brain is spinning faster than the teacup ride."

"Shut up, and stop making fun of me because I can't help it. I just want to know."

"You will. I promise, you will."

Kneeling, Detective Lewis stared at the skid marks on the bridge pavement. Something wasn't right here. He felt it all the way to his toenails. Although he wasn't an accident scene investigator, he could tell the tire tracks indicated more than a driver merely losing control, even if it had been raining.

He walked to the guardrail and watched as the wrecker service prepared to haul away Toni Matthews' BMW. The forensics team had done a preliminary examination at the scene. Whoever had been in the car had broken the window from the inside.

A dive boat rocked in the middle of the river, kept in place by a tether to the shore. They were searching for a body now. Neither the men on the force, nor the group led by Mark Ross, had found anything to indicate Miss Matthews was still alive.

Was it his fault?

When she had come to the station begging him to look further into Scott Chadwick's death, he thought she was just in denial, that it was part of her grieving process. Now, he wondered. Within the span of a little more than a week, three people, all related in some way, had turned up dead. Chadwick, the pretty red-haired real estate agent, and now Matthews.

His radio crackled to life. The call was for him, one of the officers at the station.

"Go ahead," Lewis said.

"The man you asked me to locate, Brian Chadwick, he's already checked out of his hotel."

"When did he leave?"

"Early this morning."

After she finished eating, Toni had gone into the guest room to take a nap. She didn't sleep long, little more than an hour. She lay there another thirty minutes with her eyes closed, but remained awake.

How could Jill do this? Pretend to be her closest friend? She had played the part so well. Toni remembered their twice-weekly lunches, shopping trips to Atlanta and New York, the late nights spent discussing the merits and foibles of the male species over a bottle of wine. She hadn't been that open about her life with another female since Kellie Snow.

Kellie's family had moved into the house across the street from Toni when they were both in kindergarten. She was the only girl Toni had ever talked to about her mother. They remained best friends throughout high school, but lost touch when Kellie left for college out west and Toni chose to stay in Alabama with her father and attend Auburn.

Over the years, Toni had made several casual friends, but had never allowed herself to form any strong bonds with anyone. Trust was something she didn't give freely. But after she met Scott, she began to change. He had been able to break down many of the walls she had built around herself; he made her believe it was okay to put her heart out there again. So she had let down her guard and allowed a friendship to grow with Jill. A friendship she thought was rock solid.

Although she never discussed her mother, she had shared her feelings about Scott, her beliefs about life, and the dreams she had for the future. And what about all the details Jill had shared about her life? Were they all lies?

Toni wondered whether Jill's mother had really suffered from cancer and committed suicide and if her father had really died of a heart attack. The part about being an only child was obviously not true. She thought she knew Jill well, but the woman she had known didn't even exist.

Waves of sadness and frustration rippled through Toni. How could she have been so stupid? How could she have allowed Jill to get so close? She should have known that one way or another, she'd just get hurt again.

And how did Clint fit in? Had Jill played him as well? Or was he another character in this charade? Playing his own devious role?

One thing was certain. For as long as Toni had known him, Clint had been all about the money. He always had to be first to own the newest electronic gadget. Had to trade up to a new car every year, live in the most exclusive neighborhood, throw the most lavish parties, and be known for giving the largest annual donation to his church. The emphasis on the *be known* part. Clint didn't believe in giving anonymously.

Maybe Toni had been right earlier. What if Clint had embezzled funds from Chadwick & Shore to purchase those apartments? He could have killed Scott on his own. Jill might not even be aware of it. There was only one problem with that theory.

Gloria.

Jill had said she didn't know her. She had said it so easily. Toni had never suspected for one second that she was lying. If Jill had nothing to do with Scott's death, then she would have no reason to hide her sister.

Toni rolled over and opened her eyes. There was no use in lying there awake, but she just couldn't get her mind to turn off. Brian was probably sleeping soundly in the next bedroom. She should make the best use of the time, go downstairs and do some more investigating online.

When she entered the den, Toni found Brian awake on the sofa, his computer in his lap.

"You couldn't sleep either?" she asked.

"Nope, and I really should. I've been up more than twenty-four hours now. I just can't get comfortable." He gestured toward his bandaged arm.

"I'm really sorry, I was just so scared—"

"I know. It's okay. If I had been you, I probably would have gone for my chest."

"Oh, I thought about it."

He smiled, and she saw Scott again. The resemblance tore at her heart. She had to look away. Had to get out of the room. "You want something from the kitchen?" she asked.

"No thanks."

Toni opened a Coke and leaned back against the refrigerator.

It had been so much easier when she thought Brian was guilty. As long as she hated him, she could ignore all the little mannerisms he had in common with Scott. Tell herself the two brothers were nothing alike. Now she knew that wasn't entirely true. The more time she spent with Brian, the harder it was to be around him.

By the time she found the courage to look at Brian again, she had sipped more than half the bottle of Coke. He was still staring at his computer screen.

"You really should go up to bed," she said.

"I know. I wish I could take a shower. That would probably help, but I can't get these stitches wet."

"I just might have a solution for that."

Toni left the room. She returned a few minutes later with a roll of plastic wrap and some first-aid tape. "Hold out your arm," she said.

Starting at his wrist, she began wrapping the plastic around his arm, all the way up to his elbow and then back again. Once she was satisfied his wound was properly encased, she sealed off the edges of the plastic wrap with the first-aid tape. "That should keep the water out," she said.

"What gave you this idea?"

"Well, that's a bit of a story. When I was little, we lived on a cul-de-sac, and I used to ride my bike up and down the street. My father never would let me get out on the main road of the subdivision because he thought there was too much traffic. Well, one day when I was around ten years old, I decided I was big enough to go anywhere in our neighborhood I wanted. So off I went. I was doing pretty well too—using my hand signals when I turned, making sure I was far enough over to the right so the cars had plenty of room to pass me. I was feeling invincible—until I came to the big curve. I looked up and there was this huge truck right in the middle of the road. It looked as if it was coming straight toward me, and I panicked. My tires went off the edge of the pavement and I ended up hugging a tree."

Brian couldn't help but laugh. "How badly were you hurt?"

"Not too bad—no broken bones or anything like that. But I did get a pretty good gash in my right calf and the doctor had to give me five or six stitches. I refused to go to school the next day without taking a shower, so my dad came up with the plastic wrap fix."

"Did you get in trouble?"

"No, not that time. Dad was so glad I was still alive, he let it slide."

She hadn't thought about that day in years. And why in the world did she tell Brian about it? She could easily have said she'd had stitches once and left it at that. She'd be glad when all this was over and he was back in Washington.

"Are you from around here?"

"No, I grew up in a little town just outside Auburn, Alabama. I didn't move to Nashville until after college."

"What brought you here?"

"Well, my father died, and I just couldn't live in that house anymore. I had to get away, you know?"

"Yeah, I do." Brian hesitated for a second, and then motioned toward the stairs. "I should go shower."

After Brian went upstairs, Toni picked up his laptop. She searched the tax records for Sylvia Keith but didn't find any property listed under that name. Then an idea hit her. She typed in the address for the house where Nico lived. She wasn't a bit surprised when she read the property owner's name: AlquilaCorp. And as she suspected, the tax bill went to Chadwick & Shore.

She clicked back to the main search page. She typed AlquilaCorp into the property owner's name field and was about to hit enter when a phone rang.

Brian's cell phone.

She wasn't in the habit of answering another person's phone, but what if it was his friend Sam? What if he had figured out the spreadsheet? She put down the computer and picked Brian's phone up off the coffee table. She glanced at the caller ID.

The number on the screen was one she knew well.

Jill's private line.

31

Shocked, Toni stared at the number.

Why was Jill calling Brian?

Maybe it didn't mean anything. It could be completely innocent. She probably just wanted to let him know Toni was missing. Find out if he had seen her.

The phone rang four more times before switching over to voice mail. Toni waited a few seconds to see if a message alert popped up. When none did, she opened the menu and scanned through the call log. Brian had received six more calls from Jill's various phone numbers during the past few days. He had dialed her private line twice.

Why would he be talking to Jill? As far as Toni knew, they were not exactly friends.

A knot began to form in the pit of her stomach.

She returned to the call menu and pulled up the text messages. As she feared, there was one from Jill, sent on Wednesday at 4:28 p.m. Two little words that made her heart rate spike.

"It's done."

Jill had typed the message within fifteen minutes after Toni crashed into the river.

What she originally suspected, but didn't want to believe, had now turned out to be true. Jill had been checking in, shouting the all-clear.

Letting Brian know Toni was dead.

So Brian was guilty too. He was involved with Jill, Gloria, and Nico.

After everything Toni had uncovered, why had she allowed herself to trust Brian? In her heart, she knew the answer. She had let his physical resemblance to Scott impair her judgment. She had made it easy for Brian to con her.

No wonder he hadn't wanted to brainstorm ideas about the rental properties. He didn't want her to figure out the connection. If she had hit on the truth, his eyes or his body language might have given him away.

"Let's just wait on Sam," he had said. Sam probably didn't even exist. Brian most likely sent the e-mail to Jill. A slick way to let her know exactly what Toni had found out.

Cold sweat broke out on the back of her neck. Why was she still alive?

Brian could easily have killed her when she came back to Josh's that morning. There had to be a reason he let her live. Maybe they hadn't decided what to do with her body yet. The police had found her car in the river. Maybe Brian was waiting for the cops to clear out. Then he could drown her and let her body wash up on the bank. There would be fewer questions that way. Her death would be ruled accidental. But if she just disappeared, people might start to wonder.

She had to get out of there.

Brian still had her car keys. She would have to leave on foot.

Toni popped open the DVD drive on Brian's laptop computer. Scott's disk wasn't there. She had to find it. That was the only piece of evidence she had.

Brian had stowed the computer carrying case underneath the coffee table. She slid it out and noticed a bulge in the outside pocket. She stuck her hand in and pulled out a spiral notebook. A loose paper was stuck to the back.

Brian's hotel bill.

She glanced at the charges and realized something was off.

When Brian agreed to come to the wedding, he said he would be arriving in Nashville the afternoon of the rehearsal dinner. That night at the restaurant, he acted as though he had just flown in. But according to his bill, he had checked into the hotel a full week prior.

What had he been doing all that time?

She was about to unzip the main compartment of the carrying case when she heard footsteps on the stairs. She crammed the notebook and bill back into the pocket.

"The plastic wrap worked," Brian said. "Thanks."

"You're welcome." She struggled to keep her voice calm. "You should go back upstairs and try to get some sleep. You really need the rest."

"I will, in a bit. I'm actually kind of hungry. Do you want any more of the chicken?"

"No, you eat it."

Choke on it.

Mark turned the shoe over in his hand. A woman's brown leather loafer, size eight. One of the volunteers had found it caught in a brush pile along the edge of the river. Jill had recognized it immediately. His worst fear was confirmed. Toni had been in the car.

The search party had continued their quest throughout the day. After scouring the river for several miles, they had gone door to door asking the residents in the area if they had seen Toni. No one had.

Now, as darkness approached, the divers had come to shore. They avoided Mark's eyes as they passed. He knew what they were thinking. He didn't care. He wasn't ready to give up hope. Not yet. He wanted to believe there was still some chance Toni had survived.

Until they found her body, he would refuse to accept that she was gone.

Act normal.

Toni had repeated the phrase in her head over and over since Brian came back from taking his shower. She had to make it seem as though nothing had changed. That she still trusted him. Just make him feel comfortable, let him fall asleep, find the computer disk, and get the hell out of there.

There was no way she could risk talking with him. She was sure he'd be able to read her thoughts through her eyes. Instead, she had turned on the television and pretended to be engrossed in an old movie. She appeared focused on the screen, but in reality, she had no idea what was going on. She was too worried Jill would call again. Call and tell Brian it was time to kill her.

Why was he still awake? Was he afraid she would slip away? If he had been up as many hours as he'd said, he should be dying to shut his eyes. Yet he refused to go upstairs. Was he really watching the television, or was he studying her?

The urge to bolt from her chair and tear through the back door was almost more than she could bear. She had to calm down. Without Scott's disk, she had nothing to show the police.

"That movie was pretty good," Brian said. "I don't think I've ever seen it before."

Toni realized the film credits were rolling. She began flipping through the channels.

"What's wrong with you?" Brian asked.

"Nothing." She hoped her voice hadn't sounded too sharp.

"Look at me."

Toni tried to keep her heart from pounding.

Take deep breaths. He doesn't know you're on to him.

"I'm okay," she explained. "I'm just tired, and I want all this over with. I guess the wait is eating away at my nerves."

Brian moved to the edge of the sofa and put his hand on her chair. "I'm sorry it's taking so long. But I promise you, we will find out who killed Scott and why. And once we do, I'm going to make sure they get put away for life."

Toni wanted to scream. Grab him by the collar and shake him. She didn't just want him put away. He deserved to die for what he'd done. She bit down on her tongue until she tasted blood. If she opened her mouth, she would be the one who ended up dead. Instead, she turned away and continued her channel surfing. How could he have looked her straight in the eye and vowed to punish Scott's killer? Brian was an expert liar. Just like Jill.

"Hey. Wait," he said. "Turn that back."

Toni flipped back a channel. The local news was on. Mark stood next to the river talking to a reporter. He hadn't shaved, and his face appeared haggard.

"She may be disoriented. It's possible she doesn't remember her name," Mark said. "If you think you've seen her, please call."

"We hope she's found soon," the reporter said.

The broadcast switched back to the studio. Toni's picture flashed on the screen, her name and the police department's telephone number below it.

"I hate putting Mark through this," Toni said.

"I know, but you can't call him. Nobody can know you're alive. It's too dangerous."

Somehow she knew Brian would say that.

His cell phone rang, and Toni jumped.

Brian cut her a strange look before answering.

"Hello? Okay . . . great . . . I'll be waiting." He ended the call. "That was Sam. He just got in and read my e-mails. He said he'd probably know something in a few hours."

So they weren't quite ready to kill her yet. Or were they? What if it had really been Nico calling to say he was on the way over? Was that what Brian was waiting up for? She couldn't take that chance. She had wasted too many hours hoping he would go to sleep so she could search for Scott's disk. That didn't matter anymore. She had to get out of there. Now.

Toni fought the impulse to run.

"I'm going upstairs to get some rest," she said. "Wake me when Sam calls."

She made sure Brian wasn't following her and then slipped into Josh's study. She grabbed the phone book off his desk before heading upstairs to the guest room.

Several cab companies were listed in the yellow pages. She took her cell phone from the nightstand and started to dial, but stopped. Brian might be lurking in the hallway. It would be best to wait until she got outside to call.

Toni tore the page from the phone book and stuck it in the pocket of her jeans, then locked the bedroom door and switched off the light. She sat on the bed letting her eyes adjust to the darkness. Once she was able to see, she went to the window and raised the blind.

The guest bedroom window overlooked the sloping roof of the covered patio below. Toni popped out the screen, climbed through the opening, and then pulled the window back down. She didn't want the cold air rushing into the house and alerting Brian. Sitting down, she scooted her way across the asphalt shingles to the edge of the roof. She looked down. The distance to the ground seemed a lot farther than she had imagined.

Great plan, genius. You've come this far. Now you're going to fall and break your neck.

Toni tossed her purse from the roof. After saying a silent prayer, she rolled over onto her stomach and dropped to the lawn. She sat still for a moment, hoping Brian hadn't heard her.

The den light went out.

32

Toni flattened herself against the ground.

Why had the light gone out? Did Brian hear her slide off the roof? Was he peering through the blinds, scanning the lawn for any sign of movement?

She lay just a few feet from the raised patio. She doubted her body was visible from the angle of the window. But if Brian came outside, he would be sure to see her.

The knife.

She had left it in the bedroom. There was no going back for it now. If Brian opened the back door, she would have to take her chances and run.

Toni remained motionless for several minutes, the cold seeping up from the ground and spreading throughout her body. The wind whipped the grass around her, and the soft rumble of thunder echoed in the distance. Rain was on the way. Her muscles tense, she listened to the sounds of the night—crickets and tree frogs, and a bird she didn't recognize—alert for any warning that Brian was in the yard. Finally convinced he was still inside, she crept from tree to tree until she reached the driveway.

Once at the street, Toni phoned a cab company. She gave the address of the house across from Josh's and said not to pull into the driveway. Crouched between two evergreen bushes, she waited nearly thirty minutes before seeing the taxi's lights approaching.

She jumped into the backseat, gave the driver her street name, and asked him to hurry. By the time they reached Toni's neighborhood, the sky had opened, sending down a steady shower.

"Stop right here," she said.

The cab driver pulled over a few houses down from where Toni lived and she handed him his fare. "I'll give you an extra hundred if you'll wait here for me. I won't be long."

Toni pulled up the hood of her jacket and ran across her neighbors' lawns and then around to her own yard. The rain stung her face like tiny needles and made it difficult for her to see. Squinting her eyes, she headed for the back door. She couldn't believe she had been stupid enough to give Brian her keys. Thankfully, she had put the spare house key back under the patio table.

Once inside, she ran to Scott's study. He was bound to have saved a copy of the spreadsheet on his computer. She would print out the file and take it to the police station. Demand to speak to the police chief, tell him everything she had discovered, and refuse to leave until he agreed to reopen Scott's case.

She would also request police protection. After dodging two attempts on her life and then getting caught by Brian, she had no other choice.

Toni sat down at the computer and opened Scott's documents file. The folder was empty.

What the . . .

She clicked on her own folder.

Empty too.

Someone had erased all the files. Had Brian been in her house after he checked out of his hotel? He was the only other person who knew about the spreadsheet.

What now? How would she convince the police to help her with no evidence?

The safe.

She had seen computer disks when she took out the money. Maybe Scott had made a backup file. As far as she knew, he had not told anyone else about the secret safe behind the bookcase. She didn't even know it existed until after they had moved into the house.

One by one, Toni put the disks from the safe into the computer's DVD drive. She searched through all the files. They were mostly architectural drawings and random notes Scott had made on the various projects he had completed. Nothing even remotely resembled the spreadsheet.

She felt like crying as she removed the last disk from the computer. She knew there were ways of recovering deleted files from a hard drive, but that would probably take days. And she would have to find someone with the expertise to do it.

Where would she go until then? In order to get far enough away so Brian couldn't find her, she would need more money. She went back to the safe and pulled out the metal box containing Scott's cash.

Then she saw it.

A flash drive.

It had been behind the money box. Scott had written her name on the drive with a black marker, the same as he had the computer disk. Toni plugged the drive into one of the computer's USB ports. Using the same password that had opened the spreadsheet, she gained access to the flash drive files.

The words she read amazed her. Everything made sense now. The abbreviations on the spreadsheet columns, the amounts, and the addresses. Scott had laid it all out.

She realized now he had meant for the information on the disk he left in the car to be cryptic in case someone else had found it. Scott knew she would end up searching the safe.

Toni burned a copy of the files onto a CD and then returned the flash drive to its hiding place. She now had enough to put Jill and Clint away for a long time.

There was one thing she didn't understand. Why hadn't Scott gone to the police?

She bet it was because of the wedding. It was her own fault Scott didn't confide in her. If she hadn't been so set on having the wedding of her dreams, if she hadn't been so selfish, things might have turned out differently. Scott would have done just about anything to keep from spoiling her special day. He always put her feelings first, above everything else, never being concerned for himself. All he ever cared about was protecting her and making her happy. In many ways, she knew she was also to blame for his death.

The arrest of a well-known businessman like Clint would be big news. The press would be all over it—and all over Chadwick & Shore. Scott probably planned to wait until they got back from their honeymoon. He wouldn't have been able to leave town once Clint was apprehended. Scott would have had to stay behind and handle the fallout. Again, she knew he'd been thinking about how everything would affect her.

Jill and Clint must have figured out he was onto them. Their solution: get rid of him. But they needed someone to help with their scheme, Toni reasoned. Someone who hated Scott, but at the same time, someone he would trust. So they had obviously contacted Brian and made a deal.

Brian could have used Clint's keys to enter the hotel construction site early that morning, before anyone else arrived. It would have been easy for him to lure Scott up to the penthouse.

After the murder, as the only surviving relative, Brian probably thought he would automatically inherit his brother's fortune. Then he would sell his half of Chadwick & Shore to Clint. Jill and her husband could continue their business with no one the wiser, and Brian would be a multimillionaire.

Everybody would win.

Except for Scott and Toni.

So when she started asking too many questions, they decided to take her out of the way as well. Only this time, she would make sure they failed.

Toni grabbed an umbrella and headed back out into the night. When she reached the street, she found the taxi had left. She had taken too long to locate the files. The driver must have decided she wasn't coming back.

Returning to the house to wait for another cab seemed a bit too risky. She had no way of knowing how long it would be before Brian discovered she was gone and came looking for her. She needed to keep moving. She could have a taxi pick her up on the next street over.

As Toni flipped open her cell phone, a gust of wind caught her umbrella, whipping it up and forcing it inside out. Knocked off balance, she slid off the shoulder of the road and dropped her phone into the rain-filled ditch.

"Dammit!"

Toni pulled her arm out of her jacket, pushed up her sleeve, and fished around in the ditch until she found the phone.

It was dead.

That's what she got for buying a cheapie. She thought about going back into the house to make the call. Then she remembered: Brian had tapped her phone line.

Now she was stuck. She couldn't walk all the way to the police station. It would take her all night. No, but she could walk to Mark's house. He lived only a few miles away.

Toni threw the useless cell phone back into the ditch along with her broken umbrella.

The phone rang.

The ringing cut through the haze of Brian's dreamless sleep. He sat up on the sofa. "Hello?"

The voice on the other end confirmed what he already knew.

It was time.

After a long trek, hiding every time she saw headlights and cutting through more back yards than she could count, Toni finally made it to Mark's condominium complex. Cold and muddy, her wet jacket hood plastered to her head, she rang his doorbell.

The door swung open. Mark stood at the threshold. Clad in a bathrobe, he stared at her as though he'd never seen her before.

"Toni!" His arms engulfed her, pulling her off her feet. "Thank God! I thought I'd lost you. Where have you been?"

She had so much to tell him. Where should she begin? Toni let out a huge sigh.

"Never mind," he said. "Just come inside. You're soaked."

He ushered her into the foyer and helped remove her coat. Finally she felt safe. The proof she needed was in her hands, and now nothing could stop her from getting justice. She glanced down at the dirty footprints she had left across the tile floor.

"That's it!" Toni grabbed Mark's arm and jumped like a schoolgirl. "I know how he did it!"

33

Brian knocked on the bedroom door.

"Toni?"

Receiving no answer, he knocked again.

"Toni, it's time to wake up." He listened for movement in the room. Something was wrong. He tried the knob. Locked.

Brian kicked the door open and flipped on the light.

She was gone.

"Calm down," Mark said. "You know how who did what?"

"I know how Brian murdered Scott."

"Toni, honey." He pushed her wet hair back out of her face and spoke to her as though she were a child. "We've already been over this. Brian didn't kill Scott."

"I know what I'm talking about and you're wrong. Please, Mark, if you'll just listen—"

"All right." He held up his hand. "You win. I'll listen to whatever you have to say, but first, let's get you dried off and into some warm clothes. You're shivering."

Toni looked down at her legs. Her jeans were soaked all the way up to her knees. "Okay, but you have to believe me."

Mark's eyes locked with hers, revealing a deep empathy. "Your pants need to go into the washer. I'll get you some sweats to wear for now."

She slipped off her shoes and followed him into the utility room. A basket of freshly laundered clothes sat on top of the table next to the dryer. He pulled out a gray sweatshirt and matching pants, along with a pair of sport socks. "I know these are a little big, but at least you won't be cold."

Mark gave Toni a bath towel for her hair, and she went into the powder room to change. The reflection in the mirror startled her. She looked terrible. Even with makeup, her face was pale, and dark circles ringed her eyes. The events of the last week had taken their toll on her body as well as her emotions.

She wondered if Brian would search for her here. She knew Mark would defend her with his life. She hated putting him in danger. She hoped Brian would assume she had left on foot. If that were the case, he would think she was still somewhere in Brentwood, not Blanton Hills.

The sweats felt good against her icy skin. She pulled the drawstring tight and then slipped on the shirt. It fit like a dress. She rolled up the sleeves until they fell just above her wrists.

After drying her hair with the towel, Toni scrubbed the smudged makeup from her face. She hoped washing her jeans wouldn't take too long. Showing up at the police station in Mark's clothes would make her appear light-years away from credible.

When she was finished in the powder room, she found Mark in the kitchen. He had changed into a T-shirt and gym shorts and had switched the coffeemaker on. Two cups sat on the counter. "Thanks for the sweats," she said

He laughed and shook his head. "You look nice."

"Hey, I'm a fashionista." She carried her own clothes into the laundry room and threw them into the washer. When she came back into the kitchen, Mark was pouring the coffee.

"Let's take this into the living room," he said.

Toni settled on the sofa, closed her eyes, and let the steam from the coffee warm her face. She opened her eyes. "Do you have a gun?"

"Why would you ask that?"

"Just tell me."

"No, I don't have a gun. Do I need one?"

"Yes, you might."

He put down his cup. "What exactly is going on here? And where have you been? I've driven myself crazy worrying about you."

"I know, and I'm sorry, but I couldn't call you."

"Why not?"

"I couldn't drag you into this mess for your own safety. I didn't want to get you involved, and I really shouldn't even be here now."

"Well, you are. So start explaining."

Cradling her cup with both hands, she took a sip of the coffee. "Since the crash, I've been hiding at one of my listings in Brentwood. I needed everyone—you, Jill, Clint, Brian, the police—to think that I was dead."

Mark looked as though he'd been slapped. "You mean no one was in your car? The whole accident was staged?"

"Oh no. I was in the car when it crashed into the river, and I almost drowned. But it was no accident: I was forced off the road."

"Brian ran you off the road?"

"No, a man Brian hired, Nico Williams, was driving the other car."

"How do you know that? How do you know it wasn't some drunk driver?"

"Because I've been to Nico's house and I've seen the car he drove—a dark green Audi sedan."

Mark shook his head. He didn't believe her. "Do you realize how many of those cars there must be in this county alone?"

"There's only one with red paint from my BMW on the fender."

He seemed to ponder that information. "Okay. Let's say you did find the car that hit you. Why do you think Brian is responsible?"

"Because he killed Scott, and now he's trying to kill me."

"Toni—"

"I know you think Scott jumped from the balcony, but he didn't. He was thrown over the wall. Brian threw him over the wall."

Mark rubbed his unshaved chin. "How do you know?"

"The day of Scott's funeral, after you left, Jill and I went back to the hotel site. I had to get it clear in my mind exactly what had happened that morning. While I was there, I found his pen—the one he had with him the night before he died—on the floor of the construction elevator. At the time, I thought he had fought with somebody and lost it that way, but I was wrong."

"Go on."

"Everybody thinks Scott went into the hotel by himself, but that's not what happened. Brian carried him into that elevator, probably over his shoulder, and the pen fell out of Scott's pocket because he was turned upside down."

Mark just stared at her.

"You think I'm crazy, don't you?" she asked.

"I know you're not crazy. But I talked to the police that day. Brian wasn't even there when Scott died."

"Oh yes, he was there, but at the time nobody realized it."

"You think he was hiding in the hotel?"

"When I first found out that Scott had arrived at the hotel alone, I thought Brian was already inside, but now I know better."

"You're not making sense. If Brian had been at the construction site, someone would have seen him."

"People see what they expect to see."

"Meaning?"

"Alvin Harney, the lead superintendent, was at the site that morning when Scott arrived. He stood just a few feet from Scott's car and he saw the same thing he was used to seeing every morning. His mind had become conditioned to see the same thing."

"Which was?"

"He saw his boss driving a silver BMW. Only this time, Mr. Harney's eyes lied. Scott wasn't behind the wheel that morning. Brian was.

Mark scratched his head, raking his fingers through his uncombed hair. "How did you come to this conclusion?"

"You can't deny the resemblance between them. If I saw Brian wearing Scott's hard hat, driving his SUV, I would be fooled, and I knew Scott better than anyone else."

"Okay, you're right. They do look alike, but that still doesn't mean it's true. And where was Scott? Tied up in the back?"

"Yes."

"What you're describing sounds like something out of a bad movie. Not real life."

"So you still don't believe me?"

"I'm sorry. I just think you've been hurt so deeply, you're not thinking clearly."

"Oh, my mind is crystal clear. Do you remember the night before Scott died?"

"Of course, I do."

"Rain poured down so hard that on the way home from the rehearsal dinner, Scott had to pull over twice because he couldn't see the road."

"I remember the weather. I had to pull over once myself."

Toni readjusted herself on the sofa, leaning closer to Mark. "After the funeral when I went to the hotel, I parked in the exact spot where Scott's car was found. I followed the same path he would've had to take to get inside, and I know beyond a shadow of a doubt that there's no way he walked into the building."

"How?"

"Even though I parked on the gravel, the only way I could get up to the hotel was by crossing damp ground—heavy red clay."

"So?"

She cocked her head to the side. "When I received all of Scott's personal belongings from the morgue, there was no mud on his shoes."

Mark sat back in his chair, silent for a moment. "Maybe they cleaned them at the medical examiner's office."

"No. No, they couldn't have. When I took his shoes out of the bag, I noticed a layer of street dust on the tops. They wouldn't just clean the soles and not the uppers, and after a night of heavy rain, if Scott had walked, his shoes would have been caked with that red clay."

Mark looked stunned.

Toni smiled. "You're starting to believe me."

"Well, I have to give you credit. You've made a good case. But if you're planning on taking this to the police, you might not be too successful."

"Why do you say that?"

"They'll have to admit they made a huge mistake. They should have caught something that obvious. They'll probably claim they scraped the mud off for evidence."

"Fine, it doesn't matter. Let them say whatever they want because I know the reason Scott was murdered, and they won't be able to shut me up."

"Right: Brian's lawsuit over the will. But the police will see Scott's money as a motive for you too. If Brian is convicted of murder, you get the whole estate. They could think you're trying to frame him so you don't have to split the inheritance."

Toni shook her head. "No, you don't understand. I actually have real proof now, from Scott's own hand, that he was murdered."

Toni told Mark about the files Scott had left for her that detailed Clint and Jill's illegal activities. She also related her last visit to Gloria's apartment and explained how she had found the Audi in Nico's garage. She concluded by summing up her encounter with Brian.

"Do you have the computer disk with you?" Mark asked.

"It's in my coat pocket."

He nodded. "I never pictured Brian as a killer, but you've convinced me. With everything you've discovered, the police won't have a choice. This will force them to reopen Scott's case." Mark reached for her hand. "Scott would be really proud of you right now."

A tear slid down her cheek, and Mark brushed it away.

He stood up. "Let me run upstairs and take a quick shower. Then I'll drive you to the police station."

Toni watched him walk up the stairs. It was almost over. The truth would soon be out, and Scott would be vindicated. She picked up her half-empty coffee cup and carried it to the kitchen. From the adjacent laundry room, she could hear the washer making its final spin. She waited for the machine to stop and then transferred her clothes to the dryer. After topping off her coffee, she returned to the living room.

She nestled into the sofa, putting her feet up. Exhaustion permeated every cell of her body. Maybe now that someone she trusted knew what had really happened, she could start to relax a little.

She had just started to drift off to sleep when a sharp whack echoed from the direction of the laundry room.

Was that the dryer? Had it gone haywire?

Toni peeled herself from the sofa and went into the kitchen. The door to the patio stood wide open. Rain splattered the floor.

Don't panic. It was just the wind.

The door wasn't shut all the way. That's all.

Brian is not here.

She pushed the door closed and engaged the lock.

Before she could turn around, a searing pain ripped through the back of her head.

34

Mark checked his watch before going downstairs. Almost eleven o'clock. He imagined Detective Lewis was enjoying his Friday evening at home with his family. They might even be in bed by now. It didn't matter.

There was no way Mark would let Toni give her statement to some flunky on the night shift, unfamiliar with Scott's case. Whatever the hour, he would demand the detective come down to the station. Even if he had to threaten his job.

Mark had more than a few friends in high places. He suspected Lewis knew that already.

The living room was empty.

"Toni?"

Mark headed into the kitchen. His feet slid across the wet tile. Why would she go outside? He flipped on the exterior lights. The patio and courtyard appeared deserted.

A sick feeling rushed through him.

He jerked open the door and ran out into the rain. As he rounded the corner of the building, a car tore out of his driveway and disappeared into the night.

Toni struggled in the darkness, trying to free her hands. Whoever attacked her had bound her wrists behind her body and then hog-tied them to her feet. She lay on her side, the back of her head throbbing with pain. How long had she been unconscious?

The stale air pushed in around her, heavy and still. Her first thought was that she was inside some type of makeshift coffin. They had left her to die.

Then she realized she was moving, slowing down. She recognized the familiar sensation and the faint smell of oil and exhaust fumes. They had locked her inside the trunk of a car. But whose trunk?

She hadn't seen the face of her attacker. Was it Brian or Nico? And where were they taking her? And what about Mark? Had they killed him?

He had been upstairs taking a shower. What if he had heard the commotion? He never would have let them take her. Not without a fight. Why had she involved Mark in the first place? She should have just walked to the police station no matter how long it took. If he was dead, it was her fault. First Scott, then Dana, and now Mark.

Toni wrestled with her restraints. She had to find some way out. And if Mark was still alive, she had to find a way to save him.

Nico Williams waited in the dark.

She was running late, as usual. Normally, her dawdling didn't bother him; he was used to it. It was one of the many allowances he afforded her. After what she'd been through, he felt he owed her, but tonight was different. Tonight their timing had to be perfect.

He was about to go in after her when the car door opened. She was wearing the red wig. The length was a little off, but it would do.

She slid into the passenger seat. Even with the disguise, she was stunning.

Throughout the years, his baby sister's beauty had been a source not only of his pride but also of his fear. He realized she was special early on, when she was little more than a toddler. She'd follow him around mimicking his every move, then stare up at him with her big blue eyes and angelic face. Her wavy blonde hair fit her like a halo.

As she grew, she made it known he was her hero. And he tried his best to live up to the title. But her carefree childhood didn't last long. She blossomed early, needing her first bra when other girls her age were still playing with Barbie dolls.

That was when his fear began.

He saw the way his mother's boyfriends leered at her. Bringing her candy and other gifts and asking to be called "uncle." Nico was always quick to step in, making it clear that any man who dared even think of touching his sister would pay with his life.

And the day finally came when one of them did. The twentieth of January.

Many years had passed since that bleak winter day, but for Nico, it sometimes seemed only moments.

Warned of an approaching snowstorm, the principal of his sister's school made the decision to send the kids home a few hours early. Jake Gardner, their mother's flavor of the week, was alone in their trailer, left there to sleep off the previous night's whiskey.

If only his sister had known Jake was still there; she never would have gone inside. But she didn't know, and Nico had not been there to protect her. Jake had raped the innocent girl and then beat her until she was unconscious. She had been just twelve years old.

Jake was the first person Nico had killed. There were witnesses who saw the fight. They testified Jake had been the first to pull his knife. It was a lie, of course. Nico had gone to the bar with one goal in mind: to end Jake's life. Even if it meant he too had to die in the process.

Nico suffered a few cuts and bruises, but other than that he was fine. He never even stood trial. The killing had been ruled self-defense. However, his sister didn't fare quite as well. Her physical wounds had long since healed, but emotionally, she had never fully recovered. In many ways, she would always be the same frightened child who had come home too early.

But unlike that January day, Nico would always be there to shield her—as he had done in the past and was doing now. He vowed to protect his family. Even if it meant someone else had to die. Strike before you were stricken. That was the true meaning of self-defense.

"You know what to do?" he asked.

Gloria smiled at her brother.

35

The trunk lid popped up.

Toni's back was toward the opening. She lifted her head in an effort to see who was there. Cold steel pushed against her cheek.

"Now I'm going to cut your hands and feet loose, but if you move a single inch, I won't hesitate to shoot you. Do you understand me?"

It was Jill's voice. All hope that Toni had been holding—her wish that by some miracle her friend wasn't really involved—disintegrated.

The gun pressed harder into her face. "I said, do you understand me?"

"Yes."

Once her bonds were cut, Toni rolled over and sat up. They were at the hotel site. As usual, the night security lights were on. Jill had parked inside the fence, around a hundred feet from the main entrance to the building. As far as Toni could tell, neither Nico nor Brian was there yet.

"Now get out of the car," Jill commanded.

Toni swung her legs out of the trunk. She realized the rain had stopped.

Still pointing the gun, Jill threw Toni's clothes into the trunk. "Put these on."

"You took my clothes from the dryer?"

"Just shut up now, and do what I tell you."

Toni stripped off Mark's sweats and pulled on her damp jeans and shirt. It was clear Jill aimed to kill her. She needed to buy herself some time and try to figure out a way to get the gun. "What's your plan, Sylvia?"

Jill smiled. "So you know who I am."

"Yes, I know everything—not just your name. I know all about the money and the dummy corporations."

"Well, let's just give you a gold star."

"There never was a problem with the construction of the hotel, was there?" Toni inched away from the car. "Scott never had a reason to commit suicide. He found out the truth about AlquilaCorp, so you had him killed."

"That's right, and it's a shame you couldn't keep your nose out of my business. We had such good times together, but now I have to kill you too."

It was as if Toni was seeing Jill for the first time. Her mask had fallen away, revealing a soul of ice. "I thought you were my best friend, but you've never cared about anyone but yourself."

"There's no way you could ever understand me in a million years. You grew up with a father who loved you, but I never had anything even close to that. Nico and I were born just a year apart, and we never had anybody to look out after us. Our mama was always drunk and she'd stay gone for days at a time. There was never enough food in the house. We did anything and everything just to survive."

The revelation came as a shock to Toni and she wondered what else lay hidden in Jill's past. "How did your mother really die?"

"What, you think I killed my own mama?" Jill laughed. "In the real world, my mama is very much alive, but she's dead to me, and that's all I care about. Now as unpleasant as this is, I do have to get rid of you, so quit stalling. There's not anything you can do to stop it anyway."

"If you're just going to shoot me, then why bring me all the way out here?"

Jill pulled something out of her coat pocket. It looked like a plastic zip bag with a paper inside. "I suppose I could put a bullet in you right here and now, but I've got something better in mind."

She held up the bag. "You see this?" Jill asked, "It's a note written on your stationery, and it tells a very sad story. It's all about a sweet young woman who lost her husband-to-be. When that happened, the poor thing just couldn't go on living, so she decided to go out the same way he did, by jumping off the top floor of his hotel."

"Nobody will ever believe I wrote that."

"Now that's where you're wrong. The signature on this letter is a perfect match to yours, and everybody who knows you will recognize it. I doubt that even you could tell the difference, and while you were unconscious, I took the liberty of putting your fingerprints all over the paper."

"What about Mark? Did you kill him?"

"Not yet. Is there a reason I should?"

"No. No, I didn't tell him anything," Toni lied. "I was going to, but I didn't get the chance." At least Mark was safe. She hoped he had already made it to the police station with the disk.

"We're wasting time now, so get moving."

Toni took a step toward the building. "You've set yourself up quite an enterprise here. How much money are you making? Millions?"

"Now why do you care about that?"

"I just don't get it, that's all. Scott built Chadwick & Shore into a virtual gold mine, and he did it legally. Clint has all the money he could ever need, and he had to know that eventually you'd be caught. Even without the murder charge, he'd be facing serious prison time, so why would he risk it all? Is he that greedy?"

"I guess you don't know everything after all."

"I know enough. I admit that it took me a while to put the pieces together. When I found out Gloria collected the rents for all of Chadwick & Shore's leased properties, I thought she might be underreporting the funds, but it was the exact opposite. The bank deposits are for far more than the actual rental income should be. Who are you laundering the money for? And who owns all those companies? Clint's fishing buddies down in Mexico?"

Jill laughed.

"What's so funny?"

"Now do you really believe that Clint has the balls to orchestrate this kind of a deal?"

"You mean he's not a member of your drug cartel?"

"Where did you get the idea that I was a drug dealer? I simply manage the finances for a very profitable organization of businessmen. How they make their money is not my concern."

"And Clint has no idea?"

"Clint knows exactly what I want him to know, and that's all."

"Do you even love him?"

"*Love* is such an abstract word, don't you think? Let's just say I'm fond of him, and I find him useful."

"You had this all planned out before you even married him, didn't you?"

Jill smiled. "If you must know the truth, I had my eye on Scott first, but then I realized Clint was much easier to manipulate. All I really had to do was stroke his ego. You should be glad I decided to take the quickest route; otherwise, I'd be Mrs. Chadwick right now."

Toni wanted to slap her. "Scott never would have fallen for you, and I don't believe he dated Gloria either, did he?"

"Now how could he? I went out of my way to make sure the two of them never met each other. Your knight never cheated on you. I know that's all you really care about, and now I've given you the answer, so move."

"You can kill me, but it won't solve your problem. Before he died, Scott put together a detailed file on all your transactions, including the bank records. It's all on a computer disk."

"Are you talking about the disk you left in your jacket? The one that's on the backseat of my car?"

Acid rose in Toni's throat. She swallowed hard. Mark didn't have the disk. Even if he was still alive, how could he prove anything? Would the police act on his word alone, or would Detective Lewis brush him off the same way he had Toni? "That's not the only copy."

Jill gave her a suspicious look. "I guess I'll have to take my chances on that." She shoved Toni forward. "Now go!"

After walking a few steps, Toni slid her foot across the gravel and pretended to stumble. She lunged toward Jill, knocking her to the ground.

The gun went off.

36

Nico stopped the car at the end of Toni's driveway. "You remember the alarm code?"

"By heart," Gloria confirmed.

"Good. I'll call you on your cell and let you know when to phone the taxi. After you get in the car, try to keep your hair across your face and keep looking out the window. Don't make eye contact with the driver. When you get to the construction site, have him drop you off at the end of the access road, and make sure to tell him you own the company building the hotel. Then give him the five hundred dollars."

"Got it."

When the gun fired, Toni froze.

Her hesitation, though brief, proved to be a mistake. Jill slammed her fist into Toni's jaw. The blow thrust Toni to the side, off of Jill, but she managed to hang onto Jill's right wrist, keeping the gun above their heads.

Toni had never been in an actual fistfight before. She had come close once in junior high, but other than teenage hair pulling, she had no experience with hand-to-hand combat. She struggled to regain her position on top of Jill, but Jill held her back.

Seeming equally matched, the two women continued to wrestle for control of the gun. As they fought, Toni became aware of another car pulling up to the hotel. Jill must have heard the car as well. As if bolstered by the thought of reinforcements, she shoved her elbow into Toni's neck and then pinned her down.

Jill's arm trembled as she put all her weight into bringing the gun level with Toni's head. Her strength waning, Toni realized she had to act fast. Still pushing against Jill with her right arm, she brought her left arm down to the ground.

Toni scooped up a handful of gravel and rammed it into Jill's eyes.

Jill cried out in pain, and although she never let go of the gun, Toni managed to break free. She leaped to her feet and ran toward the gate. She almost collided with Mark.

He wrapped his arms around her. "Are you okay?"

"It's Jill—she's got a gun. We have to get out of here."

"You're not going anywhere," Jill said.

Toni turned around. Jill had recovered from the attack. She held the gun steady.

Mark took a step toward Jill. "You don't want to do this," he said. "There are other ways out."

"Like what?" Jill asked. "You think I can just leave here and start over somewhere else? Because I know you can't expect me to just give up and spend the rest of my life in some prison."

"Just let Toni go, and I'll help you. We'll work out all the details. You can live anywhere in the world, and no one will ever find you."

"Now why would I do that when I have everything I could ever want right here?"

Jill swung the gun back toward Toni and fired.

37

When Mark saw Jill swing her arm, he knew what was coming.

He threw himself in front of Toni.

The bullet ripped into his chest, and he felt as though he'd been hit with a sledgehammer. He slumped to the ground and pressed his right hand against the wound. As the initial pain begin to subside, a tingling sensation spread throughout his body, followed by a feeling of numbness.

Toni knelt beside him, her eyes filling with tears.

"Don't cry," he said.

Toni stroked his hair. "You're going to be all right. You are. She has the disk now, so she can let us go, and I'll get you to a hospital as soon as I can. Please try to hang on."

Jill circled the pair. "She just has no idea who she's crying for, does she?"

Toni looked up at Jill. "What are you talking about?"

Jill reversed her circle.

"Mark," Toni said. "What is she talking about?"

He wanted to deny everything. Wanted to spare her the grief of his betrayal.

"Why don't you just go ahead and tell her?" Jill said.

He owed her the truth. That was all he could give her now.

The cloud of hatred that began to creep into Toni's eyes pained Mark far more than any bullet ever could. "I'm sorry," he said.

"You're sorry?" Toni asked. "Scott is dead, and all you can say is, you're sorry? He was your best friend. Did you know all along that they murdered him? Did they pay you to keep quiet?"

"I never wanted to hurt you."

"Then why didn't you save him? If you knew about Jill's scheme, why didn't you tell the police?"

Jill started laughing. "You know, for somebody who is so smart, you really can be dense at times. Who do you think introduced me to Clint and all my friends down in Mexico in the first place?"

Toni seemed to ignore Jill. She kept her focus on Mark. "Is it true? Were you involved from the very beginning?"

Mark nodded. "I arranged the shell corporations." He coughed. "I dated Jill for a while, and I met her family. I knew what they were capable of, and I knew she could get close to Clint."

"Why would you ever let them kill Scott? All those years, he treated you just like you were his brother."

Mark noticed the night air becoming colder. He wanted to shut his eyes. Forget about his past sins, but it was time he confessed.

"The morning it happened," Mark said. "Scott came to my house. He woke me up around four o'clock. He said he had something important to tell me, and it couldn't wait until daybreak. About a week before, he was working on a bid for a new apartment complex. When he started putting the numbers together for the investor, he noticed something seemed off with Chadwick & Shore's property management accounts. He thought Jill and Clint might have altered the books, so he kept quiet and started digging. He had just managed to put all the pieces together when he came to see me. He wanted me to go to the police station with him right then."

Toni blinked back tears. "He didn't know that you were in on it with them?"

"No. Jill found out he'd been snooping through the files and realized he was suspicious. Without telling me, she sent Nico here to pose as a construction worker. He was supposed to arrange an accident."

"You didn't know they were planning to kill Scott?"

"No. I had no idea Scott even suspected something was going on with the accounts. Not until he came to see me that morning."

"Why did you have to tell Jill about it? Didn't you know what she would do—what would happen to Scott?"

Mark shut his eyes. Hurting Toni was the hardest thing he had ever done, and he hated himself for it.

"Answer me," Toni said. "Why didn't you stop Brian from killing Scott?"

"Toni, I've been trying to tell you. Brian is not responsible. He didn't kill Scott. I did."

38

In an instant, the man she had trusted, had leaned on, had loved like a brother, ceased to exist. In his place lay a vile and deceiving monster. Toni wanted to put her hands around Mark's throat and steal the life from his body the same way he had stolen Scott's. "You're even lower than Jill," she said. "You deserved to be shot, and you deserve to die."

"I'm sorry. I know there's no excuse for what I did," Mark said.

"How could you murder someone who loved you like his own flesh and blood?"

Mark tried to shift his position on the ground, and then winced. Toni noticed that the scarlet stain on his white shirt had widened. "When Scott told me he knew about the money laundering, I panicked," Mark said. "He turned his back, and I hit him over the head. It knocked him unconscious, but he was still alive."

"So you think you showed him some kind of strange mercy by finishing him off?"

"No. Right after I hit him, I was actually sorry. I made the decision to call for an ambulance and then leave. I already had an escape plan in place just in case we were ever caught. I had everything I needed to leave the country."

"Then why didn't you? Was it the money? Was your greed more important than a man's life?"

"I was about to call 911, but before I could get to the phone, it rang. And then . . . everything changed."

Jill kicked at the gravel. "Why in the world are you taking the time to tell her every little detail?"

"I need her to know," Mark said. "I need her to understand."

"Understand?" Toni said. "I will never understand how you could take away the only person, outside of my father, I have ever truly loved."

"I don't expect you to forgive me," Mark said. "But I need to tell you. Think of it as my last request."

Toni glanced at his chest. He had lost a lot of blood. It was true: he might not make it. Then she reminded herself that only the just men died young; the evil ones seemed to live forever. Like drunk drivers. You read about them in the newspaper and see them on television all the time. They plow into another car, and all the innocent passengers die. But somehow the drunk driver always seems to survive.

Still, Toni wanted to know. She needed to hear the truth just as much as he needed to tell her. "What happened?"

"You've met my mother. You've seen the hell her life has become. Scott told you about her accident, but did he tell you what was really going on in that house?"

"What do you mean? Your mother was cleaning, and she tripped and fell down the stairs."

"No, she didn't."

"Don't you dare try to blame Scott for her accident. He told me he wasn't even in the house when she fell."

"No. But his father was. They were having an affair. Charles Chadwick promised my mother he would leave his wife, Ellen, but he never did. They were arguing about it that day. He's the one who caused my mother to fall down those stairs."

Toni shook her head. "Whatever happened between your mother and Mr. Chadwick has nothing to do with Scott."

Mark cleared his throat. "It was my mother's nurse who called me. My mother was having another spell, and I could hear her screaming over the phone. I looked down at Scott lying on my living room floor, and I realized I hated him."

Mark paused, catching his breath. "First, Charles Chadwick destroyed my mother's life. And then Scott threatened to take away everything I've built here. Everything I've worked so hard for. He had it easy his whole life while I've had to struggle. For years, we were always competing. For girls, for grades, for everything. And Scott always won. So now that I've finally made a future for myself, why should I have to give it all up for him? Why should I let him beat me again? Do you realize what living on the run is really like?"

"I don't give a damn what your life would have been like. As far as I'm concerned, you don't even deserve to have a life anymore."

"Remember the first time Scott asked you out? You said no."

"Of course, I remember, but what does Scott asking me out have to do with any of this?"

"I thought you turned him down because of me. I thought I had a chance with you."

His words cut through Toni's chest. She didn't want even more reasons to blame herself for Scott's death. "Please tell me that you didn't kill Scott because you had some wild idea that if he was out of the way, we would be together."

"No. But you are one more reason I hated him."

"Even if I had never met Scott, nothing ever would have happened between the two of us. Back then, I thought of you as a customer. That's all. And if you somehow thought I was sending you different signals, you were wrong."

"Don't blame yourself. He'd be dead even if you weren't in the picture. The only difference is, I wouldn't have gotten caught."

For the first time in her life, pure hatred radiated throughout Toni's entire body.

"You were right about the construction superintendent," Mark said. "He saw exactly what he expected to see. He didn't suspect a thing when I drove Scott's SUV through the gate. Of course, Nico was there to make sure nothing went wrong."

"Was Scott still alive when you got to the hotel?"

"Yes, but he never woke up. I carried him to the top floor. After it was over, I hid in the building until the superintendent found his body. Nico stood as a lookout while I sneaked back through the gate. Then I cut across the field, through the trees, and Jill picked me up in the parking lot behind the mall."

Toni sat motionless, fighting the image in her mind: Mark on the balcony hurling an unconscious Scott to his death. Nausea grew in her stomach. It was one thing to speculate about what had happened. But now, hearing the words, knowing the actual details, made it all too real. The truth was almost more than she could bear.

And then Toni realized Mark must have called Jill when he went up to shower. "You wanted to kill me too, didn't you?" she said. "Are you the one who hit me over the head and loaded me into Jill's trunk?"

Jill started laughing. "Do you know how many times Mark threatened to kill me if I so much as laid one finger on you? He gave me so much hell when you went missing, I thought he'd actually go through with it. Can't you even see what's right in front of your face? He thinks he's in love with you."

"If he loved me," Toni said, "he would have left the country that morning and Scott would still be alive."

"I never would have let them hurt you," Mark said. "I would have driven you to the police station. When I knew you were safe, I planned to head to the airport."

Knowing he didn't want her dead was only a small consolation. Although he hadn't harmed her physically, he'd destroyed the most important part of her life. Even if she lived through the night, she would never recover from losing Scott.

Jill pointed the gun at Mark. "Well, now that you've made your last confession, let's get on with this. Take out your cell phone, and toss it over here."

Mark struggled to get the phone out of his jacket. He handed it to Toni. She was tempted to throw it at Jill's head, but the risk of getting shot was too great. She pitched it on the ground.

Jill picked up the phone. "Now get up, Toni, or I'll shoot him again, and then I'll shoot you too."

"No," Mark said. "Let her go. I'll take all the blame. I'll say I forced you into helping me. You still have time to leave, and I'll tell everyone you're dead. The police won't look for you."

"I don't think you'll be able to talk much with a bullet in your brain," Jill said.

Toni knew Jill would kill him. As it stood, Mark still might have a chance of living. Even though she hated him, even though he didn't deserve one more second on this earth, Toni couldn't let Jill shoot him in cold blood. "Leave him alone," she said. "I'll go with you."

39

Toni felt the barrel of the gun pressing against the small of her back as she walked into the building. She thought about Scott. About his final trip to the hotel and the way he had died. She was thankful he had remained unconscious. By not waking up, he had been spared the fear of the fall and, she hoped, the pain.

They reached the construction elevator. Although the car had an interior light, Jill switched on a flashlight before shoving her inside. Toni remembered the last time they had been at the hotel together, when she thought they were friends. If she had known then what she knew now, she probably would have pushed Jill over the wall.

"What are you going to do with Mark?" Toni asked. "Do you plan to get him some help, or will you kill him too?"

"Well, I really haven't decided yet, but the way he looked, I may not have to worry about it anyway."

"You managed to keep a lot hidden from him too. He said Brian wasn't responsible for Scott's death, but I know he was working with you. I saw your private number on his cell phone."

"You think he was helping me just because of a few phone calls? I was just working out a deal for him to sell us Scott's share of the business if he got the estate—you know, covering all the bases."

"So Brian played no part in any of it?"

"Now why would I trust the brother of a man I just had killed? Do you really think I'm that stupid?"

"Then why did you send him the text message that said, "It's done"? You sent it right after Nico ran my car into the river."

"You really do have a wild imagination, don't you? You want to know why I sent that message? I was letting Brian know that the appraisal on the business was finished."

Brian had been telling the truth. She should have listened to him instead of jumping to conclusions. If she had, chances were that Jill would be in jail right now instead of holding her at gunpoint.

Toni hoped Jill wouldn't wonder how she had seen Brian's phone. If Jill realized Brian knew about her and Nico, his life would be in danger as well.

The elevator rumbled to a stop, and Jill pushed her out into the hallway. The beam from the flashlight panned the floor. Toni noticed the workers had hung drywall since her last visit. The dust hung heavy in the air, visible in the flashlight's glow.

She glanced around looking for a trowel or other tool she could use as a weapon, but she saw nothing. "The police are going to wonder how I got here, since I don't have a car," Toni said.

"Now don't you worry about any of that. It's all been taken care of."

"Really? How?"

"Does it really make any difference to you now?"

"No, but if I'm going to die, you could at least tell me how you plan to pull it off."

"I guess it wouldn't hurt to tell you. You see, Gloria will be acting as your double, the same way Mark was Scott's double. She'll be dressed up in that emerald green coat of yours and a red wig, and she'll take a taxi here from your house. I'll put the suicide note in your coat pocket and leave it on the balcony, so nobody will ever doubt that you killed yourself."

As they passed the door to the maintenance room, Toni caught the reflection of something metal on the floor up ahead. A soda can. A ladder stood near the entrance to the rear penthouse suite.

"What if Mark dies?" Toni asked. "Won't it be a little too coincidental having so many people turn up dead in such a short time?"

"Mark won't be a problem for me. I can make his death look like a random shooting just as easily as I can make yours look like a suicide. Do you know how many people are carjacked in this country every year?"

"It sounds like you have our murders all figured out."

With her next step, Toni kicked the soda can across the hallway. Startled, Jill jerked toward the noise. At that moment, Toni knocked the ladder down and ran.

40

"There's no use in hiding," Jill called out. "There's nowhere for you to go but down."

Toni crouched beneath a bank of scaffolding, letting her eyes adjust to the darkness. Instead of going into the rear penthouse suite when she knocked the ladder down, she had slipped into one of the rooms on the front side of the hotel.

She could still hear Jill's footsteps in the hallway, moving from door to door. It was apparent that Jill wasn't sure which way Toni had fled.

"You know, you're only making things worse for yourself," Jill said. "Nico will be here in just a few minutes, and he's not a very nice man. I was planning to knock you out before I threw you off the balcony, but he'll probably want to rough you up a little first. You'll be saving yourself a lot of pain if you just come on out now."

The flashlight beam swept the room where Toni was hiding. She held her breath.

Jill stopped at the doorway, stood for a few seconds, and then went back out into the hallway.

Toni knew she had to move. If she stayed still for too long, she'd be caught. As she made her way out from under the scaffolding, she bumped her head on a platform so hard her jaw rattled.

Dammit! It hurt like hell. She sank back to the floor and hoped Jill hadn't heard her.

Toni waited and watched for her to reappear in the doorway. After a few minutes had passed and Jill still had not come back, Toni realized she probably wouldn't. At least not for a while.

Dust from the platform fell from Toni's hair, threatening to make her sneeze. She rubbed her nose and then crawled to the other side of the room. She had to figure a way out of the building. Not all of the drywall had been put up yet. It was possible she might be able to pass through the adjacent suite and circle back around to the entrance.

Taking the elevator would be too noisy. Jill would be on her before she could even get it started. Toni needed to reach the stairwell. But to get there, she would have to cross the hallway. That could be a problem. Since Jill hadn't come in to search the rooms, Toni suspected she was standing guard in the hall, blocking the exit and waiting for Nico to arrive.

If only there was a way to lure Jill into one of the suites. Toni might be able to sneak past her and make it down the hallway without being seen.

She crept back to the doorway, took a deep breath, and peeked around the wall. Jill was right where she expected her to be. Pacing the floor at the end of the hall near the elevator. She was still holding the flashlight. That was good. That meant her eyes had probably not grown accustomed to the darkness yet.

Toni moved through the suite looking for something she could use to get Jill's attention. She finally found it next to the whirlpool tub in what would become the master bathroom. One of the workers had left behind a measuring tape. Small but weighty. Perfect.

Toni returned to the doorway. She checked Jill's position again, and then hurled the tape measure across the hall into the rear suite.

She heard the smack of the initial impact, and then a loud crash. It sounded as if she'd knocked over something big.

Jill took the bait.

The glow from the flashlight came into view. Toni pressed her back against the wall. She waited until she was sure Jill was inside the rear suite and then silently escaped into the hallway.

She started to run. She had to make it to the stairwell before Jill realized she'd been tricked. But Toni forgot about the ladder. It was still lying across the hall floor. By the time she saw it, it was too late to jump over.

The ladder snagged Toni's shoe.

She hit the floor hard.

The fall onto the bare concrete skinned her palms. The pain in her left elbow was so intense she thought the bone might have cracked. Her shins were bruised as well. Toni pulled herself up and staggered down the hallway.

A firecracker exploded next to her ear. Only it wasn't a firecracker at all. Her left shoulder stung. She'd been shot. Toni ducked into the maintenance room before Jill could fire again.

Jill called out to her. "I tried to make this easy for you, but you just wouldn't listen."

Toni hugged her left arm. Strangely enough, falling on her elbow had hurt far worse than the gunshot. She figured that could mean one of two things. Either the wound wasn't serious, or that the bullet had done so much damage, she was going into shock.

She touched her sleeve. It was wet with blood. Not a good sign. She leaned against the wall, closed her eyes, and tried to keep her breathing deep and even. The last thing she needed to do was panic.

Jill's footsteps were getting closer. Toni knew she was trapped.

The elevator cranked to life and started to descend. Nico had finally arrived.

"Do you hear that, Toni?" Jill asked. "It's all over, so come on out now, and I'll tell Nico to go easy on you."

The maintenance room was empty except for a five-gallon bucket filled with trash. As Jill approached the door, Toni picked up the bucket. She swung it as hard as she could.

The blow took Jill by surprise, knocking her backward.

The gun clanked across the floor and down the hallway, sliding out of sight. Toni needed that gun. How else could she protect herself from Nico? Even if she managed to get down the twelve flights of stairs, he was sure to catch up with her before she could make it out of the building.

She grabbed the flashlight and scanned the hallway floor. She had just spotted the gun when Jill slammed into her. They both went down.

Toni whacked Jill across the head with the flashlight and then crawled toward the gun. She was almost there when Jill yanked her back by the hair. She had a fist full and was not about to let go.

This time Toni beat her with the flashlight so hard the light went out.

With Jill fighting to pull her back, hanging onto her shirt, Toni inched closer to the gun.

It lay just beyond her reach.

The construction elevator began moving upward. In mere minutes, Nico would be there.

Toni wriggled and kicked her legs in an attempt to keep Jill off her. She stretched her arm out as far as she could, and her fingers closed around the butt of the gun. It was heavier than she'd imagined.

A rush of power flooded her body. She twisted around and pointed the weapon at Jill. "Get up, or I'll kill you."

Jill laughed. "Oh no, you won't," she said. "You're way too soft, and we both know it, so just go ahead and give me the gun, and I'll make sure you don't suffer."

The moan of the elevator grew louder. It had almost reached the top floor. Toni's time was running out fast. "I mean it, Jill. I will shoot you. Let go of me! Now!"

Jill started to get up, but then dove on top of Toni and grabbed for the gun.

Toni squeezed the trigger.

41

Toni shoved a stunned Jill off her.

The bullet had torn into Jill's left shoulder. At such close range, the slug was bound to have caused some permanent damage. But unless she bled out before help arrived, Jill would live. Not that she deserved to.

Toni had to get out of the hallway before Nico reached the penthouse floor.

She ran into the stairwell. When the door swung shut, total darkness enveloped her. There were no windows here. No glow from the moon to guide her. Without the flashlight, she would have to move more slowly than she wanted. She gripped the railing and began the descent.

The numbness of her own wound had been replaced by a burning pain. She wondered how much blood she had lost. She was afraid to touch her shoulder—afraid of what she might find.

She had to keep her mind focused on getting down the stairs. Block out the pain. Concentrate on outsmarting Nico.

He'd be in the stairwell soon.

Toni counted off the floors in her mind. Two flights of stairs for each level. She was almost to the ninth floor when a wave of dizziness hit her. She clung to the handrail.

There was no time to stop. She had to keep going. She closed her eyes and willed the vertigo to pass. If she could just make it to the ninth floor, she could hide in one of the rooms.

A thought popped into her head. What if she was leaving a trail of blood behind? Then no matter where she hid, Nico would be led right to her.

And what had caused the dizziness? Was it from going around and around in the stairwell? Or was she bleeding to death?

Her foot missed the next step.

Toni slid down the stairs. The gun slipped from her hand and tumbled downward, clanking across the treads. She had to get up. She had to find the gun.

Her head was spinning, and her hands felt clammy. She tried to pull herself up, but her muscles refused to cooperate.

A noise echoed through the stairwell. Someone yelling. She thought she heard her name.

And then Toni realized: she was going to pass out.

42

Toni!"

Brian's calls went unanswered. Maybe she was already out of the building, or maybe Jill had lied. Jill had been surprised when he'd emerged from the construction elevator. She'd been expecting Nico, who would probably be arriving within the next few minutes.

Brian had to find Toni fast.

Although he had shoved the Beretta in Jill's face and threatened to splatter her brains across the floor, she might not have been telling the truth when she said Toni had gone into the stairwell. He thought about turning back and searching the penthouse floor just to make sure.

And then he heard a noise. It seemed to come from a few flights below. He hurried down the stairs careful not to outrun the beam from his flashlight. He was almost at the ninth floor when he heard another noise. A familiar clicking sound. He shone the light into the corner of the landing.

Toni sat on the floor, a gun aimed at his head.

"Toni, don't shoot. It's me, Brian."

She seemed not to hear him at first. For a second, he was afraid she would squeeze the trigger. But then she smiled and lowered the gun.

"The police are on the way," he said.

She slumped in the corner, her head down. He knelt beside her. "Toni?"

She had passed out. Blood soaked her shirt; she'd been shot. He cradled her in his arms and tried to get her to come around. How much blood had she lost?

He was thankful he'd had the foresight to place a GPS tracking device on Mark's car. Otherwise he never would have known she was at the hotel site. When his friend, Sam, had called to say he'd discovered Mark's name linked to AlquilaCorp, Brian hadn't been the least bit surprised. Although his initial suspicions about Toni had proved wrong, he still had never trusted the attorney.

He only wished he'd shared his uneasy feelings about Mark with Toni. Maybe then she wouldn't have run straight to the enemy. He hoped his omission wouldn't prove to be a fatal mistake.

He had no family left. No real connection to anyone. But in the short time he had known her, Brian had begun to feel a sort of kinship with his brother's fiancée. They shared a common bond. They had loved and been loved by the same person.

If Toni didn't make it, he would always blame himself.

He was good at that. He'd had years of practice.

When his sister, Caitlin, died, Brian knew he was at fault. She had depended on him for help, and he had let her down. Her blood was on his hands, the same as if he himself had performed the fatal procedure.

And then there was the death of his parents. Losing their only daughter had taken a huge toll on his father's heart. Brian still had nightmares of his parents' car soaring over the cliff. If he hadn't taken Caitlin to that quack of a doctor, they would all still be alive. He had caused so much pain for his family. He had become a poison in their lives.

After his parents' funeral, Brian decided it would be best if he left town. If he stayed, he knew he would only end up hurting his brother even more. He staged an argument. He pushed Scott away. In his then eighteen-year-old mind, putting distance between them was the only way he could ensure his brother's safety.

Now he wished more than anything else that he had stayed. He had lost too much time, years he could never get back. Ironically, it seemed he had done his brother more harm by leaving. Scott's death might have been partially his fault too. If he had been here, maybe he could have prevented it.

Brian scooped Toni up and carried her toward the elevator.

He prayed it wasn't too late.

• • •

The scream of sirens grew closer.

Nico recognized the wail of an ambulance and two, maybe three, police cars. There must have been a wreck on the nearby interstate. At this hour, the majority of streets running throughout Blanton Hills were deserted.

He glanced at the dashboard clock as he turned onto the gravel road leading to the hotel. Everything was going as planned. Right on schedule.

Jill was waiting for him just up ahead. Earlier, he had bound Toni's hands and feet and stuffed her into the trunk of his sister's car. He hoped she was still out. If she woke up, she'd try to get free. He didn't want any bruises detectable on her wrists. Of course, as dumb as the cops on the Blanton Hills PD were, they probably wouldn't notice.

If she was conscious, he'd knock her over the head again. Then untie her and help Jill change her clothes. It wouldn't take long to carry Toni up to the penthouse and throw her over the balcony. Then he could call Gloria.

The two taxi companies in town closed up shop at one in the morning. To try to make sure all their cars were back in the garage by then, they refused to take any calls after twelve thirty. It was now three minutes past midnight. He had plenty of time.

The squeal of emergency sirens continued to grow louder. Too loud. Like they were right on top of him.

And then he knew.

Something had gone terribly wrong.

Nico checked his rearview mirror. Blue lights streaked down the highway toward the hotel. He started to make a U-turn, but it was too late. A police cruiser was already turning onto the access road.

He took out his cell phone. Gloria answered on the first ring. Nico had only one word to say.

"Run."

43

She felt a presence. Someone standing over her.

Toni opened her eyes. Detective Lewis was beside her hospital bed. She wondered how long he'd been there, waiting for her to wake up. She managed a smile. "So, do you still think I'm crazy?"

The cop shrugged his shoulders and then chuckled. "Okay, I admit it: I was wrong." He turned serious. "I'm sorry that I didn't believe you, and it's something I'll always regret."

Toni thought about everything that had happened that week. She thought about Dana Dawson and her family. If Detective Lewis had listened, if he had investigated Scott's death further, would her friend still be alive? There was no way to know for sure. But Toni could tell that the detective was wondering the same thing. She could see the pain of guilt in his eyes. She wasn't the only one feeling blame.

There was really nothing she could say to soothe him. "Have you already arrested Jill and Mark?"

"Not yet. All three of you were in surgery when I got here last night, and the Feds are involved now. They'll be doing the honors. As of this morning, my part in the investigation is pretty much over."

"Then why are you here?"

"I wanted to thank you."

"Thank me?"

His smile was back. "For not listening to me."

Toni attempted a laugh, but felt the soreness radiate from her shoulder. "My father always told me that I was too hardheaded."

"Sometimes that's not such a bad thing—especially in this case. I don't know if you realize it or not, but thanks to your stubbornness, the lid's been blown off what looks to be the largest known money laundering operation in the South. Maybe even the whole country."

"Scott's the one who figured it all out. I was just trying to find the person who killed him. Nothing else really mattered to me."

"Well, you've got a hell of a lot of determination. Most people would have given up once they realized their life was in danger."

"I couldn't give up. I didn't have a choice. I knew Scott was murdered, but no one else could see it. I was the only person left who could find a way to prove it."

The detective shuffled his feet. "That's my fault. After you came to see me, I should have taken another look at the evidence and asked more questions, but I didn't. When you've been in law enforcement as long as I have, you start to compare each new case to one you've had before. You pick out the similarities and start to focus on them. You develop this need to categorize everything into neat little piles. Ninety-nine percent of the time, you're right, and the cases end the same. What looks like a duck is usually just a duck. After a while, it becomes routine. But every once a decade or so, a case comes along that's not what it seems. Everything points to the wrong conclusion—like this case did. I thought you were too close to the situation to see it clearly, but the truth is, I was too detached. I won't make that mistake again."

"What about Nico and Gloria?"

"They're both in jail. We caught Nico trying to run away from the construction site last night, and the Feds picked up Gloria at the airport early this morning. She was about to board a flight to Belize."

There was a tap on Toni's hospital room door. She looked up and saw Brian carrying a vase filled with peach-colored roses.

"Am I interrupting?" Brian asked.

"No, not at all," Detective Lewis said. He shook Brian's free hand. "I need to get going anyway. I've got a week's worth of paperwork waiting on my desk." He turned back to Toni. "You take care of yourself, and from now on, leave the criminals to me."

"I'll be happy to," she said.

Brian found a spot for the flowers and then gave her a quick hug. "How's your shoulder?" he asked.

"It's a little achy; I think the painkillers must be wearing off."

"Do you need me to call a nurse?"

"No. No, that's okay; they're in here torturing me every five minutes anyway. They keep checking my IV, my blood pressure, my temperature, and anything else they can think of."

"You sure?"

Toni nodded. "I'm sure."

Brian pulled a chair closer to her bed. A memory flooded her mind. For the first time, she recalled waking up in the ambulance the night before. She remembered Brian beside her. Felt him holding her hand.

"You were at the hotel last night," Toni said. "You're the one who found me after I'd been shot."

"That's right."

"You saved my life."

"That's not how I remember it. I seem to recall you almost shot me."

"I did?"

"Yeah, you did. You were just waiting for someone to come down those stairs so you could blow them away."

"I thought you were Nico. I was waiting in the corner for him, and I think I really would have killed him too, even if he'd shot me first. It feels strange to say this, but I don't think I would have given up until I knew he was dead."

Brian didn't say anything. He just looked down at the floor. She wondered if he was thinking about Scott.

"How did you find me?" she asked.

"Remember when I told you I had installed a GPS system on your car? Well, I was tracking Mark too. When you disappeared, I figured you'd run to him because he was the only one you still trusted."

"He killed Scott."

"I know. You told me on the way to the hospital."

Exhaustion had seeped into her bones and she let her head fall back against the pillow. "I don't remember."

"It's because of all the sedatives. Once you came to in the ambulance, we couldn't get you to shut up. You kept talking about a computer disk you had made and files locked in a safe."

Toni tried to push herself up. "The files are on a flash drive in Scott's study, in a safe behind the bookcase. You have to go to my house and get it. The complete spreadsheets are all there, along with notes that explain everything."

"Lie back down. The police don't need those files."

"Yes, they will."

"No they don't. Didn't Detective Lewis tell you? Mark had records of every transaction they had ever made in the trunk of his car. They found detailed accountings of all the money that had been collected and paid out. Jill disguised the dirty money as rental income and then deposited it into Chadwick & Shore's property management account. Once the funds were all nice and clean, they were transferred to accounts belonging to the dummy corporations. The majority of the money went right back to the owners of the corporations in Mexico, but they paid Mark and Jill millions of dollars for their services. Mark had set up numbered bank accounts for the two of them in the Caymans. It was all there. The names of all the people involved, the account numbers—everything. He planned to take the information with him when he ran."

"He said last night he was going to leave the country."

"That would have been easy for him to do. The police also found passports and credit cards for him under five other names."

"That's just as unbelievable to me as the thought of him killing Scott. At least now he'll pay for what he's done. At least now, instead of living the good life on a tropical island somewhere, he'll be spending the rest of his years in prison."

A strange look crossed Brian's face.

"What?" she asked.

"I thought you knew."

"You thought I knew what?"

"Mark died last night. During surgery."

Toni's stomach tightened. Although she had realized Mark was seriously injured, somehow she had thought he'd be okay. That she'd see him again. She reminded herself that he had murdered Scott. Mark deserved to die, didn't he? So why did she feel like crying?

She hated Mark for what he had done. But part of her heart still loved the person she had believed him to be. The man who had stood beside her—who had been her friend. If only that man had been real.

Toni rubbed her eyes. "The bullet that hit him," she said. "It was meant for me. Jill was aiming at me, and Mark jumped between us."

"I wondered why she would shoot her partner."

"He tried to talk her into leaving the country last night and letting me go. I guess he set up a bunch of fake passports in her name too."

"Probably. And I'd bet she has other bank accounts the Feds won't ever find."

Toni bit her lip. "Is she still . . ."

"Alive? Yes, and she'll be fine. As long as she stays away from me."

"I hope she never gets out of prison. Then it won't matter how many fake identities she has or how much money is hidden away."

A man wearing green scrubs and a white coat came into the room. He had Toni's chart in his hand. "Good morning," he said. "I'm Doctor Brandon, and I performed your surgery last night."

"It's nice to meet you," Toni said.

"How are we feeling today?" he asked.

Toni wondered why doctors always used the term *we.* It wasn't as if he was lying in the bed with her sharing her pain. She wanted to say, *I don't know how you feel, but I feel like hell.* Instead she replied, "I'm doing okay."

"Any pain?"

"A little."

"We don't want to give you anything too strong right now, but let one of the nurses know if it becomes too uncomfortable for you to rest."

"Okay."

"Your vitals are all good, and the surgery went very well. Fortunately, we were able to remove the bullet with no problems. You're a lucky woman. When the wound heals, you'll regain full use of your shoulder."

"Does that mean I can go home soon?"

"I'd like to keep you at least another day to let you recuperate, but don't worry about the baby. All the tests indicate that everything is normal and progressing just as it should."

"What are you talking about? What ba—Oh my!"

Tears streamed down Toni's face.

This time, they were tears of joy.

44

Toni placed her foot on the steel rung and pushed the For Sale sign down into the lawn.

It was the first step.

One of many that were yet to come.

She brushed the hair from her face and stared up at the house. She remembered the first time she'd seen the five-acre lot. She and Scott had walked the perimeter, holding hands, talking about their dreams for the future. The day they finally moved into the home he had so lovingly designed, she felt they were well on their way to making all those dreams come true.

With Scott gone, her dreams had changed. Her future would be different from the one they had planned. But now, as on that very first day here, her heart was again filled with hope.

Only three weeks ago, her spirit had been broken. Desperate to find a way to hold on to the love she'd found with Scott, she had decided to stay in the huge family house he had built for her. Alone. Pretending he was still there. Imagining him in another one of the many empty rooms. It was only in the past few days that she'd come to understand that a love that strong would follow her wherever she went. She didn't need to pretend.

Toni slid her hand across her stomach and smiled, amazed by the tiny life growing within. The words Scott had spoken in the nightmare came back to her.

"*I will always be with you.*"

She realized now those words were true—not just in spirit, but in flesh as well. Part of Scott would be with her. Would live on in their child. Together they had made something far more precious than a structure built of mere brick and wood. They had created a miracle. Another living soul. One she would protect and nurture and cherish the rest of her days.

Although she now had hope for the years ahead, the pain of her loss remained fresh. Like a jagged cut. She'd been told that acceptance would eventually come. But Toni knew the hurt would never completely go away. Still, for the sake of her child, she would be strong. She would go on.

One step at a time.

The blue Mustang convertible pulled into the drive. Brian got out and walked across the lawn toward her. "I'm on my way to the airport," he said. "I didn't want to leave without saying good-bye."

"Good-bye? I thought you would be able to stick around a few more days."

"I was, but this morning I got a lead on a story. One I can't pass up."

Toni hated to see him go. He had come to feel like her own brother. They walked back to his car. "Can you at least stay for lunch?" she asked. "I actually have healthy food in the house."

Brian laughed. "I wish I could, but the plane would take off without me."

Toni sighed. "I'm going to miss you."

He pulled her close and held her. In that moment she knew: Brian considered her a member of his family.

Although he had refused to accept any part of the inheritance, Toni had transferred half of Scott's assets into a trust for any children Brian might one day have. After all the paperwork was signed and he couldn't do anything to stop her, she would tell him about it.

"Oh, wait," she said. "I have something for you."

Toni ran into the house and returned a few minutes later with the leather-bound album. "Scott would want you to have this. I found it in his study when I was going through his stuff."

Brian placed the scrapbook on the trunk of the car and opened the cover. One by one, he flipped through the pages. By the time he reached the end, there were tears in his eyes. "I never imagined . . ."

"That he kept up with everything thing you were doing all those years?"

Brian nodded. "He followed my career. From the very beginning."

"Scott was proud of you, and he had every reason to be. He loved you more than you could ever know, and I think that's the reason he never told me the details about your fight and about what happened to Caitlin. I think he was afraid I might hold it against you, and he never would have wanted that."

"I should have come back here earlier. Years ago. Things might be different now."

"We can't go back, but even if we could, there's still no guarantee that things would turn out any differently in the end."

"I know. I still wish I'd come home, but there were so many ghosts here. I haven't told you this, but I even flew into Nashville a whole week before the rehearsal dinner. I visited my parents' grave and Caitlin's. I walked through the neighborhood where we used to live, and it all came back to me. All the pain. I still wasn't sure I was ready to face Scott. I thought about backing out right up until the moment I saw him at the restaurant. Now I'm so glad I got to talk to him again, even if it was only for one night."

"I'm glad too, and I know Scott was as well."

"I threw away my relationship with my brother all because I was scared. I was afraid I'd somehow hurt him again or, honestly, that I'd be hurt. But I've had a lot of years to think, and now I realize that's just part of caring about somebody. You have to take that chance. You have to be willing to get hurt in order to enjoy all the good things. People aren't perfect, especially not me. But some of them are worth the risk."

They hugged again and Toni promised to take good care of his little niece or nephew. Brian promised her he would visit at Christmas.

She stood and watched the blue convertible until it disappeared over the hill.

The sun had pushed away the morning clouds and burned high in the sky now, promising a warm afternoon. Toni pulled off her jacket as she walked up the drive to the house. She thought about what Brian had said.

He was right. If she continued to spend her whole life trying not to get hurt, she wouldn't really be living. She would be cheating herself out of experiencing all the truly wonderful moments the world had to offer.

And more important, she would be cheating her child.

After eating a salad with grilled chicken and drinking a tall glass of milk, Toni drove to her office. Her desk was a mess. She rifled through the various stacks of papers and pink message slips. Finally, under a pile of mortgage rate sheets, she found the small cream-colored card.

Toni's fingers trembled as she dialed the phone number. To her surprise, the call was answered on the first ring. The voice on the other end made her heart stand still. A flood of doubt surged in her mind.

Did she really want to do this?

Was she ready?

Tears started to well in her eyes, and she considered hanging up. After a moment's silence, she let out the breath she didn't even realize she was holding.

She forced the words from her throat.

"Mom? It's me. Toni."

ACKNOWLEDGMENTS

My deepest thanks to my outstanding agent, Noah Lukeman, whose guidance is invaluable, and to my amazing editor, Lauren Spiegel, whose enthusiasm for the book was a constant source of encouragement.

I'd also like to thank the wonderful team at Touchstone: publisher Stacy Creamer, associate publisher David Falk, publicity director Marcia Burch, publicity manager Shida Carr, marketing manager Meredith Kernan, publishing assistant MacKenzie Fraser-Bub, director of subrights Marcella Berger, associate director of subrights Marie Florio, art director Cherlynne Li, designer Renata DiBiase, production editor Josh Karpf, copy editor Beverly H. Miller, production manager Larry Pekarek, managing editor Kevin McCahill, and managing editorial assistant Amanda Demastus. I'm truly grateful to each of you.

Warmest thanks to my parents, Milton and Joyce, and to my loving husband, Tim. Your support means more than you will ever know.

Deed to Death

For Discussion

1. There are a series of plot twists and shocking discoveries throughout *Deed to Death*. Which of these developments surprised you the most?

2. After Scott's funeral, everyone moves quickly to secure his financial assets. Brian, his estranged brother, wants his estate, while Clint wants his business. Did these actions arouse your suspicions? Who did you suspect might have an ulterior motive, and why? Were your suspicions correct?

3. Scott designed their custom-made dream house. What does the house symbolize throughout the novel? What does it mean to Toni?

4. Almost all of the characters in *Deed to Death* have secrets. How do these secrets influence each character and their actions? Are any of the characters able to overcome their past demons?

5. Why don't the police believe Scott's death could be a homicide? Did you ever believe Toni was in denial, or did you think she was on the right track all along? In real life, do you think it's important to question the police's conclusions?

6. After his death, Toni finds out about a number of secrets Scott had been keeping from her. Do you think her reaction would have been the same if he were alive? Or do you think it's easier to forgive someone who is dead?

7. Gloria Keith claims to have been Scott's lover. What kind of reaction does this spark in Toni? When does Toni realize that Gloria might not be telling the truth? How does Gloria's true identity impact the narrative?

8. Toni breaks the law on more than one occasion while investigating Scott's murder, including breaking into Josh's house, taking his license plate, and stealing information from Chadwick & Shore human resources. Do you think her actions were justified? Why or why not?

9. Do you think Mark's feelings for Toni were genuine?

10. Throughout *Deed to Death*, Toni's trust in others is consistently broken. Whom can she actually trust? Why? What does she learn about herself through this ordeal? And does it change her?

11. Toni calls her mom at the end of *Deed to Death* in an attempt to mend their relationship. Discuss how family is a recurring theme throughout *Deed to Death* and what role it plays in the characters' motivations, conflicts, and resolutions.

12. Do you think we can ever truly know the people we love?

A Conversation with D.B. Henson

Where did you get the idea for *Deed to Death*?

One day I was touring a high-rise building under construction, and as I looked down from the top-floor balcony, I thought about how terrifying it would be to fall. It was late in the day and all the workmen had gone home. With the site deserted, I realized it was the perfect place to stage a fictional murder.

How does your experience as a former real estate agent and director of marketing for a construction company inform *Deed to Death*? Does Toni's professional experience reflect your own?

The only thing I really have in common with Toni is her occupation. I worked in the real estate industry for many years and know it so intimately that it was a natural backdrop for my first novel. The day-to-day activities Toni engages in are true to life and do indeed mirror my own experiences.

You originally self-published *Deed to Death* as an ebook. Why did you decide to go the self-publishing route initially?

When I was writing the final draft of *Deed to Death*, I came across a blog post by another author detailing his success self-publishing on Amazon. Before reading the post, I had never even considered self-publishing. In fact, I had already made a list of agents to query. However, I knew that going through the list of agents would take months and I might only end up with a pile of rejection letters. I wasn't even sure my novel was saleable. Since it was my first book, I decided to take a chance and publish it on Amazon. I was shocked when *Deed to Death* landed on the bestsellers list.

The characters in *Deed to Death* are complex and three-dimensional individuals with distinct personality traits and flaws. Who was your favorite character to create, and which character do you like the most?

I think Mark was probably the most fun to create. Despite his many sins, he actually sees himself as a good man. Deep down, there is a sliver of good in him. This is evidenced by the fact that he sacrificed his own life for Toni.

My favorite character is Toni. She's strong, loyal, and determined, but she's definitely not perfect. She doesn't mind breaking the rules for what she feels is a just cause. She also has a few lessons to learn about trust and forgiveness.

Why did you choose to set the novel in Nashville?

Nashville is a dynamic and diverse city with a small-town atmosphere. The residents are friendly and welcoming. Strangers on the sidewalk will smile and say hello as they pass. It's exactly the kind of city Toni would seek.

When did you first start writing? What is your creative process like and who are your favorite authors?

I started writing short stories when I was around six years old, but never considered having any of them published. I began writing *Deed to Death* in 2009.

Before I begin writing a novel, I create a complete biography for each major character that will appear in the story. I know everything that has happened in their lives—when they were born, where they went to school, and even their favorite color. Then I begin working on the plot. I like to have the entire storyline mapped out before I write a single word.

My favorite authors are Harlan Coben, Greg Iles, and Tess Gerritsen.

What advice would you give to aspiring writers?

I would advise them to read everything they can in the genre in which they wish to write. Study the characters, the pacing, and the sentence structure. Dissect the plot. Get a feeling for what makes a story work and what doesn't. I would also recommend keeping a journal. Writing about daily experiences can often lead to a story idea.

***Deed to Death* is full of lies, deceit, and betrayal. How did you keep track of who was double-crossing whom? Were any of these characters based upon people in your life?**

Before I began writing, I made an event log for each character, which helped me stay on track. None of the characters in the novel are based on actual people.

If *Deed to Death* were made into a film, whom would you like to be casted to play Toni, Jill, and Mark?

I was a fan of the television show *Lost*, and I think Evangeline Lilly would be great in the role of Toni. Kate Hudson would be perfect for Jill, and I can see Ashton Kutcher as Mark.

Enhance Your Book Club

1. Toni lives in a beautiful house built by her fiancé, Scott. Have you ever thought of what your dream house would be like? Write down some notes and share with your book club.

2. *Deed to Death* takes place in and around Nashville, Tennessee, which is known as "Music City." Research this iconic city and bring one unique fact about Nashville to share with your book club.

3. Check out www.moonpie.com and www.googoo.com to order some tasty Nashville MoonPies and GooGoo Clusters for your group!

Printed in the United States
By Bookmasters